Katie Reus is the *New York Times* bestselling author of the Red Stone Security series, the Moon Shifter series and the Deadly Ops series. She fell in love with romance at a young age thanks to books she'd pilfered from her mom's stash. Years later, she loves reading romance almost as much as she loves writing it. However, she didn't always know she wanted to be a writer. After changing majors many times, she finally graduated with a degree in psychology. Not long after that she discovered a new love – writing. She now spends her days writing dark paranormal romance and sexy romantic suspense. You can find out more about Katie and her books at www.katiereus.com, www.facebook.com/katiereusauthor, or Twitter @katiereus.

Praise for Katie Reus' mesmerising Moon Shifter series:

'A wild, hot ride for readers. The story grabs you and doesn't let go' Cynthia Eden, *New York Times* bestselling author

'Sexy alphas, kick-ass heroines, and twisted villains will keep you turning the pages' Caridad Piñeiro, *New York Times* bestselling author

'Explosive danger, and enough sexual tension to set the pages on fire' Alexandra Ivy, *New York Times* bestselling author

'Reus' passionate and protective alpha-warrior shifters come alive on the page . . . Expect a fast-paced, action-packed read including battle scenes and nail-biting suspense' *Happy Ever After USA Today Blog*

'Reus' worldbuilding is incredibly powerful, as she seamlessly blends various elements of legend and myth . . . The romance between a shifter and a human is the real highlight – it's lusty, heartfelt and shows that love can conquer all' *Romantic Times* (4 Stars)

'Ms. Reus ⟨...⟩ ng short of heart-pou⟨...⟩

By Katie Reus

Katie REUS

HUNTER REBORN

headline
ETERNAL

The right of Katie Reus to be identified as the Author of
the Work has been asserted by her in accordance with the
Copyright, Designs and Patents Act 1988.

Published by arrangement with NAL Signet,
a division of Penguin Group (USA), LLC.
A Penguin Random House Company.

First published in Great Britain in 2015

by HEADLINE ETERNAL

An imprint of HEADLINE PUBLISHING GROUP

ISBN 978 1 4722 1235 1

Offset in Times by Avon DataSet Ltd, Bidford-on-Avon, Warwickshire

Printed and bound by CPI Group (UK) Ltd, Croydon, CR0 4YY

MIX
Paper from
responsible sources
FSC® C104740

Headline's policy is to use papers that are natural, renewable and recyclable
products and made from wood grown in well-managed forests and other
controlled sources. The logging and manufacturing processes are expected to
conform to the environmental regulations of the country of origin.

HEADLINE PUBLISHING GROUP
An Hachette UK Company
338 Euston Road
London NW1 3BH

www.headlineeternal.com
www.headline.co.uk
www.hachette.co.uk

To all my wonderful Moon Shifter fans,
this one is for you.

Chapter 1

Aiden leaned against the front door of the SUV, arms crossed over his chest, as he waited for some of his other packmates to join him. Connor, Jayce, Erin, and Noah had already left for Winston-Salem, which was only a couple of hours away. Barely. With the aggressive way Erin drove they'd probably arrive sooner than expected.

At the soft sound of approaching footsteps, he straightened. When he saw Teresa enter the parking structure, he grinned. Her knee-high heeled boots barely made a sound on the hard ground as she strode toward the SUV.

Her dark eyes flashed in annoyance when they landed on him, the normally indiscernible flecks of amber seeming brighter under the soft glow of the moonlight streaming in through the skylights. "Don't even start," she growled. The petite dark-haired shifter clenched her jaw tightly as she eyed him.

"Start what? You look hot. . . . Did Natalia dress you?" he asked teasingly, knowing it was probably the truth.

"I wish I could be offended, but yes. She left this dress plus a threatening note on my bed that I'd better be wearing this tonight." Teresa looked down at herself, then grimaced. She had on a short leather jacket over the dress that did little to hide how fitted it was. "Do I . . . look ridiculous?"

Aiden was surprised by the very real thread of insecurity that rolled off her. Teresa was truly a beautiful woman, but a sharp scent spiked in the air. The female was closer in age to Ana, her cousin and their pack Alpha's mate, so he knew she was around seventy—even though she looked like she was in her twenties. As lupine shifters they aged a hell of a lot slower than their human counterparts. But Teresa had been born in a different time, unlike her younger sisters, and he'd never seen her in anything other than jeans, T-shirts, and work boots.

"No, you look—"

"What the hell are you wearing?" Ryan called out as he entered the parking structure, Kat hot on his heels.

The four of them were heading to Winston-Salem together as part of their pack's recon mission of a supernatural club they suspected of trafficking vampire blood. Aiden loved Ryan like a brother, but he wanted to beat the shit out of him for the stricken look he'd just put on Teresa's face. The warrior male was a computer genius but when it came to Teresa, he was an idiot.

She paled and looked down at the impossibly tight

black dress that was secured by some sort of chain thing around the back of her neck. It hung a little looser around her chest—Aiden was pretty sure that was called a cowl—showing off all sorts of cleavage he knew Ryan didn't want the world to see. But Ryan was too big of a coward to make a move on Teresa and Aiden wasn't going to let the bastard hurt her feelings because of some territorial vibe the guy had going on over her.

Aiden whirled on the tall cowboy. "What the fuck's your problem? Teresa looks like sex on heels so pull that stick out of your ass." Without waiting for a response, he opened the back door to the SUV and motioned to Teresa. "Come on, sweetheart, you can sit in my lap. We need to get ready for our role as a couple. It probably wouldn't hurt if we kissed as practice—"

On an angry growl, Ryan dropped the bag he was carrying and rushed him, claws already unsheathed. Teresa let out a yelp as Kat dragged her out of the way. Aiden had been ready for the attack. He didn't want Teresa in a sexual way—he didn't want *any* female other than the one he'd lost—but he liked to rile up his jackass packmates fighting their mating instinct. Ryan had a future mate literally dropped into his lap but the male was too damn stubborn to embrace the gift he'd been given with Teresa. For that alone Aiden wanted to slice him up. Provoking him allowed Aiden to let loose his beast.

Aiden didn't try to avoid the attack, but embraced Ryan's tackle. Letting the other lupine grab him, Aiden slammed his fist into Ryan's ribs. As he started pummeling his packmate, Ryan turned and slammed an elbow across Aiden's face.

Instead of fighting the pain, he savored it. Nothing could compare to the agony he'd been carrying around for decades. He might put on a happy face for pack-mates, but every morning he woke up and that invisible knife embedded in his chest was still there.

Time was supposed to lessen the pain of loss. Or at least that's the bullshit he'd been told. And that's exactly what it was. Bullshit. Time just made it worse. He died a little every fucking day. Right now he wanted to make someone else hurt and Ryan was a convenient target.

Rolling into the face slam, he came back strong, plowing his other fist across Ryan's jaw. His packmate flew back against the SUV with a loud thud, but bounced back immediately.

Before Aiden could attack him again, something hard slammed against the side of his head. What the hell? He turned to see Kat with a long wooden sparring stick in her hands.

Ryan laughed, then held up his hands protectively as Kat brought down the stick on him too. It rapped against his knuckles, making the other male cry out in annoyance.

"What the hell is wrong with you two? We've got shit to do and you're acting like cubs!" Kat held the sparring stick firmly in one hand as she glared at both of them.

She'd been turned only a few months ago and was just in her twenties. She was young by human and shifter standards. Considering both he and Ryan were close to two hundred years old, their behavior was that much more shameful.

Out of the corner of his eye Aiden kept tabs on Ryan, but watched Kat warily. He deserved everything she had to dish out. They shouldn't have been fighting right before a mission. Before either of them could respond, she held up a hand in warning.

"I don't even want to hear it! Both of you, get in the car. Ryan, front seat, Aiden back seat with Teresa. *I* am driving."

Aiden could tell Ryan wanted to argue, but he nodded instead. His expression dark, the other shifter grabbed the laptop bag he'd dropped and rounded the vehicle without looking at Teresa. Aiden, however, wrapped an arm around her shoulders and squeezed. She looked close to tears, but she didn't say anything as she got in before him.

Most of his male packmates thought he was a flirt and a player. Nothing could be further from the truth. He just hated seeing any female in pain, especially someone as sweet as Teresa.

The drive to Winston-Salem was long and awkward. Thankfully Kat turned on the radio, but that was pretty much the only conversation. Normally they all played around with one another, but after what had happened, Aiden wasn't surprised at the silence. He also wasn't sorry for what he'd instigated.

He was fucking tired of scenting Teresa's pain whenever Ryan gave her the cold shoulder or said something to hurt her feelings. It didn't even matter that it was unintentional. The thing was, Ryan was one of the most decent males that Aiden knew. He'd taken in an abandoned cub and adopted him as his own. And it was clear he had feelings—strong ones—for Teresa. It wasn't like he went out of his way to hurt her, but it seemed like he did more often than not lately.

"We're almost there," Ryan said quietly as he clacked away at his laptop. He was going to stay behind and monitor their movements in the secret club that catered to supernaturals.

Most of the others had already arrived and planned to break in to the nonpublic area of the place, but Aiden, Teresa, and Kat were going to infiltrate the club and place hidden cameras wherever they could. Natalia was meeting them there and she and Teresa were going to be more of a distraction than anything, if necessary. It was why Teresa was dressed so skimpily.

Without turning around, Ryan reached back and held out two small earpieces. One for Aiden and one for Teresa. The technology was impressively small and undetectable to the eye because of how they settled in the ear canal. Everyone had already tested these so they were ready to go once Kat parked.

The energy in the SUV shifted as they continued down a long dirt path surrounded by woods on either side. It was time to work and everyone knew it. No matter what conflict Aiden had with Ryan at the moment, he wasn't worried about his packmate being unprofessional. Up ahead, Aiden could see the taillights of another vehicle that must have turned off the highway before they had.

Once they reached the end of the path, it opened up into a giant field where the industrial-building-turned-nightclub sat. High-end vehicles were parked everywhere around the makeshift gravel parking lot.

"Everyone have what they need?" Ryan asked as Kat maneuvered to a dark corner.

The vehicle stopped and they all murmured affirmations. Kat and Teresa each had six small video cameras in the lining of their clutch purses—in case they were searched on the way in. That didn't seem to be the norm, based on previous experiences, but they weren't taking any chances this time.

"Everyone, turn on your earpieces," Ryan said.

Once they made sure they were all on the same feed, everyone opened their doors except for Ryan, who remained glued to his laptop. The rest of the group had gone completely dark per their Alpha's orders. Connor didn't want his team to have any distractions or any possible way for them to be discovered. Plus, Jayce and Kat could communicate telepathically, so if there was an emergency Kat would just let the other team know through Jayce.

Teresa hovered outside her door; then her chin tipped up almost mutinously as she slipped her leather jacket off. It was February and freezing cold with a dusting of light snow on the ground, but as shifters they had much higher body temperatures. He knew that wasn't why Teresa was taking off the jacket though.

Without looking at Ryan, she tossed it onto her seat, then slammed the door. Aiden's eyes widened when she sauntered away. The back of the dress dipped dangerously low, all the way to the top of her butt. One wrong move and she'd be showing off everything.

Grinning, Aiden threw an arm around her shoulder. Since Ryan could still see them and hear every word they said, he tugged her closer. "You should let Natalia dress you more often," he murmured.

Teresa nudged him with her elbow, but she smiled. A real one. And that painful scent wasn't rolling off her anymore. He hated seeing any female in pain and that smile soothed his inner wolf immensely.

As they drew closer to the front doors, he straightened and so did Kat and Teresa. They might be posing as partygoers, but everything about this mission was serious to them. There'd been mass reports of humans doing violent and illegal things while under the influence of vampire blood. The humans—who were still alive—all said they felt as if they weren't in control of themselves, as if someone else was pulling their strings.

After some research they'd discovered reports of vamp blood deals going down here. Winston-Salem was too damn close to Aiden's pack's ranch in Fontana Mountain. And Connor Armstrong wouldn't let any of that shit encroach on his territory.

Next to Aiden, Teresa pulled her buzzing cell phone out of her pocket. "Natalia's on her way. She'll be here in twenty minutes," she said after glancing at the screen.

"Good—according to Jayce, everyone else is inside. They're slowly searching the place but haven't run into any snags," Kat said.

If they did, at least there was enough of the pack here as backup. With supernatural beings there was never any telling when a threat could escalate out of control. If someone was dealing vamp blood out of this club and they got wind that the Armstrong pack was looking to shut them down, there was no telling what could happen.

Chapter 2

Raw energy hummed through Natalia Cordona as her boots crunched over the gravel of the crude parking lot. There were too many vehicles to count outside the industrial building that had been turned into a club. She was running late because one of her sisters had had some sort of crisis so she'd gotten stuck on the phone. While she loved her sisters, her Alpha Connor had given her a chance to be part of this recon mission and there was no way in hell she wanted to screw this up. Not when she was one of the youngest—translation, coddled—of the pack. As she stepped inside the entryway, she scented another shifter nearby.

Next to a vintage elevator a tall shifter with a military-short buzz cut stood waiting, his arms crossed over his huge chest. He flicked her a quick, dismissive glance.

She frowned as she headed his way. Not standing too close as to crowd his personal space, she didn't hide that she was studying his profile. He was a lupine like her and there was something oddly familiar about him. Which was strange for her since she hadn't spent much time off the ranch except for when she'd been away at college.

His jaw clenched once and she realized she'd been staring too hard.

She averted her gaze forward when the elevator jerked to a halt. Even though it looked vintage on the outside, once the doors whooshed open it was all sleek and shiny on the inside. Whoever owned this place had definitely refurbished part of it. Her boots clicked on the flooring, but his were silent.

Natalia couldn't help another sneak peek at him as they stepped inside. "You look . . . Have we met before? Did you go to Duke?" That was where she'd gone to college. She hated not being able to figure something out, and this guy was seriously making her radar ping.

He snorted and looked at her as if she was disgusting. "Not interested."

Her eyes widened when she realized what he meant and she laughed. "Go fuck yourself. I wasn't hitting on you." That was when it clicked into place. He looked like Jayce-freaking-Kazan, Kat's mate. "You just look like my friend's mate Jayce, but . . . okay then, whatever." She trailed off and turned to face the doors when it was clear that 1) the guy was ignoring her and 2) there was no way Jayce Kazan had any relatives.

Or she didn't think he did. He'd never mentioned any—not that he would ever have a reason to talk to *her* in a one-on-one situation. He was hundreds of years older and an enforcer for the Council. But Kat hadn't said anything either and Natalia and the tall, gorgeous female shifter had become friends ever since she and Jayce had moved permanently to the ranch.

Natalia pulled out her cell phone to text Kat to let her know she'd be arriving in a minute when the elevator jerked to a halt and an alarm blared. Whipping her head around, she glared at the tall jackass who'd pressed the emergency stop. He wasn't putting off any hostile vibes or attempting to crowd her and it was the only reason she was containing herself. "What's the matter with you?"

His eyes narrowed. "Did you say Jayce?"

"I swear to God, if you don't release that button I'm going to flay you alive." If some asshole thought he could trap her in an elevator he was in for a surprise. She knew she probably shouldn't have started in with the threats right away but she couldn't help it. Before her mom died she'd always told her she needed to get ahold of her temper—and her sailor mouth. Natalia didn't bother trying to watch her mouth. And her temper, hell, she came by that honestly. Her mother had no one to blame but herself for that trait.

Taking her by surprise, the giant shifter's mouth quirked up. "You're quick-tempered for such a little thing."

Her canines and claws descended. "You want to find out what this little thing can do?" She had no idea why she was getting so worked up but this guy was bringing out the crazy in her. She felt edgy and restless being near him. It was unsettling and she didn't like it.

He let the red button go, but eyed her as the elevator jerked into motion again. "Were you referring to Jayce Kazan a moment ago?" *Now* he was all politeness and civility. But she wasn't fooled. This guy was a class A predator. She could see it in every taut line of his muscular body.

The truth was, she hadn't been hitting on him but now she noticed that he was actually pretty good-looking. Okay, more than pretty good. And for some reason, that annoyed her. "So what if I was?" Turning away from him, she shoved her phone back in her pocket and watched the numbers fly by on the elevator and pretended to ignore him.

"He's mated?"

God, what rock was this guy living under? Okay, maybe it wasn't exactly common knowledge so she should give the guy a break, but he rubbed her the wrong way. And he'd been rude to her so he could suck it. She shrugged noncommittally.

The elevator stopped on level nine and she could feel the pulsing beat of the club music even before the doors whooshed open. Hell yeah, time to work. Her entire body hummed with anticipation. She couldn't believe her Alpha had okayed letting her be part of this mission and there was no way she'd screw it up. She was tired of life on the ranch. Her old Alpha had tried to keep the entire pack sequestered from society, and it wasn't like she was happy he was dead, but she liked Connor as an Alpha a hell of a lot better. He understood that they needed to interact more with humans and he seemed to genuinely like the other species. She did too.

Humans were amazing. They were fragile compared to supernatural beings but so many lived like they'd never die. It was inspiring.

"So what are you doing here by yourself, little wolf?" the guy asked as she stepped out of the elevator.

Immediately she was blasted with too many sensory things. Music, smells, voices . . . it was all so much. This place was supposedly owned by someone supernatural so why did they have the music so loud? With their sensitive hearing it was aggravating. Most supernatural-owned places she'd been to in the past had been conscious of their clientele and kept the music at a lower level.

She glanced up at the male, but didn't stop walking toward the entrance where a security guy stood next to a roped-off entryway. It actually wasn't a condescending question—though the "little" part annoyed her. Most shifters traveled in packs so maybe he was just being curious. "I'm not by myself." Well, she wouldn't be in a few minutes. She was meeting Aiden, Teresa, and Kat. Jayce, Connor, Erin, and Noah were also here, but they weren't going to interact with her group. They were doing their own reconnaissance and breaking into the offices and back rooms of this club while she, Aiden, Teresa, and Kat were simply hanging out, drinking and pretending to party while they surveyed the club surroundings. She almost asked this shifter why he was by himself but she didn't want to open herself up for any more conversation.

The bouncer—who was definitely a vampire—didn't even card them as they approached, just smelled them.

It was subtle but Natalia recognized what he was doing. He gave them a quick nod, then unhooked the heavy, velvet rope and let them pass.

"Let me buy you a drink," the male said as he kept pace with her.

"No, thank you." She glanced around the expansive room. It was three stories and the first floor had three bars and a dance floor. High-top tables surrounded three sides of the dance area. From her position she could see private areas on the second floor—which was technically the tenth floor overall of the industrial building. But supposedly no one could get to the lower floors except through internal stairwells from this dance area.

The sectioned-off rooms looked like opera boxes. Some had curtains pulled back, revealing that they were empty, while others blocked whatever was going on inside. Natalia could only guess for what. On the floor above that she saw flashes of purple strobe lights, but glass encased the balcony areas overlooking the first-floor dance area. She couldn't hear any extra music so maybe that floor was insulated well.

As she scanned the crowd she spotted Aiden and Teresa dancing among the throng of shifters, vamps, fae, and some other creatures whose origins she didn't even want to guess. Kat was sitting at one of the high-top tables and when she spotted her, the tall female smiled.

The male next to her sighed. "Listen, I just . . . do you seriously know Jayce Kazan?"

Natalia looked at him, assessing him. She had no clue who this stranger was or what his intentions might be and she sure as hell wasn't leading him to Jayce's new mate. Kat could take care of herself but Natalia wasn't going to point her out to anyone. She shrugged. "Kind of. I met him a while ago. It's not like we hang out or anything. What's your deal? And what's your name?"

The male watched her as if he didn't believe her. Which he shouldn't since she was lying. Sort of. She'd worded her answer so she wouldn't put off that metallic scent associated with lies.

"My name's Aldric." Now he watched her even more intently, those grayish green eyes turning mercurial. He stared as if he expected some sort of recognition. She just raised her eyebrows, unsure how to respond. She didn't want to give him her name. After a few long moments, he stepped back. "I'm sorry I bothered you. Enjoy your evening." Then he disappeared into the crowd.

Natalia watched him walk away, then glanced at Kat. Instead of fighting through the crowds she texted her friend. *Something weird just happened. Going to the restroom on the west side. Meet me there in ten minutes.*

Kat checked her phone, answered okay, and didn't look in Natalia's direction again. They were going to act as if they didn't know each other. Which was all part of their plan if anything out of the ordinary happened. It wasn't like her conversation had been particularly strange but it had been odd enough and she wanted to let Kat know. Then Kat could easily let her mate know through their telepathic bondmate link.

This floor of the club was thick with supernatural beings. The scent of sex filled the air and as she walked past the dance floor she realized there were actually people having sex on it. Vamps, of course. Hedonistic maniacs. She shook her head and kept her pace steady, but not too fast as to draw attention to herself.

As she made her way through the crowd she passed a couple of vamp cocktail waitresses on roller skates carrying trays of drinks—some of which she could tell were blood. They wore skirts that might as well be Band-Aids and had little pasties over their nipples. Why even bother wearing them?

At the west side exit, she pushed open a heavy metal door and stepped into a brightly lit hallway. When the door shut, all the sound and scents from before faded. Damn, that was some serious insulation. From the recon her pack had done and the map Ryan had given everyone a couple of days ago to study, she knew there was a bathroom down this hallway on the right side. There were a lot of other doorways though and the pack wasn't yet sure what was behind them.

She quickly ducked into the bathroom and was relieved to find the three stalls empty. The place was all marble, mirrors, and gold finishing touches. After a few minutes passed she sat on one of the cream tufted settees and checked her phone again. No message. She was supposed to get an earpiece from Kat, but until then she was in the dark.

When she realized she'd been tapping her booted foot against the tile at a rapid rate she forced herself to stop. Another glance at her phone told her ten minutes had passed. Feeling uneasy, she stood and started to head for the door when the sound of a woman screaming outside the bathroom rent the air.

Natalia raced out the door to find a half-naked

woman covered in blood running down the hall. Her eyes were wide and her blond hair was tangled all around her face. "Help me!" she screamed.

Out of an instinct to help, Natalia unsheathed her claws. When the human woman saw them, however, she screamed even louder and jerked to a halt. Cringing, Natalia drew them back in and held up her hands to show she meant no harm. "I can help you. What's—"

She stopped talking as two angry-looking vampires rounded the corner at the end of the hallway, blood dripping down their faces and bare chests. They slowly stalked down the hall, looking like rabid but very deadly predators. Something was wrong with their eyes. They glowed bright amber in the way of vamps, but . . . something was off about both males. She just couldn't figure out what it was.

Oh, shit.

The woman looked back and forth between the vamps and Natalia, raw fear in her eyes. Natalia wanted to move between the female and the two males but didn't want to spook her. She held out a hand. "Come to me." The human just stared at her, as if frozen in a state of shock.

At the sound of a door opening, Natalia swiveled. Her claws once again unsheathed as she turned to face the new danger. Instead of a threat she found Kat slipping into the hallway. Her pale blue eyes widened and went pure wolf as she saw the woman and the vamps. Without pause, she unzipped her black jacket and tossed a blade to Natalia.

With her quick reflexes she caught it midair.

"Take the human to the restroom!" Kat ordered. "Jayce and the others are on their way," she murmured low enough for only Natalia to hear.

Holding the blade tightly she nodded and faced the human again. "We can help you."

The female took a jerky step forward, her eyes still wide and a little manic, but it was clear she'd decided to trust them. Probably thought they were the lesser of two evils. Holding out her blade-free hand, Natalia wrapped an arm around the bleeding woman and started to usher her down the hall. As soon as she got her to relative safety she was coming back to help Kat.

She knew for a fact that the enforcer's mate could take care of herself—she trained with her mate and his enforcers-in-training almost every damn day of the week—but Natalia would do anything to help a pack-mate and she wouldn't let Kat fight alone.

As she practically dragged the now-sobbing human down the hallway another door burst open. A male vampire with descended fangs appeared in the doorway. Natalia shoved the human behind her. The vamp moved like the wind, slamming Natalia against the wall.

Her back ached as plaster splintered behind her but before she could move, the vamp's eyes widened, turning bright amber as he looked down between their bodies.

The blade Kat had given her was embedded in his chest. Natalia shoved forward deeper and twisted it hard. Shock registered on his face—right before he turned to ash.

Chapter 3

A iden casually leaned back against the edge of one of the polished wooden bars. It was the only one not in use on this floor of the club. He had a drink in one hand as he surveyed their surroundings. Though his stance was casual, he was wound tight.

Kat had disappeared a few seconds ago, telling him and Teresa that she was meeting Natalia in one of the restrooms. He knew Teresa wanted to go because Natalia was her youngest sister, but she'd stayed with him to give Natalia the space she'd been craving. Teresa's sister was starting to assert her independence and his Alpha wanted to give it to her. Something Aiden respected. Not all Alphas were like that. No, they still had ridiculously archaic ideas about how their pack members, especially the females, should be treated.

Teresa came in from the dance floor after having been dancing with a couple of female vamps, her eyes alert even though she fake-stumbled once for show as she headed toward him. Tonight, they were just party-goers. Technically Aiden could have come in here and put all the cameras in place himself, but without a cover date, he'd known females would have been coming on to him all night. It wasn't arrogance, just experience. The thought of any strange female sidling up to him made him nauseous and they couldn't afford to be noticed.

As Teresa reached him, she snuggled in close and wrapped her arms around him as he placed the final video camera on the underside of the lip of the bar. With her covering his movements, there was no way anyone would see what he was doing. The device was small and the same dark color as the bar. Ryan had chosen them specifically for this mission. "Visual?" he asked Ryan through the earpiece once he felt the camera lock into place with the fast-acting adhesive.

"Once Teresa moves . . ."

Teresa gracefully stepped around Aiden, moving to the other side of him where she leaned against the bar next to him. Now that the last camera was in place they didn't have to playact anymore. She took the same casual pose as Aiden as she watched the dance floor.

"Perfect angle," Ryan said. "Good work, you guys. When Kat and Natalia get back you all can get out of there."

With the nearly undetectable cameras in place Ryan would be trying to get shots of anyone and anything they could use to figure out just who the hell was selling some weird type of vamp blood that was having a strange effect on humans. "Kat?" he murmured.

When she didn't respond, he inwardly frowned. "Can you hear her, Teresa?"

"No."

"Neither can I," Ryan muttered. "I think it might be some sort of interference."

Aiden straightened, ready to go find both her and Natalia. But he wanted Teresa out of there first. "Teresa, why don't you head out . . ." Aiden trailed off as a flash of dark hair caught his eye.

The blue-black color shimmered under the moving strobe lights. All he could see was the back of the female's head, but something inside his chest started to tingle.

The sensation was odd, almost painful. Ignoring it, he pushed off the bar, as if pulled toward her by a magnet.

"Aiden?" Teresa asked, her voice filled with concern.

He ignored her and kept walking. Right now he needed to see the woman's face. His inner wolf clawed at him, more agitated than he'd ever been, demanding that he hunt down the dark-haired female. It didn't matter that he knew *she* was dead. That whatever the hell he was thinking was fucking *impossible*. He was like a puppet on a string as he shoved his way across the dance floor. Or more like a possessed madman.

He could have circled around it, but didn't want to waste the time. Heart pounding, he pushed right through a vamp couple screwing on the dance floor. The male shouted at him, but Aiden turned on him, canines bared. He was barely leashing his inner wolf at this point.

Whatever he looked like was enough to make the

male back off and scramble away. When Aiden looked back across the dance floor, he couldn't see the female anymore.

No!

A small part of him knew that he was completely risking the mission, but he couldn't stop his actions. His heart beat out of control and that odd sensation had intensified. It wasn't just a tingling anymore, but full-fledged adrenaline raging through him, punching out to all his nerve endings like a battering ram. Everything around him was out of focus as his wolf threatened to take over. He'd never been out of control like this. Not even as a cub. The crushing hope intermixed with the agony of reality telling him this wasn't real. What he was seeing simply couldn't be. Maybe he was having some sort of breakdown.

As he reached the edge of the dance floor, he jumped onto the nearest high-top table. Oh yeah, his Alpha was going to be pissed about this later, but Aiden didn't care. He had to find the female. Where had she gone . . . ? His gaze landed on her profile. And there was no mistaking who he was looking at.

Larissa Danesti. His dead bondmate.

Everything around him funneled out as he stared in awe. Even his wolf went completely still for a few heartbeats. Everything around him fell away. The club, the patrons, the scents and sounds, until all he could see was Larissa. Grief tightened his throat. He hadn't even dared to think her name for over sixty years. It hurt too much.

Her blue-black hair fell in soft waves halfway down

her back. Exactly the same length it had been the last fateful day he'd seen her. From one of the purest vampire bloodlines, Larissa was a bloodborn. A daywalker. Impossibly strong.

Both her parents had been royalty and she'd been everything to them. Until he'd come along and she'd dared to sully herself with a mindless animal—as they'd considered him. Royal bloodborns like that considered anyone *not* a vampire beneath them.

But she'd died. He hadn't seen it, but he'd felt the bondmate link between them shatter into a million pieces. Even that hadn't stopped him from searching for her, from following her and hearing from her parents that she was indeed dead. The best part of him had died that day. If he hadn't joined Connor's pack when he did, he'd probably be dead by now. He'd been on a dark path of destruction for years after her death and his own demise had been inevitable.

As if she felt his stare, Larissa turned to look at him. The indigo-blue eyes he remembered as being fierce were filled with confusion . . . and fear as they locked on him.

The fear was too much. He tried to take a step forward, but his surroundings rushed back in an instant and that adrenaline surge slammed right into his heart. He wasn't sure what was happening. All his muscles pulled tight as he half shifted to his lupine form.

Larissa clutched her chest, staring at him as if she didn't know him. When her eyes rolled back in her head and she collapsed he could feel her pain shooting through him just as agonizing as his own.

Shit. It was the bonding link clicking back into place. He had no doubt in his mind that was what had happened. He might not know how the fuck it had happened, but that wasn't some look-alike. The female was Larissa.

His.

His wolf clawed at him, demanding he go to her, protect her. He was in complete agreement. His clothes tore and he cried out in pain, but it was more of a growl as he tumbled from the table. He barely felt it as he slammed against the hard floor. Writhing in pain as he struggled for control of his wolf, he was vaguely aware of the music shutting off and everyone around them scattering.

Except Teresa.

She was there, staring down at him in concern as she spoke to someone. Must be Ryan. Or maybe Kat.

"We have a big problem," Teresa said, as if from the other end of a tunnel.

He ignored his packmate.

Right now he didn't care about anything or anyone but his *bondmate*. He needed to get to Larissa. Forcing himself to sit up, he took a deep breath and got his wolf under control. The fur that had sprouted on his hands receded. For a moment he was completely in charge. That adrenaline rush that had spiked in his system was evening out.

Until a male picked Larissa up from the club floor. Daring to touch what was Aiden's.

Then he lost his shit.

Giving up control to his beast, he roared in rage.

Though it felt like an eternity, only seconds passed as his bones shifted and realigned and his wolf took over. By now everyone had been smart enough to scatter.

Except the stupid vamp trying to take Larissa away. He held her limp body in his arms, using her as a shield as he slowly tried to step backward.

There was nowhere to go, nowhere to hide. Keeping a pulse on his surroundings so he wouldn't be ambushed, Aiden stalked toward the male and Larissa. He swatted a stool out of the way with a large front paw. It splintered, the pieces clattering to the floor noisily.

The fear rolling off the vamp was pungent. Aiden snarled and jumped onto a large round table barely fifteen feet away from them. It creaked, but held his weight. It wouldn't take much for him to reach the vamp now. And he had no doubt he could kill that fucker without grazing a hair on Larissa's head. Because he'd die before hurting her.

The vamp must have sensed his intent because he dropped Larissa and ran, sprinting through the club with a preternatural speed. The predator in Aiden wanted to give chase, to hunt him down, but he reined it in for the stronger impulse to protect what was his.

Using all the strength in his hind legs, he jumped from the table and landed right next to Larissa's still form. Her chest rose and fell steadily and she appeared unharmed. But he wouldn't be satisfied until he knew for sure.

"Aiden, look at me." He heard Teresa's soft voice nearby, but he couldn't look at her. He refused. All his attention was on Larissa.

"You need to shift back," Teresa whispered urgently.

He ignored her. That wasn't happening. Stepping closer to Larissa, he stopped only when her body was completely under him. No one could get to her without going through him. They'd have to kill him first.

"Aiden!" a strong, familiar voice shouted.

His head whipped around to see Connor and Noah moving around the middle bar. Connor had something in his hand. A gun. But that didn't make sense.

"Aiden, snap out of it. Shift back. Now!" his Alpha commanded with authority.

Part of him was compelled to listen, but . . . no. He could protect Larissa better as a wolf. His inner animal latched on and dug deep, refusing to give up control. Aiden snarled at Connor, baring his canines in a clearly aggressive, defiant display.

The room, which had already quieted down, went deathly silent. Connor's eyes went wide in shock before they narrowed. He thought he heard someone murmur something about him going feral.

Feral? That's when it registered what he must look like. Drawing on strength he didn't know he had, Aiden forced the change. No matter how much he needed to protect Larissa he had to explain to his pack what was going on. So they would protect her. She was all that mattered.

Agony pierced through him as his bones shifted against his wolf's will until he was crouching naked over Larissa's still unconscious body. He attempted to stand when something slammed into his chest. He stumbled back from the force of it and saw the raised gun in Connor's hand.

The deepest sense of betrayal ricocheted through him until he looked down and realized it was a tranquilizer dart. Connor was trying to control the situation, not kill him. It meant he could be trusted. Something his human side knew completely, but his wolf was agitated and wanted to take Larissa far away from everyone and everything. Including his Alpha.

"Bondmate," Aiden managed to rasp out before a bitter blackness engulfed him.

Chapter 4

Teresa stared in horror as Aiden fell back, unconscious. The scent of his link to the female vampire was unmistakable. It reminded her of a cold winter night. Crisp, fresh, and . . . powerful. Whoever that female was, she retained a lot of power. Teresa didn't understand how this was possible when Aiden had never been bonded before. It was clear Connor was just as confused so she didn't question him.

Before any of them could move, six huge vamps jumped down into the middle of the dance floor from one of the balconies above and faced off with her and her packmates. She controlled her fear as the few stragglers who'd been lingering after Aiden's freak-out scattered toward the elevators.

"Ryan?" she said quietly through the earpiece, but got no answer.

Connor, Noah, and Erin, who'd appeared only a second ago, were the only ones here. She wanted to know where Jayce, Kat, and more important, her sister Natalia were. Natalia was so young and she hated that her youngest sister had insisted on coming tonight. But their Alpha had allowed it so she'd had no choice.

It was clear her earpiece wasn't working so Teresa did the only thing she could. She strode toward Connor and lined up next to him along with their other packmates. They were all warriors, unlike her, but that didn't mean she was going to tuck tail and run if these vamps wanted to challenge them.

Because that's what it appeared these vamps were doing. Their posture was tense, their vibes hostile. Of the six, one stepped forward, his boots thudding ominously against the wood dance floor as he glared at Connor. He was clearly the leader. "Connor Armstrong." He practically spat the name, his amber eyes glowing bright and unnaturally dilated. He looked almost stoned, but she wasn't sure if vampires could even get high. Something was off about the tall male.

Her Alpha just stood there, perfectly calm, though she could feel the power radiating off him. She'd seen him in action only a couple of times, but it was enough to know that he could rip most of these vamps apart with ease. "Do I know you?" Connor's voice was a deadly blade.

"We haven't met." And it was clear the vamp didn't plan on introducing himself as he continued. "But I'm going to give you the courtesy of getting the fuck out of my club in the next sixty seconds unharmed. Take your wolf and go, but the female vamp stays."

"They're bondmates. She comes with us." It didn't

matter that Connor had never met the female, that none of the pack had known about her—if she was Aiden's, she was one of theirs.

Simple as that. It was one of the reasons Teresa was proud to have Connor as an Alpha. The male was absolutely loyal.

"Then it seems we have a problem." The vamp made a quick gesture with his hand and his warriors fanned out.

Teresa turned to the left, keeping her focus on one of the vamps. He watched her closely and made a gross flicking gesture with his tongue as he grabbed his crotch.

Ugh. She kept her expression cool, not wanting anyone to know she was afraid.

"Why do you want the female?" Connor asked, his voice still calm, though his stance was tense.

Instead of answering, the lead vampire took a menacing step toward Aiden and the female.

In the span of a heartbeat Connor shifted to his wolf form. Teresa followed suit, letting the change come over her. She bit back a cry of discomfort as her wolf took over, shredding her barely there dress. Everything around her came into sharper focus. By the time she'd shifted, so had the others—except for Erin, who remained in her human form. With two blades in her hands, it was clear the female enforcer knew how to use them.

Teresa focused on the snarling vampire closest to her. His claws and fangs had extended and she could see the hilt of a blade peeking out from his partially unzipped jacket. So he had at least one weapon, probably more.

"One more chance to leave—"

Clearly done listening to threats, Connor lunged at the vamp. All hell broke loose. Out of the corner of her eye Teresa could see her Alpha and Erin taking on two vamps while Noah grappled with one. Knowing they were more than capable, Teresa kept her focus on the vampire in front of her.

He wore dark pants, a dark shirt, boots, and a leather jacket. His black hair was cropped close and he had that same bleary-eyed look in his bright amber eyes as the other vampires. "Why don't you shift back, little wolf? You and I can have some fun," he crooned in a creepy singsong voice.

Gross. She had no doubt what kind of fun he referred to. Baring her canines, she growled low in her throat. She may be small for a shifter, but she could take on one vamp.

Whipping out the blade with an impressive speed, he lunged at her. She dodged to the side, missing what would have been a blow to the chest. Dancing away from him, she tried to tune out the growling and cries of pain around her. It sounded like the vamps were losing.

When the vampire rushed her again, she jumped onto a tabletop, using it to propel herself away from him. She landed on the far side of the dance floor and spun to face him. If she could tire this vamp out she would. Or at least frustrate him enough into letting his guard down. Then she'd strike hard and fast. It was something her deceased father had taught her and her sisters. Even though she wasn't the strongest she could fight smart.

Though it felt like an eternity passed as she dodged his attempted attacks, she knew it hadn't even been a full minute when the vampire started to show annoyance.

Letting out a snarl of rage, he rushed at her, fangs descended and blade held firmly in his hand. This time she wasn't going to evade him. Crouching low, she prepared to strike when a large dark brown wolf came out of nowhere, slamming into the vampire.

Ryan.

The male wrapped his jaws around the vamp's neck and cut all the way to the bone, ripping the creature's head free in seconds. The vamp hadn't even had time to struggle or fight. If she'd been in her human form, she would have gasped at the beauty of Ryan's impressive display of power.

In her peripheral vision she was aware that the fighting was over and her pack had dominated, but she had eyes only for Ryan. For so damn long she'd wanted him, hungered after him, and for a brief moment when their two packs originally joined she'd thought there might be something there. The sexual tension between them was off the charts and she knew for a fact that he'd warned a few males away from asking her out—but he'd never made a move.

He didn't glance back at the dead vampire as he hurried to her. Taking her by surprise, he nuzzled his nose against hers before he circled her body, checking to make sure she was unharmed. She didn't even think to stop him, though his actions were those of a mated male. Ryan drove her insane with his hot and cold routine, but right now her adrenaline was pumping and she didn't mind a little overprotectiveness. Unlike the others here she wasn't used to fighting. Technically she hadn't even fought the vamp, but her insides were shaking something fierce and Ryan's presence comforted her. She wished they were in human form so he could hold her, but she figured he probably wouldn't anyway. Not if his past behavior was any indication. Even when she'd been poisoned he'd stayed away from her. That sudden thought brought up a rush of pain and she automatically tried to back away from him.

But Ryan wouldn't let her. Once he was sure she was okay, he sidled up next to her and stood so that their shoulders touched as they faced the others. His ears were pricked forward. Clearly he was alert for more danger. Dragging her gaze away, Teresa looked at the others.

Erin stood with her blade against one vampire's neck and Connor had his jaws wrapped around another male's throat. Still in wolf form, Noah growled menacingly at the vamp Erin had pinned. Three more vamps lay dead at their feet.

Connor made a growling sound low in his throat and Noah immediately moved to stand near him. Her Alpha released the vamp and shifted back to his human form. The vampire seemed as if he was in shock as he slumped against the floor.

"Change back," Connor ordered everyone.

Though Teresa wasn't keen on being naked in front of Ryan, she didn't have a choice and knew she had more important things to worry about anyway. Her packmates had just killed some unknown vamps and she still didn't know where her sister was.

After she'd shifted, she stood up and was surprised once again when Ryan went to stand in front of her. Reaching back, he held on to her hip as he tugged her close against him. With their bare bodies, her breasts rubbed against his back and a sharp spark of arousal shot through her like a lightning bolt. She placed her palms against that muscular expanse of skin and tried to step around him, but he growled. This new territorial display should have annoyed her, but she'd been craving this from him from the moment they'd met.

"Stay." A subtle demand.

That one word rolled through her, making her entire body tingle in awareness. She knew exactly what he was doing. He didn't want the others to see her naked. As shifters it was inevitable that packmates would see one another naked often and nudity wasn't that big of a deal among their kind. But right now he was staking some sort of claim. She could feel it in a bone-deep way. Considering the way he'd been acting the past few months it should piss her off. Hell, she shouldn't be feeling anything right now other than worry, but with the feel of Ryan pressed up against her, it was hard to think straight or to stay mad at the confusing wolf. So she did the one thing that felt right. Leaning forward, she wrapped her arms around his front, pressing her body close to his.

Shuddering, he laid his hands over hers and squeezed gently.

"Who the hell are you?" Connor asked one of the vamps, his voice low and deadly.

Teresa peered around Ryan's body to see Connor, Noah, and Erin facing off with the two remaining vamps. Aiden and his bondmate were still unconscious on the floor. Worry for them made her antsy so she tightened her grip on Ryan.

"What . . ." The mouthy vampire from before looked around at all of them, confusion on his face. He didn't have that strange, glassy-eyed look as before either. "What the hell happened? You killed my friends!"

Before anyone responded, one of the doors burst open and Jayce stalked in. And he looked pissed. At his presence, the vamps took off, racing toward the nearest exit. Using impressive vampiric speed they were gone in a flash.

Without pause Noah and Erin took off after them. Connor started to leave but Jayce held up a hand. Teresa knew the Alpha didn't follow anyone's orders, but it was clear Jayce knew something.

"We have a problem. Natalia killed a high-ranking vampire with one of my blades. I gave them to Kat as extra protection tonight. The male . . ." He glanced at Teresa before focusing on Connor. "His brother's a member of the Brethren."

The Brethren was a group of four ancient vampires who more or less ruled over all vamps. They were old, powerful, and all bloodborns—and her sister had just killed one of their relatives?

Shit.

Teresa swallowed hard at the ramifications. Ryan took her by surprise by turning around and grabbing onto her hips in a firm, immovable grip. With them naked, the way he tugged her close was impossibly intimate. Need rose up inside her like a wave. She tried to shove it down, but it was impossible.

Reaching out, Ryan cupped her cheek, his dark eyes flashing with too many emotions to define. As she leaned back to look up at him, it registered just how tall he was. The male was even bigger than their Alpha. Right now he had a fierce, determined look on his face.

"Nothing will happen to Natalia. I swear it." The words were a sincere vow.

She nodded, more than a little stunned by the way Ryan was acting. "Okay." This was a side to Ryan she'd wanted all along, but now that he was being so possessive she didn't trust that it would last much longer than the dangerous situation.

It didn't matter anyway. Neither did his vow because if her sister had just killed someone incredibly important, it affected their pack and their immediate family. Teresa had already lost too many packmates, she refused to lose anyone else.

Chapter 5

The sound of Connor's voice drifted over Aiden. He struggled to surface from the consuming haze around him. Panic drove him toward consciousness as he tried to remember what was so important, why he felt so different.

Larissa.

His eyes snapped open and he realized he was sitting in the middle seat of one of the pack's SUVs. And his bondmate was next to him. She was still unconscious, but alive. Without thinking, he wrapped his arm around her shoulders and pulled her close. He was still naked except for the jacket Connor must have thrown over his waist.

Larissa buried her face against his neck and sighed. Which told him she was more or less sleeping rather than unconscious. His inner wolf immediately quieted at the feel of her and it took all his restraint not to haul her into his lap. Just holding her soothed every part of him. Through her clothes he could feel her body heat, though her core temperature was much cooler than his or even humans. But not as cool as regular vamps. As a bloodborn she had a slightly higher temperature. Leaning down to her neck, he inhaled her familiar scent and let it roll over him. She smelled like the forest in winter. And all his. She called to him on the most primal level—had from the moment he'd first seen her.

Connor was driving and he flicked Aiden a quick glance in the rearview mirror as he set his cell phone down on the center console. "Glad you're awake. How're you feeling?"

"Like I got run over by a truck." His chest ached and something told him it was because of the newly cemented bonding link, not the dart hit he'd taken. He looked out the window at their surroundings to see that they were driving down a quiet two-lane highway that wasn't familiar. The moon and stars illuminated the road and it was almost three so he'd been out for a few hours. "Where is everyone?"

Connor's expression was grim. "Natalia killed a Brethren member's brother and we killed a handful of vamps but two got away—Erin and Noah are tracking them. Ryan and Teresa have taken Natalia back to the ranch. Kat and Jayce are taking a human who was kidnapped by those asshole vamps to a friend of Jayce's who can scrub her memories. The shit has hit the fan. Now how the hell is it that you have a bondmate? You told me she died."

He snorted. "I've never said those words to anyone." Sure, he'd insinuated it, but he'd never flat out said it. Deep down he'd never been able to admit that Larissa was gone forever even though on an intellectual level he'd known it had to be true. Without seeing her body with his own eyes, he and his wolf had rebelled at the thought of her being dead.

"It was implied." The angry edge to Connor's voice had Aiden straightening.

He remembered how he'd snarled at his Alpha in the club, basically challenging him. "I wasn't challenging you earlier."

Connor let out an exasperated sigh. "I know. Now . . ."

Aiden couldn't answer what he didn't know himself. He turned to look at Larissa. Her dark hair spilled over one of her shoulders in a soft cascade, covering the front of her black top. She snuggled closer to him. "I don't know how this is possible," he murmured, staring in awe at the female who had captured his heart so long ago. Even when he thought she'd died he hadn't been able to let go of her. Now he was glad he hadn't.

"That bondmate scent is strong. I don't understand how it appeared all of a sudden."

"Neither do I. It snapped before and I thought she was . . ." Yeah, he couldn't say it. The only way bondmates were separated was in death. "But clearly she's alive." And he wasn't questioning it. The link was firmly in place, he could feel himself tethered to Larissa in a way only bonded mates could be. And every supernatural being could scent their joining. Hell yeah, no males would even think about looking at his female now.

"I'm taking you to one of our out-of-town cabins. I

wasn't sure what the deal is with her and, no offense, whether she can be trusted. I want to make sure she gets inside before sunrise."

"She's a daywalker." Aiden spoke before he could think to rein himself in. A proprietary, primitive urge to protect Larissa from everyone, including his Alpha, rose up inside him.

"Damn," Connor muttered. "What bloodline is she from? Whose coven does she belong to and how long were you two bonded before . . . What the hell happened, man? How did your bondmate link reappear all of a sudden?" The last part was more of a statement than a question.

Aiden shifted uncomfortably in his seat. He loved his Alpha, but he wasn't sure how much he should reveal about Larissa. Not when she was from one of the strongest lines. And not when he still had too many unanswered questions about where she'd been the past sixty plus years. "She's from a royal line and we were bonded for less than a month." Though it had felt like an eternity.

The first time they'd met, he'd amused her with his arrogance. At least that's what she'd told him later. She'd thought he was an obnoxious little pup and had planned to teach him a lesson in humility—until they'd kissed. The erotic dance between them had been earthy and raw. Days later under the full moon they'd been bonded.

Neither of their families had forgiven them, especially since it had been assumed she'd eventually mate with another strong vampire line. It had been hard for both of them, but harder for her at the rejection from her family. At five hundred years old she'd been entrenched in the politics and life of her coven. Not to mention she'd been the apple of her parents' eye. They'd turned her out because of her choice of mate. Deep down he'd always wondered if she'd regretted bonding with him, or even resented him. He'd never felt anything through their link to indicate she did, but he'd lived with the fear.

Connor let out a curse. "She's royalty? Are you fucking kidding me? What . . . ? How . . . ?" He let out another curse, this one more annoyed than angry. "When she wakes up we'll talk and see about taking her back to the ranch. There's a lot of shit going down that I need to figure out, and right now I can't worry about a vamp's presence there. Not with the cubs around," he said almost apologetically.

It should have offended Aiden, but he understood. Connor was Alpha and had to look out for his entire pack, especially the cubs. He couldn't just bring an unknown vampire into their midst even if she was Aiden's bondmate. Not without knowing more about the situation.

He ran a hand over Larissa's back, and cursed his shaking hand. He was terrified he'd wake up and find out this was all a dream. "How's Natalia doing?" The sweet shifter was young and a little outspoken, but killing someone for the first time could be jarring.

"Okay. I've got Ryan running all the video he took to scan the faces of those who left and we also snagged recordings from the security room."

"You know who owns the place?"

"Not yet but we're working on it. I've already sent a couple of warriors to stake out the building, see if anyone shows up."

Under normal circumstances Aiden would be more invested in what was going on, but with Larissa in his arms he found it hard to think about anything other than her. When she shifted against him, murmuring something under her breath, he froze.

She was waking up.

One of her elegant hands slid up his chest and wrapped around the back of his neck as she nuzzled the other side of his neck. His entire body shuddered at the contact and he had to force his body under control.

Unfortunately that was impossible.

Her hand slid back down his chest and her fingers curled against his skin when she suddenly froze and pulled her head back. Her indigo eyes met his with pure confusion. She looked at him, then Connor, then back at him. It wasn't overt, but she scented the air, as if she was unsure what they were. Which didn't make sense. She knew him.

"Larissa," he whispered. "How are you feeling?"

"Who are you? Where am I?" She spoke in perfect English but with a slight lilting accent that couldn't really be linked to any country.

When he'd met her she'd spoken twelve languages, English being one of them. Hearing her talk had always brought Aiden joy, but now she stared at him as if she didn't know him. And he scented her fear.

True fear. Sharp and pungent. From the one female

he'd do anything for. Would die for. And she was afraid of *him*. There was no acidic stench of a lie followed by her words either. She didn't know who he was. Aiden felt as if he'd been gutted. "You don't know me?"

Watching him warily, she slowly backed up until she was at the SUV door. "Should I?" She seemed to finally register his state of undress. "Why are you naked?" she shouted.

"Larissa, it's me. Aiden—"

She moved with a wicked fast speed, turning and punching the whole door off the SUV. The metal groaned as it snapped off and slammed against the road with a sickening crunch behind them. Connor slammed on the brakes as Aiden lunged for her. She was too quick, diving out the door while they were still moving. She was a blur of movement, her hair fanning out behind her as she flew across the snowy embankment next to the highway and disappeared into the trees.

Aiden didn't waste time. He dove from the vehicle and had gone wolf before his paws hit the snow.

Panic thrummed through Larissa as she raced through the forest. Trees and other foliage were a blur as she called on what little reserve of strength she had left. She was over five hundred and sixty years old but after sixty years in stasis she could feel the effects on her powers and even her body. Right now the cold actually affected her. Not much, but enough that she was aware of it and uncomfortable. That wasn't normal for her. She desperately needed to feed again.

She tore through the snowy landscape, aware with every beat of her heart that she was being chased. She could feel him behind her, closing fast despite her supernatural speed. A few days ago a witch named Magda had discovered her buried deep in the Carpathian Mountains. Apparently Larissa had been put into stasis, a coma-like state that rendered her virtually dead, for her own protection. A shifter named Aiden had coveted her for his own, and when she'd rejected him he'd waged a war on her coven. Until he could be eliminated her parents had wanted her protected. Unfortunately she didn't remember any of that. In fact, she couldn't remember a lot of things.

All she knew was that her parents were dead and a shifter named Aiden had killed them. So if that shifter in that vehicle was the same Aiden, she wasn't sticking around to let him attempt to hurt her. The male had been naked so she could only imagine his perverted intentions.

It seemed impossible that her parents were dead. Her mother had been strong, ancient, but her father— his power had been unimaginable. And Larissa couldn't understand why she'd agreed to go into stasis. It didn't make sense. She would have wanted to fight side by side with them.

But the witch hadn't been lying. Larissa could sense lies in a way similar to how shifters could scent them. And the female had saved Larissa. Magda had even sent her to North Carolina to meet up with some vampires who knew about her parents' killer.

Looked like he'd found her instead.

Though she hated running from any fight, she'd sensed the power from those two shifters and she wasn't even close to top fighting form. Truth be told, she was barely hanging on to consciousness. Images from her past moved in and out of her memory bank like photographs, like she was dreaming while she was awake. Some images she remembered, some she didn't. She had no idea what was real and what wasn't. It was jarring, confusing, and more than anything, she was so incredibly hungry.

The witch had managed to get her bagged blood—a strange, new experience Larissa didn't like—but not much. And Larissa hadn't trusted herself to feed from humans once she'd arrived in the United States. She was too hungry and not quite in control of herself and she didn't want to hurt anyone unnecessarily. She needed to drink supernatural blood. It was stronger and would help her gain control in a way weaker human blood couldn't.

The wind whistled eerily around her as she continued running. She needed to come up with a plan, but first she had to put distance between herself and those shifters, then get in contact with Magda. Her friend would help her. Of course she would also have to figure out where the hell she was first. Because right now she had absolutely no clue.

A wolf howled in the distance, spurring her on faster. It was him.

That male.

She wasn't sure how she knew it was him, but she did just as surely as she sensed him somewhere behind her. He was gaining on her and he was *close*. How did she even know that? No, she didn't. She *couldn't*. That was the fear and paranoia inside her. Right?

Slowing as she entered a clearing, Larissa looked in all directions. A small, frozen-over pond glistened under the moonlight, but there were only trees in every direction. Some were still green and full, but most were bare.

As she tried to decide where to go a blur of fur hurtled through the air at her. Before she could move, the all-white wolf slammed into her, tackling her to the ground. He rolled their bodies so he took the brunt of the fall.

Surprise ricocheted through her. When he shifted to human form and she found herself pinned underneath the Adonis-looking shifter with blond hair and dark eyes she immediately struck out at him. Weak or not, if this male had killed her parents she'd gut him.

Claws and fangs descended, she slashed at his middle, ripping open his stomach.

"Damn it, Larissa!" He managed to grab her wrists in an impossibly tight grip and hold them above her head, but she didn't stop.

It vaguely registered that he said her name in a familiar way. As if he had intimate knowledge of her. Kicking and bucking against him, she kneed him hard between the legs as she twisted around to bite his forearm.

The second his blood coated her tongue, a familiar sensation flowed through her with shocking intensity. The taste made her think of raw, earthy sex. She stilled underneath him. He remained on top of her, holding her, and when she met his gaze she could sense his wariness. But he wasn't trying to hurt her. And he hadn't been attacking her, just pinning her down and taking her blows.

She tensed when she heard someone nearby, their footfalls soft against the snow, barely discernible. The male heard it too and lifted his head, but he never took his dark gaze from hers. "Stay back, I've got this."

"Why do you taste familiar?" she whispered, battling confusion. His blood was still on her tongue and it made her think of dirty, sensual things that shocked her. Even more shocking, she wanted to drink from him.

The male's eyes bored into hers. Intense. Heated. "Because you've tasted every inch of my body, drank from me, defied your coven to be with me." The longing in his eyes pierced her. He meant every word he was saying. He wasn't lying. Or he didn't believe he was lying.

If it was true, she didn't remember any of it. She fought a shiver. Everything in her brain was muddled, and the pain intermixed with desire she saw in that dark gaze was too much. She was so fucking confused right now, and sensing his pain hurt her. Even if she didn't understand why, she felt his agony bone deep and she desperately wanted to comfort him. She swallowed hard and resisted that urge. "Why can I feel your pain?"

He loosened his grip, freeing her wrists. But he didn't sit back. Just placed his hands in the light layer of snow on either side of her head, that gaze locked on hers. "Because we're bondmates."

Chapter 6

Larissa stared at the shifter named Aiden and tried to wrap her mind around what he'd said. *Bondmates?* She knew exactly what that meant for shifters. Almost against her will, her eyes traveled over his muscular, toned body. The man was truly built like a warrior. He was all sharp lines she could easily imagine running her hands and mouth over. Shifters usually had great bodies, but he was perfection. It was actually ridiculous how flawless he was. As if he'd been cut from the purest marble. There was a dark edge to him that complemented that whole blond Adonis thing he had going on. And he made her feel . . . things. As her gaze landed between his legs, she blushed.

Actually blushed. Like a virgin.

As she moved her gaze back upward, she cringed at the sight of his blood. He was almost healed, but she'd caused that. For some reason the knowledge caused her great distress. "I'm sorry I hurt you." What the hell was wrong with her? The words escaped before she could stop herself. She couldn't believe she'd apologized to a shifter for anything. She was royalty and this shifter had basically kidnapped her.

"This is nothing." He didn't even seem fazed by his already mending wounds as he continued to watch her. "You don't remember me? Us?" There was such a note of agony in his voice that it pierced her.

Or maybe . . . Was that the connection she felt to him? The bondmate link? But how could she have bonded to a shifter? Or why? It didn't make sense. She was supposed to have mated to . . . someone. Someone from another coven. The name was on the tip of her tongue, but she couldn't remember. She shook her head. "No. How do I know you're even telling the truth?"

"You can't feel the link?"

Again she felt a punch of emotional pain flow through her. Damn it. She *felt* it. So he was being honest. Disbelief surged through her, but how could she fight the obvious truth? "Can you give me a little space?" With him so near it was hard to think.

When he rolled back on his heels—not bothering to try to cover up all that gorgeous nakedness—she sat up, but didn't stand. She didn't trust her legs yet. Wrapping her arms protectively around herself, she drew her knees up against her chest. It might be a display of fragility but right now she didn't care. She'd recently woken from a decades-long coma and was just finding out that she was bonded to a shifter. A shifter who had supposedly killed her parents. Now she wondered if even that was true. But why would Magda lie to her? She'd saved Larissa and hadn't asked for anything in return. "Did you kill my parents?"

He reeled back from her question as if she'd actually struck him and for some reason, guilt punched through her that she'd hurt him. Aiden shook his head. "Not even after the way they hurt you."

"Hurt me?" Her parents never would have done that.

He frowned, as if she should know what he was talking about. "By kicking you out of your coven, by denying you your place with your people."

She instantly started to refute his words, but something tickled in her memory bank. Not to mention she couldn't scent any lies from him. "So you didn't kill them? Then who did?"

He shrugged. "I have no clue—I didn't even know they were dead. I don't exactly run in the same circle as vampires. Especially after you . . . disappeared. My own pack kicked me out for bonding with you and I haven't been on that side of the pond since I thought you died." The last word came out as a whisper.

Another shot of agony sliced through her middle. "Stop doing that!"

He blinked, still crouching close to her but not touching. "Doing what?"

"I can feel your pain and I don't like it." Unexpected tears sprung to her eyes. What. The. Hell. She *never* cried.

He shook his head, those dark eyes searching hers. "I can't help it. We're bonded, Larissa. I've loved you since the moment we met and that feeling never died, even when I thought you had. The fact that you can't remember me, remember us, *kills* me."

Something told her he hated showing such weakness in front of not only her, but also the male shifter hovering quietly along the tree line behind them. "I'm sorry." She felt as if she was apologizing for a whole lot more than not remembering. Of course, she had no clue if that was correct. Her mind was a complete mess right now.

"We need to get out of here before someone sees the SUV by the road," the other male said quietly.

Aiden didn't turn around, but stood in all that gorgeous, naked glory. He held out a hand to her. "Come with me?" That was when she realized he was giving her a choice. Or at least the illusion of one.

In the deepest recesses of her mind she knew without a shadow of a doubt that if she ran, he would follow. Right now she had more questions than answers and despite what Magda had told her, Larissa knew this male wasn't lying. She could feel it in her soul. He hadn't killed her parents. And if he hadn't, that meant Magda was either a liar or misinformed. Larissa hoped she was just misinformed.

Either way, Larissa was going to take her chances with Aiden. Logically, it was the only thing that made sense. She was in a strange place with a huge chunk of her memory missing and it was clear this shifter wouldn't hurt her. The affection he felt for her and the way he was watching her, *that* couldn't be faked. Plus the thought of running from him, of leaving him, shattered her in a way she didn't understand. The invisible bond to him was strong, even if she didn't remember him.

Holding out a hand, she shivered when his strong, callused fingers clasped hers. When he pulled her close, running his other hand down her side and hip, she didn't even think to object when he squeezed her in a possessive way. The front of his very naked body was flush against hers and she ached to lean into him, to soak up all that heat. She placed her hands lightly on his chest, curling her fingers against him. He shuddered and it took all her restraint not to jump this male.

That alone told her there was something between them. There *had* to be. She would never let a stranger touch her so intimately, but this male was different and on an instinctive level she trusted him.

This male was hers. Even if her mind wasn't ready to accept it, her body flared to life in the most vivid way when he touched her. The situation was all wrong, but feeling him hold her this way, her nipples beaded tightly and her inner walls clenched with the need to be filled. Staring up into his brown eyes, she could feel everything around them fall away, as if he was the only thing that mattered in her world.

He definitely scented her desire because he half smiled in an almost arrogant, obnoxious way that was frustratingly familiar before he turned their bodies and wrapped a muscular arm around her shoulders. "Let's get someplace safe. Then we're talking and figuring out this mess."

Larissa slipped her arm around his waist and

squeezed proprietarily before she realized what she'd done. Oh yeah, she wanted him. There was no denying that. But why couldn't she remember him?

Teresa kept her arm wrapped tightly around Natalia's shoulders as they pulled into the parking structure at the ranch. She'd already texted Ana—even though she knew Connor had likely contacted her via their telepathic link—and her cousin had prepared hot cocoa for the distraught Natalia.

Teresa hadn't contacted her other sisters though. There was no sense in waking them up and Ana had such a calming influence on Natalia anyway.

"I can't believe I killed someone," her sister murmured as Ryan put the SUV in park.

Teresa hadn't exchanged many words with Ryan since they'd left the club because she'd been comforting her sister, but she planned to hash some things out with him once they were alone.

Teresa squeezed her sister's shoulder gently. "You were just defending yourself."

"And you and Kat saved that human from being hurt worse than she already was," Ryan said from the front.

Natalia shrugged, but laid her head against Teresa's shoulder and sniffled. In that moment she seemed so young. Teresa had been the first child born to their parents. Her sisters hadn't come until decades later so sometimes she felt more like a mother than a sister to all of them. With their parents now gone, even more so. "Ana's waiting up for us."

She raised her head. "Really?"

Teresa nodded and opened the door. Ryan got out too, but she ignored him as she walked with Natalia to the main house. She was still way too confused about his behavior from earlier and didn't have time to dwell on it. Not with Natalia so upset.

Ryan trailed after them until they reached the front porch, and then Teresa heard his boots softly moving toward the single guys' cabin. She let out a sigh of relief she hadn't even realized she'd been holding as she and Natalia stepped inside Ana and Connor's house.

They jerked to a halt when they saw Vivian, the ten-year-old jaguar cub Ana and Connor had adopted, sitting at the foot of the stairs in purple polka-dot pajamas. "What are you doing up?" Teresa asked.

"I couldn't sleep, then I heard Ana making cocoa and cookies. She told me Natalia was sad so I wanted to make sure you were okay." She turned those big dark eyes on Natalia, concern etched in every inch of her expression.

Teresa couldn't help but smile. Vivian was so mischievous but she had such a big heart.

"I am," Natalia said, holding her arms out for a hug.

Vivian threw herself into Natalia's embrace and Teresa knew things would be okay, at least for the night. Well, technically morning. They still had a whole mess of crap to worry about, especially since Natalia had killed someone so powerful and connected, but she could sense the relief rolling off her sister like a potent wave.

An hour later Natalia and Vivian were asleep in front of the fireplace as Ana walked Teresa to the front door. "Come by in a few hours, I'll make a big breakfast for the pack," Ana murmured low enough that she wouldn't disturb the others.

"I will. Have you heard from Connor?" Teresa hadn't wanted to ask in front of Natalia.

Ana nodded, her expression darkening. "Yeah. Nothing about . . ." She pointed toward the living room. "But apparently Aiden is mated to a vampire and she doesn't remember him. Connor doesn't think she's lying either."

Teresa rubbed a hand over her face. "What a mess." Tonight had gone nothing like anyone had planned.

"I know. Go get some rest." After Ana gave her a quick hug Teresa stepped outside.

Exhaustion swept over her as she headed back to the home she shared with her three sisters. Halfway there she paused and looked at the guys' cabin.

The houses and cabins at the Armstrong ranch spread out in a circle around the main house. The whole place was like a village, with each home far enough from the others that everyone had privacy but that they were still a close-knit community. The light from the main living room was on in the cabin where Ryan lived with some of the guys and Lucas, the cub he'd adopted. It was just one more thing about Ryan that she adored. He'd taken in a cub when he didn't have to and was the perfect father.

Even though it was late and she was about to pass out on her feet, Teresa headed to his place instead. She had questions and wanted some answers from him. Ryan couldn't just act all possessive in front of everyone and expect things to return to normal between them. Now that she didn't have an audience, she was going to sort this out. Because if he thought he could start acting all distant again, he was out of his mind.

After almost everyone had shredded their clothes at the club they'd had to change into the backup clothes they'd brought in duffel bags. Most shifters brought extra clothes everywhere they went. It was just standard from the time you were a cub. Ryan had given her one of his button-down flannel shirts, and even though he'd surprised her with the action, she hadn't fought him and insisted she wear her own spare clothes. She hadn't wanted to embarrass him by saying no in front of everyone and the truth was, she liked his woodsy scent on her.

Even if he was driving her crazy.

Her boots thudded softly against the steps as she ascended them and before she'd knocked the door flew open.

Ryan stood there, all six feet four inches of him. And he was shirtless. Raising his arms, he held on to the top of the doorframe as he silently watched her. For a moment her brain short-circuited as she drank in the sight of his bare upper body. She'd seen him earlier at the club, but she'd made it a point to avoid staring. Because she'd known if she had, she wouldn't have been able to stop at just looking. He had a smattering of dark hair on his muscular chest and his ripped abdomen tapered down in a V that made her think all sorts of wicked things.

Swallowing hard, she forced her gaze to his. He

watched her with pure hunger in those dark brown eyes. It was like he'd just let his walls down at the club and didn't plan to put them back up. Or maybe that was wishful thinking on her part.

"Are you working on stuff for Connor?" she asked even though she knew he likely was.

Letting his arms drop from the doorframe, he nodded. "I could use the break. You want to come in?"

She did, but she shook her head. Right now they needed to talk and at least outside they were in a semi-public area, even if no one was out at this time of night except warriors patrolling. "No, I . . . What was the deal at the club? Why were you acting like that?"

She was grateful he didn't pretend not to understand what she meant. Stepping out onto the porch, he reached for her hips and pulled her close so that their bodies pressed together. If she'd had any doubts about his feelings before, the press of his erection against her lower belly told her everything she needed to know. He wasn't trying to hide his reaction. If anything, he moved closer.

The bold move took her by surprise. She spread her palms against his chest and tried to keep some distance between them, but Ryan wouldn't let her. Her palms tingled against him as she savored the feel of being able to touch him so intimately.

"I could have lost you tonight." He wrapped those big arms around her in a tight grip, his tone ragged and hungry.

To hear so much need in his voice completely undid her. Where was the cold, resisting male she'd gotten so used to? "Maybe." She started to say more when he crushed his mouth down over hers in a purely dominating move.

By now she shouldn't be surprised but this was a completely different side to the sexy cowboy hacker. They'd bickered on and off for the past few months and while she'd known he was attracted to her, she'd secretly wondered if there was something wrong with her. He'd just been so distant. Not now. She tangled her tongue with his, nipping his bottom lip playfully with her teeth.

When he shuddered against her, Teresa slid her hands up his chest and held on to his shoulders. She dug her fingers into his skin in an effort to steady herself and Ryan groaned into her mouth. She arched her back, pressing closer to him, wishing she didn't have a shirt on. Before she realized what he intended, he grasped her butt and hoisted her up. It felt so natural to wrap her legs around his waist. The feel of his hard length pressing against the juncture between her thighs was too much.

As his tongue teased hers, she was vaguely aware of him moving them inside and the door slamming behind them. He pinned her against the nearest wall. Her arousal skyrocketed as he rolled his hips against hers. Ryan slid a hand under her shirt and she knew she should protest. They needed to talk, but the feel of those callused fingers skimming her belly set her on fire.

He pulled his head back a fraction and started nuzzling his way along her jaw to her ear. When he nipped her earlobe between his teeth she arched against him.

"I love seeing you in my shirt," he murmured, raking his teeth gently against her neck.

The implication of what he was doing wasn't lost on her. Male shifters didn't graze their teeth against a female's neck unless they had serious intentions to mate them. The fact that he was doing so now, even teasingly, scared the hell out of her. Not because she was afraid he'd mark her without asking, but because of the complete one-eighty he'd done.

"Wait," she murmured at the same time she heard a shuffling of feet.

"Ryan?" Lucas's groggy voice had them both freezing.

Ryan lifted his head from her neck and she let her legs unwrap from around him. He set her down, but squeezed her hips once before looking over his shoulder. "Hey, buddy. Did we wake you up?"

Teresa pushed against Ryan's chest and stepped around him so she could see Lucas.

The ten-year-old shifter wore long flannel pajama pants and a T-shirt, his blond hair sticking up everywhere in the most adorable way. "No, I'm thirsty. I didn't mean to bother you—"

"You're not bothering us," Teresa interjected. Ryan didn't seem to want to let her go, but she didn't care. She needed distance from this male if she wanted to think straight. "I just stopped by to . . ." Her brain chose that moment to malfunction. She couldn't even think of a decent lie.

"To kiss Ryan?" the boy asked, all innocence.

Teresa felt her face flame. "Ah, no. We weren't . . . I'm just leaving but Ana is cooking breakfast for everyone in a few hours so I'll see you then." Without sparing a glance in Ryan's direction she hurried out the front door.

She should have known he wouldn't just let her run out.

He caught her hand in his and tugged her back as he followed her onto the front porch. He tugged the door closed behind him with his other hand. "Hey. He won't be up for long."

For some reason that statement pissed her off as much as the hungry look in Ryan's eyes did. "So what? You can't just change the rules all of a sudden, Ryan O'Callaghan. Once you decide to give me an explanation for why you've been a jackass the past three months, come see me. Until then, this"—she motioned between them—"isn't happening again." Ignoring the dark look he gave her, she turned on her heel and left. Maybe it was harsh but she didn't care. He couldn't just yo-yo her around like this.

So what if he all of a sudden decided he wanted her. What happened when he changed his mind again? She wasn't going to deal with some emotionally challenged male. For months he'd made it a point to keep his distance, but he'd still warned other males away from her. She wanted to know why. And jumping into bed with him without talking first was stupid. One way or another Ryan was going to come clean about whatever his issues were.

Because she wanted the whole package. A mate, a family, everything. And if he couldn't give it to her, she was moving on.

Chapter 7

Jayce sat on Cece's couch and tried to rein in his frustration at the sobbing human. He understood she was upset—rightfully so—but he didn't have time for tears. If anything, they made him edgier.

At least Kat was more sympathetic. It seemed to make a difference with the human. Kat sat on the longer couch with Cece, across from Jayce, his bondmate's arm wrapped snuggly around the female's shaking shoulders.

"I just don't understand why we can't call the police," the human wailed again.

Jayce rubbed a hand over his face. Yes, she'd been traumatized, but she was also drunk. Considering the blood she'd lost and the shock she had to be in, it made sense that she kept forgetting things they'd already told her. Still annoyed the shit out of him.

"I've already called the police, Cece," Jayce said quietly. "They'll be here in ten minutes." He didn't care if it was a lie. He needed answers. She straightened at that, even though he'd already told her the same thing half a dozen times. "Why did your friends leave the club early?"

She sniffled and wiped her red nose. Once they'd got her home, she'd showered and changed into flannel pajamas. He'd bagged her bloody clothes and told her they would go to the police. In reality he'd be keeping her clothing for his own investigation.

"They were hooking up with some shifters, but they haven't texted me back yet. Bitches," she muttered.

"Can you give me their names and contact information? I'd like to follow up with them and make sure they're okay."

She nodded and rattled off both names and phone numbers. He would put them in his notebook later, but for now he mentally filed the information away. He'd be following up with her friends very soon. Because if they'd intentionally thrown their friend to those vamps for dinner, they wouldn't like his form of justice.

"You're doing great, Cece," Kat murmured, rubbing her hand against the female's back in small circles.

"Thanks. And thank you for saving me. I still can't believe . . ." She trailed off into another fit of tears and Kat pulled her into a hug.

Jayce clenched his jaw but straightened when Kat shot him an annoyed look. He didn't have to tap into their telepathic link to know she was mad at him for not being more sympathetic. The human hadn't been sexually assaulted, so he wasn't walking on eggshells around her. They needed damn answers about what was going down at that club and why. Because he knew in his gut that the club was linked to the recent rash of vamp blood dealing and the crimes committed by those hopped-up on the stuff.

"Did the men who drank from you say anything or seem to be acting strange?" Jayce asked.

Natalia had described the vamp that she'd killed as having eerie glowing eyes. And Kat had said that with her seer ability, she'd been able to see a strange aura around the other vamps, as if they were puppets on a string.

Cece's head whipped up, tears streaking down her face. "Stranger than them attacking me and drinking my blood with no provocation? I would have given it to them!" she shouted, then seemed to realize what she'd said. Her face flushed red as she looked down at her hands. "I've hooked up with vamps before so it's not like . . . I wouldn't have *minded* feeding them, but they just attacked me. I didn't deserve it."

"No, you didn't," Jayce agreed. "Those two vamps were monsters and they're never going to hurt you again." A knock at the door had him rising. Cece started to get up, but he held up a hand. "I'll get it." Before he opened the door he scented his old friend, Nikolai.

When he opened it Niko stood there, arms crossed over his chest. "All these little favors are going to add up, wolf."

Jayce snorted and stepped back. "She's in the living room."

As he and his vamp friend entered the living room, both Kat and Cece looked up. Kat wasn't surprised because he'd told her what he was doing, but Cece's dark eyes were confused.

"Are you with the police?" she asked Niko, who looked like a biker, wearing beat-up jeans, scuffed shit-kickers, and an equally worn leather jacket.

The vamp was over five hundred years old and had more money than some countries, but you couldn't tell from the way he dressed.

Niko covered the distance to her in the span of a heartbeat and knelt in front of her. As he did, Kat stood and stepped away.

"I'm sorry for what you went through tonight, but I'm going to make it better. Okay?" he asked in that rough voice of his. It didn't matter that he was a vamp and basically immortal, his voice would never change. Right before Niko had been turned his throat had been slit and had never healed properly during the change from human to vamp.

Cece looked confused, but nodded.

As Niko talked to her, Kat hurried to Jayce's side. *You trust him?* she asked telepathically.

With my life. That wasn't something he said lightly or about many people. Which explained Kat's raised eyebrows.

You could have gone a little easier on her, she chastised.

He shrugged and wrapped an arm around Kat's shoulders. He wasn't used to being soft with anyone, except her. For her he'd do damn near anything. *That's why you're here.*

Rolling her eyes, she nudged him with her elbow. *What do we do now?*

Go home, get some sleep, and in a few hours we'll hunt down Cece's friends. I don't think they're involved, but it's a possibility.

Kat frowned and looked back at the human and Niko. Niko was staring deeply into her eyes and scrubbing her recent memories. *What about Cece?*

Niko will stay and watch over her in case she wasn't randomly targeted. Unlike a lot of vamps, Niko actually liked humans. For all his rough exterior, the ancient vamp was oddly protective of the physically weaker species. It was one of the reasons Jayce respected him.

If you trust him, I trust him. Kat leaned into Jayce, wrapping her arm tighter around him.

The feel of her lush body against his was something he'd never tire of. A few months ago he hadn't thought it possible for him to have the life he wanted with the female he wanted more than his next breath. Some days he was terrified he was going to wake up and find out this was all a dream. Or that she'd be targeted by one of his enemies. That was something he simply had to live with. Luckily he was strong and so was she. His female could take care of herself if push came to shove. And he'd continue to keep training her every day to make sure she never lost that edge.

He'd seen firsthand what happened to a male when he lost his mate. His own brother, who he hadn't heard from in hundreds of years, had lost his pregnant mate to a feral coyote. It had been bloody and horrifying. His brother had gone crazy, attacking Jayce in a fit of rage. Jayce had let him because he'd known the male was suffering worse than any physical pain could inflict.

He'd stopped his brother only because he hadn't wanted to go blind, but now he was scarred, a reminder of all his brother had lost and what Jayce could lose too. Hell, he didn't even know if his brother was alive. Some days he thought about searching for him, but fuck it. If he wanted to find Jayce, he could. His brother was the one who'd left all those years ago, turned his back on Jayce, the only family he'd had.

At a buzzing sound, Kat reached into her front pocket and pulled out her cell phone. She snorted and held it out for him to see.

If u 2 don't have curfews neither should I! Where r u? A text from Leila, the sixteen-year-old shifter they'd recently adopted.

Jayce just shook his head as Kat texted her back. Their new ward was staying with December and Liam while they were off on this mission so it wasn't as if she was alone. And what the hell was she doing up this late anyway?

She wants to see her new . . . friend, Kat said, answering the question he hadn't asked.

Jayce tensed, knowing his bondmate was right. Leila had started hanging out with a human boy. Who rode a motorcycle. Hell fucking no. *Not happening tonight.*

"No kidding," Kat muttered aloud as she slid her phone back in her pocket.

"Come on," he murmured to Kat as Niko stood up.

Cece was lying back on the couch now, her eyes closed and her breathing steady. Whatever Niko had done clearly worked.

The three of them walked outside, but Niko remained in the doorway. "I'm going to stay for a few more hours until I'm sure she's okay. Then I'll keep watch over her house for a couple days. She seemed to take the memory scrub well, but she was attacked, so she might have nightmares. She thinks I'm a gay vampire she picked up at that club tonight."

"Gay?" Kat asked, a touch of amusement in her voice.

"I planted that in her memory so she wouldn't feel threatened by me. She needs rest after her ordeal."

"Thanks, man. Call me with any updates and I'll let you know if I find out anything about the vamp blood dealing," Jayce said before he and Kat headed to their SUV.

"You're keeping him apprised of your investigation?" Kat asked once they were in the vehicle.

Jayce nodded. "Out of courtesy. This business with the vamp blood dealing could affect all vampires if it's not taken care of." Normally he didn't check in with anyone regarding his investigations except the Council. This situation was different, especially since he was working with the Armstrong pack.

"And if you keep him in the loop, he'll keep you in the loop if he discovers something interesting," Kat finished on her own.

Jayce gave her a half smile. His mate knew him so well. "Exactly."

Aiden locked the front door to the cabin behind Connor, but didn't turn around yet. He could feel Larissa behind him, watching. Waiting. Even though he couldn't see them, those indigo eyes of hers were so damn expressive.

They hadn't always been like that, but now she was confused and not acting like the Larissa he knew. She was wearing her emotions right out in the open and it was jarring. His Larissa had been strong and a little arrogant. At over five hundred years old and ridiculously powerful, she had a right to be. He wanted her back, all of her.

Taking a deep breath, he tried to get his wolf under control. He knew she'd seen his animal revealed in his eyes a few times on the drive to the two-story log cabin. He'd tried to rein himself in but it was damn hard with her sitting next to him. Alive. Real. After all these years.

Whoever had put her in stasis, had taken her from him, would pay.

When she politely cleared her throat, he turned to find her standing there with her arms wrapped around herself. Such a human gesture and so out of character . . . Suddenly it hit him. "Are you cold?"

She nodded, her face flushing slightly, as if she was embarrassed. "Just a little," she said softly, her lilting accent rolling over him, bringing up so many damn memories of the first time they'd met.

Okay, that was the Larissa he knew. Not wanting anyone to sense what she would perceive as a weakness. He hated that he hadn't sensed her discomfort, but he'd had to semi-lock himself down from their bondmate link. It was difficult after being separated for so long, but not impossible. He was still connected to her, but he was allowing his wolf a little more control than normal, letting his animal channel all those emotions he felt flowing off Larissa like a tsunami. Otherwise he wouldn't be able to function. Feeling her worry and confusion was killing him inside.

"Come on." He gestured to the living room right off the foyer. The place was maintained by a caretaker and Aiden knew Connor had contacted the woman who took care of it even though it had been so late.

The place was supposed to be stocked with food—for him, because the only food she required was blood and she would feed from him and no one else—and there should be a selection of clothes upstairs for Larissa to choose from. She was petite in height and build like many of his female packmates so something should fit. Of course he hoped she decided to just go naked, but he knew that was wishful thinking.

He strode into the room with her trailing behind him. A quick flip of a switch on the mantel of the stone fireplace and it flared to life. There was something to be said for the ease of gas fireplaces.

After turning it on he sat on the pile of rugs in front of it and leaned against the nearby couch. When she tentatively sat on the rugs, he stripped his sweater off and handed it to her. In the SUV he'd changed into one of the spare sets of clothes, but he wouldn't need it in here. More than anything, he wanted his scent on her. And he noticed the way she stared at his bare skin.

With a hunger that matched his own.

He wasn't above using her own desire against her. She clearly wanted him. The desire that sparked between them was just waiting to combust and he had no problem fanning the flames. Anything to get her naked and underneath him. It was the only time she'd let him dominate her. Then she'd remember him. He hoped. A small part of him was so fucking scared she'd never . . . No. He shut that down before it had a chance to form. No matter what, he was going to reinforce the bond between them so that she had no doubt what she meant to him.

Larissa shook her head and he realized he was still holding the sweater out to her. "That's okay. With the fire I won't need it."

"I want my scent on you," he ground out, stunning himself. *Way to play it smooth.*

Her eyes widened, but she took the sweater nonetheless. "Turn around," she demanded, taking him by surprise with her heated words.

"No." If she was taking off her shirt, he wasn't moving.

For a moment she looked shocked, but then she gritted her teeth before tugging the sweater on over the silky black top she already had on. "You're so . . . obnoxious and dominant. I can't imagine that I *liked* that."

"You liked it all right. . . . Only in the bedroom though," he growled.

Her face flushed again and a sharp pop of hunger rolled off her. Larissa had confessed that before him she'd always been the pursuer of the few lovers she'd had. With him she'd given up complete control between the sheets or whatever flat surface they'd managed to find. "So, what happens now?"

"We talk. Tell me the last thing you remember." Unfortunately, Aiden could think of a hell of a lot more interesting things to do with his mouth, but they needed to talk. He wanted his Larissa back. His strong, fierce female who would punch him in the jaw if he got out of line. God, he'd missed her. So fucking much that he ached for the touch of her.

Sighing, she grabbed some of the pillows off the couch closest to her and piled them up. Using them as a headrest, she lay sideways and turned her body so that she faced him. "Your last name is Nicholl?" she asked, though it wasn't exactly a question. He nodded, hope flaring in his chest that she finally remembered him. "In 1953, some of my coven members and me—including my parents—were on our way to Scotland. The Nicholl pack was giving us something that used to belong to my family centuries before in exchange for my coven protecting some of your distant pack members in Romania."

He nodded. All this was correct.

Her eyes narrowed a fraction and her entire body tensed, though she didn't sit up. "What was the Nicholl pack returning to my coven?"

"A shield." Made completely of gold. His pack had come across it hundreds of years before during some battle between vampires and shifters and taken it as a battle prize. Way before his time.

Her lips pursed together but she nodded and settled deeper against the pillows. "Correct."

His mouth quirked up at her haughty tone.

"What?" she demanded again and he could see the Larissa he knew returning bit by bit.

Aiden just shook his head. "Nothing."

Those piercing eyes of hers narrowed as she continued. "After that, *nothing*. I don't remember anything except waking up to the witch—Magda—and having the worst sense of . . . sadness, I guess."

"Tell me about the witch." Aiden had never met a witch he'd liked. Some were into white magic but the majority were into the dark arts. They craved power. Unlike shifters, vamps, or fae, most witches weren't born with their supernatural abilities. There were a handful that were, but those tended to be white witches. Like from *The Wizard of Oz*. "Are you a good witch, or a bad witch?" He nearly snorted at the thought of the quote. That was one of the only movies he and Larissa had seen together even though it had come out more than a decade before they'd met. She'd loved black-and-white movies. The memory calmed something inside him even as she frowned.

"She told me that she didn't even know of my existence until she stumbled across a grimoire one of her ancestors kept, detailing about my stasis. I was put in stasis to protect me from you, supposedly."

Aiden's jaw clenched. "Did you see the grimoire?" Almost every witch, or at least true, practicing ones, had a grimoire. Their textbook of magic spells.

She nodded. "Yes. It's old and I guess it could be faked, but the power from the book was real and . . . I recognized the writing. Her ancestor worked with my mother occasionally."

"And it just stated that you were being protected from me?"

She nodded again, her expression pensive.

"Your parents might have thought they were protecting you from me. They sent assassins after me after our bonding link broke. I didn't understand why, considering you were supposed to be dead." He'd assumed their hatred just ran deep. But maybe they'd wanted to kill him before bringing her back from stasis. It made sense.

She didn't comment, but he could see the wheels turning in her head. "What did you do to their assassins?"

The fact that she was asking meant she believed him. Or was at least humoring him. "What do you think?" He'd sent their heads back in a box.

Her frown deepened as she rolled onto her back, staring at the ceiling. "Magda brought me to the United States because she wanted to give me the chance to get vengeance on my parents' murderers. She didn't ask for anything in return and told me it was because her ancestors owed a great debt to my ancestors. That much I know is true—the ancestor part. She obviously wanted me here for a reason, but I don't think it was to see you."

"Why were you at that club?" There had to be a reason, and if they knew why maybe they could figure out the mystery of this witch's endgame. Because Aiden had no doubt she had one.

Larissa rubbed a hand over her face. "To meet someone who knew more about, well, you. *Supposedly.*"

"Why wasn't she with you? And where have you been staying?"

She turned to look at him. "We were staying in separate rooms at a five-star hotel in Winston-Salem, but she said she had other business to attend to. She sent two vampire escorts with me though."

Aiden snorted. One of them had tried to take Larissa from him. Yeah, that witch was going to pay. Even thinking about that made his wolf claw at the surface. "What else do you know about her?"

Her gaze turned shuttered, as if she was embarrassed. "Not much. I . . . didn't know how to investigate her. All my old coven members are gone. I don't know how to use a computer and those cell phones are just confusing. I didn't have anyone to call anyway." The sadness rolling off her was too much to bear. She looked away and he realized how exhausted she was.

Shit, she needed to feed. "When's the last time you fed?"

Pinning him with an unreadable stare, she watched him for a long moment. "I'm fine."

So she was basically rejecting his blood when it was clear she was hungry. That knowledge pierced him. Deeply. He knew that if he pushed her he could get Larissa to take his vein. But he didn't want to force the issue. No, he wanted her to come to him. "Do you want to go upstairs? There are different bedrooms to choose from."

She shook her head, the firelight playing off her delicate features. "I'd rather sleep right here. It's so warm."

Unable to find his voice, he nodded and grabbed one of the thick blankets from the back of the couch. Kneeling next to her, he placed it around her body, tucking the edges around her. He didn't want to cover more of her, especially when he was very aware of the way she was watching him. Her gaze was heated, roving over his chest in a way that made his cock harden even more.

When she met his eyes, his breath caught. He could tell she was tired, but she was also turned on. Because of him. Though he'd locked down their bondmate link as much as he could, the thread of need she put off was unmistakable.

"Can I ask you something?" she whispered.

Throat still tight, he nodded.

She licked her lips once, drawing his gaze to their fullness. "Will you kiss me? I want to see if it helps me remember."

His cock pressed against his jeans at the question. Hell yeah, he'd kiss her. "Where do you want me to kiss you?" he murmured.

It took a moment for his meaning to sink in, but when it did, her face turned scarlet. "You are such a brazen shifter."

Reaching out, he ran his fingers through the dark strands of her hair fanning out over the throw pillows. "Is that a bad thing?"

She laughed lightly. "No. I can see why you would have caught my attention. I'm surprised I didn't try to teach you a lesson though. I feel like you might have annoyed me with your brashness."

He let out a loud bark of laughter at her honesty. "I *did* annoy you. And you *did* want to 'teach me a lesson in humility,' as you put it."

Her eyes widened. "What happened?"

"This." Covering the short distance between them, he kissed her. Aiden tried to tell himself to be gentle, to ease them both into it, but it was like he'd been doused in kerosene and once their lips touched, the match was lit.

Flicking his tongue against hers, he shuddered at the familiarity, at the female he'd never gotten over. She tasted like heaven. Like his. He kept his hands on either side of Larissa's head, buried in the blankets because he didn't trust himself to touch her.

She had no such control. Larissa shoved her blanket out of the way and gripped his shoulders. Her fingers dug into his skin as her tongue and lips danced with his. She groaned into his mouth, her desire palpable. God, how he wanted to touch her, to stroke her every-where, to relearn every inch of her sweet body. Some-how he managed to stop himself. His claws unsheathed, shredding through the blankets as he maintained some control.

Surprising him, she wrapped her entire body around his, pushing him until he was flipped flat on his back on the blankets. If he'd wanted to stop her, he could have. But there was no way in hell he'd stop this. The moment her legs settled around his waist, she pulled back, her eyes wide with surprise. Breathing hard, she stared down at him. Her dark hair fell around her face and shoulders, spilling onto his chest. She looked un-sure as she sat there.

Moving slowly, carefully, he slid his hands up her covered thighs, over her hips, and around her back until he reached under his sweater and her top. Barely grazing her bare back, he stroked her soft skin. Feeling her like this soothed the darkest part of him, making his wolf go completely still as he watched her. "What are you thinking?" he asked quietly.

She bit her bottom lip then answered. "I want you. Badly. My whole body aches for your touch in a way that terrifies me since I don't know you. Or remember you. And it's not just because I'm turned on for anyone. Deep down I know that only you can satisfy me."

His inner wolf growled at that. Damn straight he was the only one who could and would satisfy her. "But?"

"I don't think I'm ready for that. Everything is so different in this world. With the Internet, those small cell phones, the mass use of credit cards . . . It's just too much. I'm probably not making any sense, but . . . I'm having a hard time adjusting to all these changes and with you, here, now, and me having no memory of you even if my body clearly does . . . Okay, I'm rambling and likely sound crazy. What I'm trying to say is that it would be easy to jump into bed with you—I want to— but I just don't think I can handle anything else now. Especially not sex."

He breathed out a sigh of relief. She wasn't rejecting him, just the situation. That, he could deal with. "I'm not pushing for anything you're not ready for, sweetheart."

She jerked slightly at the endearment, but gave him a soft smile.

He cupped her cheek, pulling her back down to him.

She didn't resist as he lightly brushed his lips over hers, savoring her addictive taste.

When she sat back up, her indigo eyes were a brighter blue, almost electric.

Turning their bodies so that she was stretched out on the blankets and pillows, he pulled the throw back up over them and tucked her close against his chest. He might want sex, but he didn't need it. He just needed her in his arms. Alive. "I know you're exhausted. Get some sleep and in a few hours I'll talk to my pack about finding out everything we can about Magda and your coven. We'll find out everything about everyone you used to know."

Sighing into his chest as she wrapped an arm around his waist, she snuggled closer. "Thank you, Aiden," she murmured.

Hearing his name on her lips just about undid him as much as the way she was burrowing up to him. He tightened his grip and closed his eyes as he rested his chin on the top of her head. Never in a thousand years had he imagined Larissa would walk back into his life, but now that she was here he was holding on for good. Only when he was certain she was asleep did he allow himself to doze too.

Chapter 8

Larissa's eyes snapped open in the darkness. The fire was out and the blinds were closed, but with her heightened senses she could easily see in the dark. Aiden stood next to the fireplace, his hand on the switch he must have just flipped off. The room was still warm, but something was wrong.

He now wore a sweater and had boots on. She couldn't believe she hadn't heard him get up. He looked tense as he held a finger to his lips. She nodded, listening for whatever had woken them. Sometimes it wasn't necessarily a sound, but a sixth sense that all beings had. Vampires and shifters were just tuned in to their animal sense more than humans. Right now, she knew they weren't alone.

She tensed at a creak from upstairs. Slowly, she rose from the blankets and moved to the opposite side of the stone fireplace from Aiden. Without making a sound she retrieved one of the sharp metal pokers. Even though the thing was gas and the pokers for display, they were real.

Larissa wasn't even close to being in her top fighting shape and didn't mind an extra weapon on hand. It was a stark reminder that she needed to feed. Soon. She should have just taken Aiden's offer before they'd gone to sleep. Well, he hadn't asked, but he'd implied. But she'd known what would happen if she'd fed from him. He would have been inside her in less than a minute. She wasn't even sure how she knew that, but it was true.

Aiden started to make a movement with his hand when a blur of motion from the entryway snagged Larissa's attention.

Three masked vampires stood there, staring at the two of them. She could easily tell they were vamps by their glowing eyes. Something was off about their gazes though. They were too bright, unnatural even for a vamp. It was weird they were wearing masks though.

Tensing, she prepared for a fight. Another appeared behind them, then another. Even with the black face coverings it was clear they were all males.

A surprising burst of dread popped inside her. Taking on five vampires under normal circumstances was no problem for her. But she'd been easily tackled by Aiden in the forest. Even now her hands slightly shook. After so many years in stasis and little blood to nourish her since she'd woken she was surprised she was even this strong.

"Do you idiots know who owns this cabin?" Aiden said defiantly. He took a few steps forward, purposely moving in her direction so that he stood in front of her.

The subtle action touched her.

One of the five stepped forward, letting his claws unsheathe. "Kill the male," he growled low, his voice unnaturally deep and guttural.

Hell no. The overwhelming urge to protect Aiden rose up inside her. Without pause Larissa hauled back and hurled the metal poker at the closest vampire. It shot toward him with impossible speed. Before the masked male had a chance to move, it embedded deep in his chest, puncturing all the way through his body. Blood spilled out of his open mouth as he fell to his knees.

Though it felt as if time stood still, everything happened in mere seconds. As the male started to fall forward on his face the rest of the vampires moved into action in a blur of motion.

Letting her claws unsheathe, she launched herself at one of the vamps. In her peripheral she saw three vampires converge on Aiden. In seconds, he changed forms, going completely wolf. He was such a beautiful lupine shifter, but she had no time to admire the shining white coat of fur as she dodged a blow to the face from the advancing vampire.

Jumping onto the nearest couch, she used all the strength in her legs to spring up and over the male. It took more energy than she'd expected, but adrenaline surged through her. No one threatened Aiden. No one.

Midair she twisted, coming back down with her claws at the ready. Using them like blades, she sliced into the male's neck on both sides. She cut through tendons, cartilage, and bone until she completely severed the head. She easily dodged the arterial spray, having killed this way many times before. Though the male she'd stabbed with the fire poker earlier appeared dead, she wasn't taking any chances. She tore the metal rod from his back, pulling it the rest of the way through his body, then ripped his heart out with her hand.

There were generally two ways to kill supernatural beings. By taking their head or their heart. Even though the poker had likely shredded this vamp's heart, she was making sure everyone here was truly dead.

Behind her she heard an angry snarl and a cry of pain. Turning, ready to defend Aiden, she stilled to see him standing over three headless vampires. Her eyes widened. He killed *fast*. He was much younger than she was, but incredibly powerful.

We head upstairs, now. She jumped back, stunned at his authoritative voice in her head.

"Was that you?" she demanded.

Yes. Come on. I don't know if there are more vamps nearby but we need to pack a small bag and get the hell out of here. This place isn't easy to find and I don't think they followed us. Which means you might have a tracker on you.

Though she wanted to question him, he was right. They needed to leave. Following him as he loped up the stairs, she was awed by how graceful he was even as such a huge animal. Once they reached the top of the stairs, he shifted back to his human form with a grunt of discomfort.

She tried not to stare at the way his perfectly sculpted backside flexed as he hurried to the nearest bedroom. Inside she could scent a lemon cleanser and other subtle cleaning products with a lavender undertone. He went straight for one of the closets and grabbed clothes big enough for him and a couple of things for her. The thought of wearing another female's clothes was odd to her, but right now she didn't care.

Once he'd shoved the handful of clothes into the bag, he turned. "Strip."

Surprise more than fear ricocheted through her. "What?"

As if he sensed her automatic resistance, he frowned. "We need to get rid of your clothes if you've got a tracker on you."

Right. Nodding, she ignored his heated gaze as she lifted his sweater and her top off. It annoyed her that he wasn't even pretending not to watch or giving her the illusion of privacy. No, this male with all his arrogance wouldn't do that. Feeling strangely modest, she turned her back to him and slipped her jeans and panties off.

When Aiden let out a soft growl she looked over her shoulder at him. His eyes blazed like a dark flame. Damn him for watching her like he had every right in the world. She started to ask him for new clothes, but he frowned and narrowed his gaze on her upper right shoulder. "What is it?" she blurted, trying to peer at her shoulder.

In the span of a heartbeat he covered the few feet to her. Placing one of his big hands on her shoulder, he leaned down and let out a vicious curse.

Feeling his anger through their bondmate link, she went cold. "What is it?"

"That bitch inked you. This is why I hate witches," he muttered. "I could be wrong, but this is likely how she tracked you. The tattoo is small, and from its position below your shoulder blade there's no way you'd be able to see it unless you were staring at yourself with a couple of mirrors."

She hadn't even known about the tat. "We don't even know it was her. How would she have . . ." Larissa trailed off as Aiden gave her another look. "She did it before she woke me from stasis." It was the only thing that made sense.

Aiden nodded and let his hand fall from her shoulder. He swallowed hard as she turned to face him. "We need to cut it out."

It would hurt but Larissa could deal with the pain and her skin would regrow. Anything to get the ink off her. If Magda had done this to her, she was definitely going to pay. Feeling more like herself since she'd woken up, Larissa turned her back to him once more. She tensed, all her muscles tightening. "Cut it out. Use your claws. Do it quick."

The tip of one of Aiden's claws grazed her skin, whisper soft. He sucked in a ragged breath and she braced herself for the pain. Instead of slicing agony, she heard his claws retract.

She swiveled to face him. "What's wrong?"

His jaw clenched tight. "I can't hurt you."

In that moment she wanted to kill whoever had stolen her memories of this fierce male. The fact that he couldn't do this to her told her so damn much about his character. She hated herself for not remembering him. Without pause she reached back and ripped away a chunk of her skin with her own claws.

Tears burned her eyes as she tore it away. Aiden cursed again and she felt the pain from their link travel through to her. She ignored it and turned around. "Did I get it?" she rasped out, the wound stinging like fire.

His fingers gently wiped away blood as he inspected the raw area. "It's gone."

Without turning back to him, she hurried to the bathroom and flushed the skin down the toilet before she started washing her hands. She could already feel the first layer of skin starting to heal, stanching the bleeding, but it didn't stop the pain. Damn, this was definitely from the blood loss. She should have healed almost instantly.

"Why are you taking so long to heal?" Aiden asked from the doorway.

Grabbing the hand towel by the sink, she started drying her hands as she turned to face him. "I'm weak. You were right earlier. I need to feed."

He didn't seem surprised by her answer. "I can feed you now," he said, but there was a question in his voice and she knew why.

"If I take your blood now, I won't stop at feeding." She was feeling primal and in her weakened state knew she'd take *everything* he had to offer. They didn't have time and she was strong enough to go on the run, at least temporarily. "I'll be okay for another day or so."

He shook his head, his expression resolved. "You won't have to wait that long. I'll put a bandage on you, then inspect the rest of your body in case she inked you somewhere else."

Once he'd covered her wound with materials from a

first-aid kit, she held out her arms and let him inspect her from head to foot. It should have been clinical as he searched her for another tracking mark, but when he lifted her full breasts, inspecting the undersides, it was hard not to be affected.

Her nipples tightened and tingled, her reaction to him clear. And if that wasn't enough, she knew he had to scent her desire. How embarrassing. She knew they needed to run. They had dead bodies downstairs and who knew how many others after them. And all she could think about was going at it with him on the bathroom floor. She wanted to see his head between her legs, to feel him stroking and licking her in her most intimate place.

"As soon as we find someplace secure . . ." He trailed off, his intent crystal clear.

Larissa didn't bother to contradict him. She didn't care what she'd said about not being ready. Her body certainly was. For this male and this male alone. Once his blood coated her tongue again . . . She swallowed hard and tried to rein in those thoughts but she was so hungry and he was so deliciously masculine.

Once Aiden was done, she quickly dressed, but was surprised when he didn't. "Why aren't you putting on clothes?"

His heated gaze raked up the length of her body and locked on hers. "I'm going to go wolf. Then we're running deep into the mountains. From here it should take us maybe half an hour to reach one of the nearby ski resorts. They've got plenty of unused cabins. We're going to break into one since none of them are connected to us and use the shelter. Then I'm contacting my Alpha again. I've already texted him, telling him what happened here. He's going to send a cleanup crew. My phone is in the duffel bag. If anything happens to me, press SPEED DIAL one. Do you know how to do that?" His voice was gentle as he asked.

Feeling stupidly embarrassed, she nodded. "Yes."

"That's my Alpha's number. No matter what, he'll help you get back on your feet if I'm—"

"Nothing is happening to you!" The vehemence in her voice shocked both of them.

His head tilted slightly to the side but he nodded. "I know you're more than capable of taking care of yourself, but I also know this world is different from the one you remember. We need to prepare for all scenarios. I'll feed you as soon as we get someplace safe. Until then, stay close to me and if we're attacked again, I want you to run."

Larissa snorted. That wasn't happening.

He seemed annoyed by her response, but just shook his head. "Come on, let's get the hell out of here."

Ignoring the ache in her shoulder, she nodded. She couldn't wait to get moving.

Magda glared at the lone incompetent male vampire standing in front of her. "You have failed us. *Again.*" And for the last time.

The male was relatively lucky it was just her berating him, not . . . *him*. Magda fought a shudder, not willing to even think her master's name. He was an ancient vampire and while not inherently strong like someone of Larissa's unique line, he'd gained massive amounts of power in the last few months using the dark arts. Meaning he made human sacrifices in exchange for his new gifts. But he still had to drink blood to maintain his impressive powers. A lot of it. The more blood he drank, the more his body became accustomed to it. It was why he needed Larissa. The last of her line, a day-walker, a bloodborn, the female reeked of power. Whoever—or whatever—he'd gained his power from had demanded a specific sacrifice. Larissa fit all the requirements.

Magda could practically taste Larissa's power in the air whenever she was near the female. It was why she'd been giving the vampire animal blood mixed with human blood, keeping her as weak as possible without tipping her hand. If she could have, Magda would have just sacrificed the female in her stasis state. That wouldn't work for the required spell, however. She'd been keeping her on a tight leash, but unfortunately Larissa must have discovered the tracking ink on her because Magda couldn't locate the vamp anymore. She hadn't been able to for the past hour. Magda might have another way though.

"They killed five of us. What was I supposed to do?" Logan snapped. In vampire years he was only two years old. A child. Having been turned at eighteen, he was incredibly young. He was also handsome and knew it. Something he probably thought would save him now. Just because she'd fucked him a few times meant nothing though. "You're lucky we decided to keep one of us as a lookout, otherwise you wouldn't have even known what happened," he continued, oblivious to her ire.

She reined in her snort of disgust at his stupidity. Of course she would have known. Her master had been watching *everything* through their eyes. His powerful gift allowed him to control almost anyone with vampire blood in their veins, even from a distance. He was their puppet master. They were just too weak and stupid to realize they weren't in control of their own bodies.

Her master could even control humans who were hopped-up on the addictive vampire blood—which was why he'd taken to selling it in huge quantities. Winston-Salem was his testing ground and so far, things were moving along smoothly enough. His control wasn't perfect with vamps, but for humans, he'd been directing them to do all sorts of nasty things, including robbing banks and other places. Her master sometimes did things just because he could, but the stealing was for a purpose. He wanted power but also money. He didn't care how he attained it.

Using her own display of power, she reached out a hand and curved her fingers as if she were choking someone. Logan started gasping for air, as if she was physically strangling the life out of him.

Eyes bulging out of their sockets, he fruitlessly clawed at the invisible hand around his neck. With another burst of power, she held his entire body immobile. This would drain her, but she didn't care. She'd been so sure these fools would bring Larissa back after the failure last night. Now she would be the one who suffered her master's wrath.

So Logan would feel hers before she endured her own agony. She drank in his fear as she choked the life out of him. While holding him immobile, she reached for a dagger on her altar. His eyes widened even more as she came near him.

When she reached him, she pressed her body to his, rubbing her breasts against his chest. Even with their clothes separating them, she could feel the fear emanating off him. The stench wrapped around her, invigorating her. "I'm going to enjoy this," she said as she stepped back and dragged the blade down the front of his shirt.

It fell away as if it was a piece of paper. He started making grunting sounds, like an animal, but she kept her tight grip on his entire body. Normally she liked to hear her victim struggle and fight, but she didn't have time for any distraction right now.

Not when she was going to attempt to put off her master's wrath for another day. Shoving the blade through Logan's chest, she twisted hard, shredding his heart. His eyes widened even further. At his young age he wasn't powerful enough to heal from this wound. And he definitely wouldn't heal from what she did next. She pulled the blade out, then shoved her hand through his chest cavity.

A ripple of arousal went through her when she grasped his heart. After pulling it out she licked her wrist and fingers as the blood dripped down her arm before she placed it on her altar. He fell to the floor, but she ignored his body. She'd deal with the cleanup later.

Clasping her hands together, she smeared his blood

over her other hand before she closed her eyes, lifting her hands out in a wide, welcoming gesture, and started chanting a locator spell she'd used many times before. Usually on humans, but Magda had to try to find Larissa. She still couldn't believe the bitch had found her tracking spell.

Magda focused all her energy on Larissa's face.

Energy drained from Magda as she chanted. The harder she tried to find Larissa, the blurrier the female's face became in her mind. It didn't make sense. She wasn't sure how much time passed, but guessed it had been close to an hour when the air in the room suddenly changed, becoming colder, heavier. *He* was here. She felt his presence even before her eyes snapped open.

"Master," she whispered, staring as he slowly descended the stairs to her basement.

"You've lost Larissa." A statement, not a question. She shivered.

He wasn't wearing the hood he often chose and his eyes weren't glowing red, which meant he was in full control of himself. He was impossibly good-looking. With dark hair and beautiful eyes . . . She locked down her thought process at his knowing smirk. He loved the effect he had on her. "A momentary setback. She must have discovered my tracking spell, but I can still locate her." Magda simply needed to try harder with her locator spell. With the vampire's heart as a sacrifice it was possible. And if not, she'd sacrifice more vamps.

As if he read her thoughts, her master looked at the

dead male on the ground, then at the now-shriveled heart on the altar. His jaw tightened. "It would seem you couldn't."

She swallowed hard, hating that familiar glint in his eyes. When they'd first met they'd been equals. She'd even revealed ancient spells from her line to him. Now he treated her like a whore. Like one of his minions. "I *will* find her."

He covered the distance between them before she'd blinked. Reaching up, he grasped her jaw in a tight, unforgiving grip. His touch was unnaturally warm. "I don't doubt that," he whispered, that red glow flickering to life once again. "Because if you don't, I'll make you regret being born."

Before she could respond, he turned her around and slammed her face-first onto the altar. The blood from the vamp's heart spread over her face. She knew what was coming before it happened. Her nipples pebbled tightly as he shoved her skirt up. Seconds later, he was inside her, his thick length spreading her. Groaning, she arched her hips up as he thrust into her over and over. Bastard wouldn't let her come. He never did when he was pissed like this.

When she reached between her legs to stimulate herself, he stopped, buried deep inside her. "Don't." The warning sent a wave of fear rolling through her.

Though she wanted to orgasm, she knew better than to defy him. By now she didn't bother fighting him. There was no point. If she stroked herself anyway, he'd let her come, but then he'd punish her afterward. She'd rather deal with no climax than with what he'd do to her later if she defied him.

He resumed thrusting and she gritted her teeth. As soon as he was through with her, she'd have to find Larissa. Or suffer far worse consequences than this.

Chapter 9

Aiden tugged on one of the sweaters he'd grabbed earlier as he took the stairs to the second floor two at a time. The cabin he and Larissa had just broken into was huge, with two fireplaces. Luckily the one in the master bedroom was gas operated so he could start it without worrying about alerting anyone to their presence.

Larissa was waiting downstairs in the kitchen while he made sure the place was secure. He hadn't even had to break any windows or pick a lock to get in the place. One of the upstairs bathroom windows had been unlocked. The window was narrow and high up, but he'd used his skills as a shifter to jump up to it. Of course it had been the very last window he'd checked.

At least they were someplace relatively safe. He didn't think anyone had followed them and after he'd texted Connor he'd turned off his phone and taken out the battery. Going completely dark for a few hours was the only option right now. Larissa was beyond exhausted and needed to feed. Once she did, he planned to make sure she got more sleep. It was the only way she'd start regaining some of her strength. Since he couldn't take her back to the ranch yet, this place would have to do.

After checking the propane tank, he turned on the fireplace and turned it up high. He wanted to get this room as warm as possible, quickly. The cabin was located right near the top of one of the mountains at the Sugar Mountain ski lodge. If they'd been here on vacation it would have been the perfect getaway spot. They could practically step out the front door and hit the slopes.

But they weren't on vacation and the woman he'd never stopped loving didn't remember him. He bit back a curse and tried not to dwell on that. It wouldn't do him any good.

As he pulled two thick electric blankets down from the closet, he paused at a slight shuffling sound.

"It's just me," Larissa whispered nearby.

He stepped out of the walk-in closet to find her hovering in the doorway, arms wrapped tightly around herself. Wearing a thick jacket over a sweater, snug jeans, and knee-high snow boots, she was still practically shivering.

Damn it, he needed to feed her and get her warm. "I've got the fireplace going and I'm going to plug in these blankets. This will warm you up, but you've got to feed." He tried to brace himself for how arousing it would be for him. In the past they'd always been intimate when she fed from him, but things were different now.

She nodded as she stepped into the room. "I know." She took off her boots and set them neatly by the door. Next went her jacket, which she hung over the back of a tufted chair within arm's reach.

As he started plugging in and situating the blankets over the bed, she fiddled with the hem of her sweater, looking anywhere but at him.

"What?" he demanded, crossing to the entryway where she still hovered like she was ready to bolt at a moment's notice.

The thought pissed him off. He'd already proved he was trustworthy, that he'd never hurt her and wouldn't take anything that she wasn't willing to give of her own free will. She might not remember him, might not remember how good it had been between them, but she shouldn't be afraid.

Clearing her throat, she looked up, her indigo eyes confused. "How do we do this? Do I take from your wrist or . . ." Her gaze fell to his throat, her eyes going heavy-lidded with an emotion he recognized clearly.

Lust.

What he saw matched exactly what he was feeling. What he never stopped experiencing in her presence.

She wasn't afraid, she was *nervous*. And she was shaking. Shit.

Aiden closed his eyes and took a deep breath. No matter how much he wanted her, there was no way he could take advantage of her. Not now. He might want to use her own desire to win her over, to seal their bond, but something told him now wasn't the right time. He needed to take care of her other needs first and that meant making sure she was healthy.

When he opened his eyes, he held out a hand, let her see he was in complete control of himself and his baser desires. "Come on."

Tentatively, she placed her smaller hand in his. She seemed surprised when he led them to the tufted chair near the window rather than the bed. The curtains were shut and he didn't plan to open them or any of the others in the house. They weren't turning on any lights either. Nothing to draw attention to themselves. The soft glow from the fake wood in the fireplace barely illuminated her delicate features, but he didn't need it to see in the dimness anyway.

As he sat, he tried to order his growing erection to stay down, but it didn't work. The thought of Larissa's mouth on him was too much. Well, he'd just have to ignore it then. Without him having to say anything, she tentatively sat on his lap, perching on the edge of one leg.

This close to Larissa, that crisp forest-in-winter scent of hers wrapped around him, making him crazy. Fall and winter were always hardest for him because the smells had constantly reminded him of her. Hell, he was reminded of her no matter what.

Now he wouldn't have to worry about that anymore. He spread his thighs wider as she turned toward him, giving her more space to move. Her breathing increased as she placed her hands on his shoulders.

"You're turned on," she whispered, stating the obvious.

"So are you."

She nodded. "I should take your wrist . . ."

He tilted his head to the side, baring his neck completely to her in a way he never had or would with anyone else. She might not remember him, but maybe she would remember this. Even if she didn't, he was showing her, the best way he could, how much he cared for her. "Take what you need."

For a split second indecision flared in her eyes, but then they glowed brighter as her basic hunger took over. He thought she was just going to pierce his neck, but she bent down and started nuzzling him. The brush of her mouth against his skin was soft and sweet and so much like the first time she'd fed from him, his throat ached with too many emotions.

Closing his eyes, he let his head fall back against the chair as she gently raked her teeth over his neck. He shuddered at the feel of her teasing him with her teeth and tongue, the erotic action pushing his control to the limit. Combined with the growing sweet scent of her arousal, it was almost impossible to retain restraint. His cock ached between his legs, but he made himself stay still, just loosely holding her. One of his hands was wrapped around her back as she sat perched on his leg, but he didn't want to screw this up.

Aiden knew she needed to feel comfortable with this, feeding from him. As a rule vamps and shifters didn't comingle much, and vamps rarely fed from shifters. Even though she'd fed from him before, she didn't remember it. This would be new to her.

To him, it was heaven and hell. He was so fucking

turned on he was afraid he'd embarrass himself. The first time he'd allowed her to feed he'd been shocked by how erotic it was. He hadn't been able to control himself and they'd started fucking before she'd taken a few pulls of his blood.

When she raked her teeth against his neck again and made a purring sound, the leash on his control slipped. He slid his hand under the back of her shirt, along the length of her spine, rubbing her soft skin up and down in a soothing gesture. With each stroke, she pressed harder against his neck with her teeth until finally she penetrated his skin.

There was the briefest moment of the discomfort of two pinpricks against him, but it gave way to a pure shot of pleasure as she started to suck. His cock pulsed each time she dragged in his blood.

He groaned and wrapped his other arm around her, needing to hold her completely. Needing to feel her body pressed against his. He hated that clothes separated them. He wanted skin to skin, his cock pushing inside her as she rode him.

Larissa made a low sound of satisfaction and shifted positions so that she was completely straddling him while she fed. As she clutched onto his shoulder with one hand, her other one slid down his covered chest and didn't stop until she reached the top of his jeans. Through their link he knew exactly what she intended. And God, how he wanted it. But not now.

"No, you don't have to," he somehow managed to rasp out, though he wasn't sure how the hell he found his voice. He put a hand on the back of her head, more to ground himself than anything.

Ignoring him, she tore at the fastening of his jeans, ripping the fabric and tearing the button free until she found what she wanted.

He settled his hands on her hips and held tight as she grasped his hard length. Somehow he had to ground himself, to stop himself from stripping her down and thrusting into her tight heat. He should stop her . . . for some reason. He couldn't remember why he needed to, much less remember his own fucking name as her fingers fisted around his cock with the perfect amount of pressure.

In tune with the way she sucked his neck, she started stroking him until he couldn't think at all. He wasn't sure how much time passed as she sucked his neck and pleasured him, but when she pulled back, only stopping briefly to lick the wounds on his neck, he let go of his control.

She stared at him, her gaze an electric blue of hunger and raw need as her fist squeezed him. It was as if all his nerve endings lit up at once. "Larissa," he growled her name, sounding ragged as his climax surged through him.

She slammed her mouth down on his, stroking and teasing her tongue against his as he came on her hand and himself. He was barely aware of moving until he had her on the hardwood floor beneath him, his cock still hard in her hand.

It didn't matter that he'd come already. That had just

taken the edge off. After sixty years without her, he could fuck her for days. Weeks. The thought of being buried inside her that long made another growl tear from him.

Only when her hands pressed against his chest did he realize she was trying to tell him something. His breathing ragged, he pulled his head back and stared down at her.

Her eyes were now heavy-lidded, her gaze soft with adoration. "Aiden . . . I wanted to do that for you, but what you're thinking now . . . I don't think it's a good idea." Blushing, she trailed off and he realized what she wasn't saying.

He'd projected his thoughts to her, his hunger. And she was exhausted. This feeding would only be the first of many. She would need a few more before she was even remotely back in top form. He couldn't just take her now on the floor like he wanted. Because once he started, he wasn't stopping. He'd tire them both out until they couldn't walk. Which would just exhaust her even further.

His wolf was edgy, needy. For her. He knew his wolf was in his eyes because she went still, watching him not exactly warily, but damn close.

The caution there killed him. He forced his animal back as he cupped her cheek gently. Rubbing his thumb against her soft skin, he couldn't fight the shudder that overtook him. "We don't have to have sex, but I want to pleasure you." He needed it. To bind her to him even more, show her how good it could be between them.

She gave him a smile then, a real one. The first since

he'd found her again and it took his breath away. "I know you do. I can feel all of your emotions right now and it's amazing and overwhelming. I just, I don't think it's a good idea. If we go any further . . ."

"We won't stop until we pass out and you need more blood." While he hated the thought of her drinking from anyone other than him, he knew that to heal her quicker, he'd need to find donors. Supernatural ones. "After we rest, you can feed from me again and then we'll find you more blood."

She slowly licked her lips, the action so erotic his cock ached as he watched her tongue move. "You taste amazing. I wish I didn't have to feed from anyone else."

"Eventually you won't. Once you've regained your strength, you'll feed only from me." He knew he sounded high-handed, but didn't care. He didn't want her drinking from anyone else. Especially another male. The thought made his wolf go rabid.

She didn't acknowledge what he said as she continued. "Now that I've taken the edge off, I can find a human to mesmerize and take a little blood from. I won't hurt anyone."

"Is that why you didn't feed more until now?"

She nodded. "Yes. Magda gave me some blood but it was weak. I was too afraid to search out humans on my own. I didn't want to accidentally injure someone."

That was definitely the Larissa he remembered. Even though she'd been haughty when they first met, she'd been so kind and considerate of others. She'd viewed it as her duty to protect those she considered weaker. Because she was a bloodborn, someone higher up the evolutionary ladder than the majority of the planet, that had surprised him. But she was so respectful about not crossing boundaries and taking what didn't belong to her. It was one of the reasons he'd fallen so damn hard for her.

Closing his eyes, he touched his forehead to hers. He knew if he pressed hard enough he could have them both naked. Using willpower he hated, he said, "Let's get cleaned up, then get some sleep." His inner wolf clawed at him, telling him to shut the hell up and get them both naked, but Aiden had to think about what was best for Larissa right now. Standing took monumental effort, but he forced himself to get off her and tuck himself into his jeans before helping her to her feet.

As they headed for the bathroom, she asked, "Why did you wait so long to tap into our telepathic link?"

"I didn't want to overwhelm you at first, especially since you don't remember . . ." He trailed off when he felt sorrow emanating from her. The scent of it filled the air and he wanted to punch himself. "I'm sorry," he said, feeling like an ass.

"I'm the one who's sorry. I should remember you," she muttered, making a beeline for the shower. "Do you mind giving me a little privacy while I clean up?" She didn't even look over her shoulder as she started stripping.

He didn't want to give her space, but knew he should. The vibe between them changed so quickly he wasn't sure what to do or say to make it right. They might have just shared something intense and intimate, but for her, they were still more or less strangers. Though he didn't want to, Aiden left the room. The place had three other bathrooms so he headed for the closest one.

After he'd showered and shaved, he found Larissa lying on her side under the electric blankets. Her back was to the doorway, but he had no doubt she was aware of his presence.

"Is the room warm enough?" he asked as he closed the door behind him, hoping to keep the warmth contained.

"It's perfect. Thank you." She turned over to face him, her eyes a bright beacon in the darkness. "Sorry if things got weird. I didn't want to make things awkward. I'm just trying to adjust to everything."

"You don't have to apologize for anything."

"I'm still sorry."

"Let's just get some sleep. Is it okay if I sleep with you?" *Please say yes.*

Her gaze landed on his bare chest and she nodded before turning back over. Her look had been unreadable and he could feel her shutting him out. Their bondmate link made it impossible to completely do that, but she was trying. Which told him she clearly wanted privacy from him and that she was getting stronger already.

He didn't intend to let her push him away that easily.

He slipped into the big bed, but instead of giving her space, he sidled up behind her and wrapped an arm around her waist, tugging her close. She was wearing a T-shirt and flannel pajama pants and already felt much warmer than she had earlier.

Sighing softly, she laid her arm over his and slid her fingers through his. "I like you holding me," she murmured, her voice already drowsy with sleep.

He didn't trust his voice so he just tightened his grip. Right now he didn't give a shit about all the unknowns in their lives, he just cared that Larissa was in his arms and wanted to be there.

Her back arched under the onslaught of his wicked, talented tongue as he stroked her to her fourth, or maybe fifth, orgasm. The male was too much. Too intense. Far too dominating. And she couldn't get enough of him.

It seemed to go on forever, the climax punching out to all her nerve endings until she collapsed boneless against the silky sheets. Staring up at the high arched stone ceiling of his castle, she tried to catch her breath.

As he started to climb up her body, his shoulder-length blond hair tickled her bare stomach, then breasts before he captured her mouth with his in a purely dominating move. His hands were on either side of her head, his body caging her in as his erection pressed against her belly.

She slid her hands up his chest, over his shoulders and linked her fingers behind his neck as she wrapped her legs around his waist. A frustrated moan escaped her lips when he pulled his head back. "Why are you stopping?" she whispered.

Sighing, he stretched out over her, though made it a point to keep most of his weight off her. "We have to get back to the main castle for the meeting."

She frowned, hating that he was right. His pack had a huge castle where the majority of his packmates lived, but they also had a few other castles on their land. And her Aiden had his own castle . . .

Larissa jerked up in bed, her heart racing. Before she'd even sat fully up, Aiden moved, his blond hair free from the tie he'd used to secure it earlier.

"What's wrong?" he rasped out, looking around the room for danger. The sun had already risen; she could see the outline of light at the edges of the dark draperies covering the windows.

"Nothing." She reached out and fingered the soft strands of his hair. "Your hair is the same as it was before, right?"

Turning into her hand, he made a soft, growling sound she felt all the way to her toes as she cupped his cheek. "Yes, why?"

It had to have been a memory. "Is your pack considered royalty among humans?"

He shook his head. "Not in the way you think. But they're very, *very* wealthy."

"They have castles?"

His eyes narrowed slightly, but he didn't pull away. "Yes. Why?"

"I had a dream. Or I think it was. Were you and I ever in a room in a castle with a four-poster bed, a high arched ceiling. . . ." She trailed off, trying to remember more of the setting. The dream or memory was fuzzy around the edges and she'd been so focused on the very naked Aiden.

He smiled, more than a hint of a wicked gleam in his

eyes as he lay back, pulling her with him. She laid her head against his chest and splayed her hand over his stomach. She savored the gentle way he stroked up and down her back. "We were in my room many times. What were we doing in this dream?" For the first time since she'd spoken to him in those icy woods last night, she could hear the tiniest hint of a Scottish accent. He must have buried it deep when he left his pack. The thought made her sad. How he must have suffered if his own pack had rejected him. She might not remember them, but she knew how shifters were. They were so family oriented. She wondered if his new pack was better than his old one. But she held off on questioning to answer him.

"I think you can guess," she murmured, feeling her face heat up.

"Yes, but I want you to tell me." There he went again, with that wicked charm.

"The dream was brief, but I distinctly remember your head between my legs and neither of us had any clothing on." She smiled against his bare chest as he stiffened.

"Did you like what I was doing?" His voice was strained as he spoke.

Grinning, she nodded. "Oh yeah."

"Do you remember anything else?"

"No, it was very brief." When he didn't respond, she continued. "What is your current pack like?" She was still learning a lot about this new world, especially since shifters and vampires had come out to humans. That alone was jarring.

"Are you asking if they'll accept you?"

She didn't respond because she wasn't sure if that's what she'd wanted to know. If she was asking that, it meant she was thinking of a future with this male.

"They will," he said quietly when she didn't answer. "My Alpha and his mate have adopted a jaguar shifter and one of our warriors just mated with a royal member of the fae. They're out of town on a brief assignment for her family, but should be back in a day or so."

At that, her head popped up. "A *royal* member of the fae mated with a shifter? Who?" Though her coven had had enemies in every supernatural community, she'd known almost all royal fae. It seemed impossible that any one of them would have mated with a shifter.

He watched her carefully. "Brianna O'Brien."

Larissa didn't bother to hide her shock. "Rory and Eoghan's baby sister?"

"You know her?"

She nodded slowly. "We were not friends, but acquaintances. I knew her brothers well, though." When he growled, his expression turning fierce, she grinned. "Not like *that*." Laying her head back against Aiden's chest, she closed her eyes and was thankful when he didn't press her for more. That was certainly interesting. When she'd been put into stasis, a shifter-vampire mating had been unheard-of. Especially for someone royal like her. But if Aiden's pack had interspecies matings, maybe she and Aiden had a chance after all in this new world.

The thought soothed something deep inside her. She wasn't ready to evaluate it yet so she let her body relax as sleep once again claimed her. The memory of drinking Aiden's blood was so fresh, she could practically taste him as she drifted off. With every second she spent with this male she grew more and more attached and that terrified her. Everything about this new world was jarring and Aiden felt like a constant, the only safe place in a storm.

And something told her that a nasty storm was coming soon.

Chapter 10

Ryan sighed with pleasure as he poured his first cup of morning coffee. After three hours of sleep he was ready to go again. Not that he really had a choice anyway, not after all that shit from the club and the recent vamp blood dealings.

Three of his laptops were running various facial recognition software programs. One that the Council of lupine shifters used for their own investigations and two human government databases he'd hacked into. He'd plugged in different photos of individuals he'd managed to isolate from the videos he'd taken last night. Most of them were probably just supernatural beings looking to unwind and have a good time. But he hoped to get a hit on something more.

Anything to guide them in the right direction. Jayce was already working an angle with Kat—though Ryan was pretty sure she and the enforcer had come back a couple of hours ago to snag some sleep too.

Needing to sleep was such a bitch.

As he stepped away from the counter he scented and heard Lucas at the same time. The ten-year-old hadn't exactly learned how to stay quiet yet. While their predatory nature was inborn, for a shifter Lucas still had a lot to learn. He stomped into the kitchen, his expression serious.

Ryan raised his eyebrows. "You hungry?"

Lucas nodded. "Yeah, but I'm heading over to the main house. Vivian called and said she was saving me a seat and some chocolate chip pancakes."

Shit, right. Ana was cooking for everyone. He didn't have time to join them. "Will you grab me a plate?"

He nodded, but instead of leaving, sat at the center island in the kitchen. Lucas watched Ryan silently for a long moment and thanks to Ryan's blasted "gift" he could sense the boy's pain and confusion. Damn it, he needed to talk to Teresa about his gift soon. Hell, he needed to tell his Alpha too. He just didn't want to.

"What's wrong, Lucas?" he asked quietly, setting his mug down and moving to the island counter, where he took a seat next to the boy.

"Are you going to mate with Teresa?" Lucas asked.

Wasn't that the question he'd been asking himself for the past three months? He sure wanted to. "How would you feel if I did?"

Lucas shrugged and another shot of pain rolled off him. Dread surged through Ryan. If Lucas didn't accept her, he had no clue what he'd do. "I thought you liked Teresa."

The boy finally looked at him and when he did, a light

sheen of tears was in his eyes. Shit, shit, shit. "I do, but if you mate with Teresa, won't you be related to Ana?"

Blinking, Ryan nodded slowly, trying to figure out why that would matter. "Sort of. Teresa and Ana are cousins." They were all packmates anyway.

"And Ana's basically Vivian's mom. And you adopted me so you're like my dad."

Hell yeah, he was. Adopting Lucas was the best thing Ryan had ever done in his life. "Okay."

"If you mate with Teresa, does that mean . . ." He cleared his throat nervously. "Does that mean I can't mate with Vivian when we're old enough?" The tears were gone, but the seriousness was there.

Ryan's eyes widened. That's what this was about? "You and Vivian will never be related by blood." They weren't even the same species so it wasn't even an issue. "So if you want to mate with her and she wants to mate with you, then when you're old enough, you can." Good God, though, Ryan didn't even want to think about Lucas growing up so fast.

"Oh." The cub slid off the chair, his boots thumping loudly on the hardwood floor. "Okay then. I hope you mate with Teresa. I like her a lot."

Relieved, Ryan followed suit and stood. "So why are you so sure you're going to mate with Vivian?"

Lucas stared up at him as if he was stupid. "She's my best friend and she already takes all my toys anyway. If we live together, we can keep all our stuff together."

Ryan bit back a smile, but it was hard. "Have you told her of your intentions?"

Lucas snorted. "No way. You don't tell a girl that." He shook his head and ran out the front door, letting it slam behind him as he left.

Before Ryan had turned back to his coffee and laptops, the front door opened again. Jacob strode in, looking exhausted. Ryan knew he'd been out patrolling the property all night. All the warriors took shifts making sure the property stayed locked down. They'd had issues in the past few months, and with the hundreds of acres of land the pack owned, sometimes it was difficult to keep every square inch secure. Luckily, as shifters, they could typically scent intruders easily enough. He nodded at the pot of coffee. "There's a full pot on, unless you're crashing?"

Jacob scrubbed a hand over his face and looked at the pot before shaking his head. "Thanks, but I'll pass. I need to snag a few hours of sleep. I've got a run planned later this afternoon." The way he said it made all the hair on the back of Ryan's neck stand up.

He tried to keep his wolf locked down, but he was agitated thinking of Jacob running with Teresa. "Run? With a female?"

Jacob's eyes widened a fraction before he grinned. "Yep."

Ryan resisted the urge to bare his teeth at his friend. "With who?"

"Why's it matter, man?"

It mattered because not too long ago Jacob had planned to ask Teresa out. The other shifter had had every right to, but Ryan had seriously considered beating the shit out of his friend for even contemplating it.

He'd settled for threatening his packmate's manhood instead.

Jacob held up his hands in mock surrender and Ryan realized he'd started growling. Damn, he needed some more freaking sleep.

"It's not Teresa, jackass. Though . . . you might want to think about speeding things up with her. That is, if you *ever* plan to make a move."

Oh, he'd made a damn good move last night. And he planned to speed things up. First he needed to tell her a few things. If she still wanted him when she knew the truth about what he was, then there was nothing holding him back. Hell, at this point he didn't know that he could hold back anyway. After the way she'd melted in his arms in this very cabin . . . "Wait a minute. Why do I need to speed anything up?"

Jacob shrugged and headed toward the stairs. "You're not the only one interested in her."

He started to go after his packmate to question him when two of his computers made dinging sounds almost simultaneously.

The same image remained static on two of his screens. As he pulled up a chair at the counter, the third pinged with the same picture. The male who had been talking to Natalia last night. She'd pointed him out to Ryan in the videos earlier. Ryan hadn't even had a chance to tell his Alpha or anyone else. Now he was glad he hadn't because the male's name was Aldric Kazan.

Jayce Kazan's brother.

Holy shit. Ryan hadn't even realized the enforcer had any relatives. Much less one with such an interesting record. He'd never been prosecuted for any crimes, but according to the human databases, he was a person of interest in a few unsolved vampire murders. He was also in the shifter database, but there wasn't much information associated with him. Just a name and a note that he was Jayce's brother.

Ryan immediately texted Connor with a 911, asking his Alpha to get to the cabin. As he set his phone down, the front door opened. When he turned and saw Jayce there, he immediately closed all three laptops. In hindsight he realized how stupid that was. He should have just changed screens. Too late to do anything about it now.

The way the cabin was set up, the living room and kitchen were all joined into one big area with little separation.

Jayce glanced at the living room area, then strode toward Ryan, his expression curious. "You all right?"

"Yeah. You?"

Jayce watched him with those eerie gray eyes, as if trying to get him to confess to something. Hell, maybe the deadly enforcer was. As a warrior, Ryan could hold his own against most, but he knew Jayce hadn't earned his reputation for being lethal without being able to back it up. Finally he spoke. "Find out anything usable from the videos?"

Ryan shrugged. Without giving a yes or no, he wouldn't put off that metallic stench associated with lies. There were always ways around answering things you didn't want to. "Where's Kat?" he asked, changing the subject.

"Busy. I don't know what you're holding back, but . . ." Jayce trailed off and headed to the living room. He flipped on the flat-screen television so Ryan followed and stood next to him as he found a national news channel.

Connor and Liam strolled in as Jayce grunted at the screen. "You guys need to see this."

A female reporter came on screen talking about how the following story wasn't suitable for minors and might offend some viewers. Most of the image was blurred out, but a man had been beheaded and his naked body nailed up onto a billboard in Winston-Salem.

Ryan frowned as he listened to the reporter talk in circles, basically saying nothing as she talked about how police weren't releasing any details except the victim's name. Ned Hartwig.

Suspected drug dealer—whose laptop Ryan had in his possession thanks to Jayce stealing it from him.

"You do that?" Connor asked Jayce wryly, not exactly joking.

Jayce snorted. "The last time I saw him he was terrified of his dealer. More terrified of him than me. I'm guessing his dealer did that."

"Nice warning," Liam muttered.

That was *exactly* what it was. When supernatural beings killed, they knew how to dispose of a body. Displaying the human's body like that was a warning to all others by whoever Hartwig had worked for. *You fuck with him, you end up dead.* If only they knew who that someone was.

"We need to follow up with more of his contacts,"

Jayce muttered, more to himself than the others as he muted the television.

Ryan nodded in agreement, then motioned toward his closed laptops. "I might have another lead." He shot Jayce a quick look before he focused on his Alpha. "Last night a male at the club made Natalia nervous as she was arriving. She told me about it on the drive back to the ranch. His picture was among the ones I ran through the facial recognition software programs."

Connor's dark eyebrows raised. "And?"

"And I just got a hit." Sighing, he flipped open the closest laptop.

As the other three males stared at the screen, reading the name and other information next to the male's picture, Connor and Jayce let out curses at the same time.

Aiden slid out of bed as quietly as possible and was surprised when Larissa didn't stir. She'd fallen asleep hard this time. Clearly she needed it and he had to check in. He grabbed his phone and the battery and headed downstairs.

Once he'd checked the place again to make sure everything was secure and that he didn't scent any intruders, he slid the battery into his phone and called his Alpha. As he sat on the long couch in the living room, Connor picked up on the second ring.

"Hey, you guys doing okay?" he asked immediately.

Aiden liked that he asked about both of them. He knew his Alpha was fair and gave everyone a chance, but he was still worried about the dynamics of bringing a vamp onto the ranch. "We're good. Holed up in an unused cabin at the Sugar Mountain resort. As soon as she wakes up though, we're heading out and I'm buying disposable phones for both of us. I'll call you from mine."

"Sounds good. How's she adjusting to everything?"

"Considering she was put in stasis the year color TVs came out, Stalin died, and our kind was still living in secrecy, I'd say pretty damn good."

Connor let out a low chuckle. "I can't even imagine waking up in this technology-filled world overnight."

"No shit." Aiden was impressed by how well Larissa was taking everything in stride.

"Listen, I don't like leaving you out in the cold like this. If you think she's safe and she's not being tracked anymore, bring her to the ranch. We can protect her."

Aiden's throat tightened for a moment at the gesture. "I appreciate it, but with the cubs . . . I just can't take the chance until we know more. I'm not worried about her, but whoever is after her." He wanted that clear. Larissa would never be a threat to his pack.

Connor let out a small sigh of what sounded a lot like relief. "I agree—I just hate you not being able to come home. If you're not coming back here, what are you planning?"

"Finding the witch who released Larissa from stasis."

"Good. Brianna and Angelo just returned. I'm sending them to meet you. Just give me the address whenever you're settled somewhere." He spoke with the confidence of an Alpha and had clearly been ready for Aiden's answer.

Normally he had no problem following his Alpha's orders. But Aiden didn't want to share Larissa with anyone for even a moment, his wolf acting more dominant than usual. But Connor was right. Whatever the hell was going on, they'd need backup if they came up against the witch. She was an unknown and Aiden hated that. "The witch's name is Magda and she's got ties to Larissa's former coven. Supposedly." The female had told Larissa that her ancestors owed hers a debt. There might have been some truth in the woman's words.

"Noted. We'll go back to that, but I've got some other interesting news." The way he said "interesting" set off alarm bells in Aiden's head. "Jayce apparently has a brother and he was at the club last night. He was talking to Natalia. This might have nothing to do with the blood dealing, but we're looking into him. I'm going to text you a picture. Show it to Larissa, see if she knows him."

He'd already known Jayce had a brother because Kat mentioned it during a conversation. Aiden hadn't thought it had been a secret, but hadn't seen the need to tell anyone about it. "Will do. Listen, uh, has Ryan attempted to look into Larissa yet?" Because he had no doubt his packmate would have done just that as soon as Connor ordered.

"You didn't give me her last name."

"Would that really stop you or him?" It wasn't exactly a question.

"No. But the answer is no. I was giving you a day to come to me. Who is she?"

Aiden rubbed a hand over his face and let his head fall back against the couch. God knew he needed his pack's help with this. Larissa didn't know shit about what had happened to her family other than what that witch had told her so the assumption was everything she'd been told was a lie. Aiden didn't run in vampire circles and after her supposed death—and after he'd searched in vain in the hopes he was wrong—he'd headed to the United States and roamed aimlessly for years until joining up with Connor's band of warriors. Somehow he didn't think Google was going to give him or Larissa what she needed to know about her family.

"She took her mother's family name, which is Danesti." Aiden waited to see if Connor would know the line.

A short pause. "That sounds familiar."

It should. It had been one of the royal lines of the House of Basarab. The Danesti line had been in constant contest with the Draculesti line for the throne of Wallachia. Which technically didn't exist anymore, but was part of the country of Romania. Connor wouldn't give a shit about the history and Aiden didn't care to enlighten him. None of that was important now. "The Danesti line was eventually absorbed by the Draculesti line. Larissa took her mother's name so it wouldn't die out. But her father is Vlad Dracul. The third."

A longer pause. "Are you fucking kidding me?"

Oh yeah, he would have heard of *that* name. "No."

"Larissa's father was Vlad Dracul? Vlad *Tepes*? Vlad the fucking *Impaler*?"

Tepes translated meant "the Impaler," something Connor clearly knew. "Yeah."

Surprising him, Connor let out a loud laugh. "Man, I bet her family just loved that she mated with a shifter."

A weight on Aiden's chest lifted at his Alpha's reaction. "You have no idea." He'd always thought their reaction was asinine considering the way her parents had mated. Two opposing vampires from warring covens that had had regular assassination attempts on the other for the better part of two centuries. They'd been like Romeo and Juliet of the vampire world and had been deeply in love. But their daughter fall in love with a shifter? Hell fucking no.

"Are her parents really dead?" Connor asked.

"Maybe. Magda told her they were, but she's not exactly a reliable source. I just don't know." Once he'd moved to the States and gone roaming he'd lost contact completely with his old life. It wasn't like he had any damn vamp contacts anyway.

"All right. I'll put Ryan on that too."

"Ask Teresa to help him. She's good with computers." His words were light.

"You're an ass," Connor said on a chuckle.

"I just wish Ryan would save us the fucking headache and mate with her already. He's been such a dick the past couple months." Aiden loved his packmate and understood why Ryan was so edgy. Constantly being near the female you wanted and not being able to have her was stressful. Except Ryan *could* have her. He was just too much of a dumbass to stake his claim.

"No kidding. Hold on. . . . Kat, damn it. . . ."

"Aiden?" Kat's breathless voice came over the line. He could hear Connor grumbling in the background.

"What's up?"

"How are you? How's your mate? Is this the vampire you said you screwed things up with? I thought she was dead. What's going on? And why haven't you *called* me?"

Aiden smiled even though he didn't have time to get into a long conversation with Kat. Since he'd turned Kat into a shifter, he was considered her maker and they had a tight, unbreakable bond—much to the annoyance of her mate. Jayce didn't care that there had never been a spark of attraction between Kat and Aiden, he was just alpha and didn't like his female being so friendly with Aiden. He didn't care though. Hell, even if he hadn't turned her, he would have adored her anyway. She was strong, funny, smart, and a good friend.

"Honey, I don't have time to get into all that now, but I promise I'll fill you in as soon as I can."

She snorted loudly. "The pack gossip doesn't have time?"

"Connor will fill you in, but I've got to go." He needed to get back to Larissa so they could get out of the cabin, find new phones and transportation. Because very soon they'd be hunting down Magda and getting some answers.

"Aiden—"

"Kat, I've gotta go." He ended the call even though he hated hanging up on her. He'd been on the phone long enough as it was. After taking the battery out of his phone he stood.

When he turned toward the doorway he found Larissa standing there with a furious expression on her face. Shit, he hadn't even heard her come downstairs. She was definitely getting stronger.

Her hands were balled into fists and her eyes spat sparks at him. "Who the hell is Kat and why are you calling her honey?"

Chapter 11

Larissa stared at Aiden, feeling betrayed, but more than anything she was raging pissed. Her claws pricked her palms, but she didn't even wince. The powerful sense of jealousy hummed through her, making her body go icy-cold. She hated that Aiden's simple endearment to another female made her crazy.

Aiden watched her carefully, his mouth curving into a half smile. As if he thought this was funny.

"Is my question amusing?" she bit out. She wanted to wipe that look right off his face.

Taking a tentative, almost cautious step forward, he held up his hands as if he were surrendering. "No, but I like seeing you jealous."

He *liked* this? Oh yes, she really wanted to punch him. She took a deep breath and tried to contain this insane feeling. Before she'd exhaled, Aiden crossed the few feet to her and settled his big hands on her hips. As if he thought he had every right to.

Though her first instinct was to lash out, she decided to let him talk first. She didn't pull back from him, but she also didn't touch him. She didn't trust herself not to claw him to shreds. Crossing her arms over her chest, she said, "Explain why you used an endearment on another female. Is she your lover?"

His expression softened. "No. Kat is a friend. A dear friend who is mated—bonded—to the enforcer, one of the scariest shifters in the world. I'm her maker, so we're close. But things between us are and always have been very platonic. I just called her 'honey' out of habit. It used to piss off her mate before they were mated, but I guarantee it means nothing beyond friendship. But I won't do it again if it bothers you." His words were sincere, but there was still a hint of something in his eyes that drove her crazy.

"You sound sorry, but you don't look it," she snapped.

His mouth quirked up even higher. "I'm sorry I hurt you. I've just never seen you quite so territorial before. *I* was the jealous one when we first met. I don't care if it's fucked up; I like that you're feeling this way. You might not remember me, but your subconscious does." And he was absolutely smug about it.

She relaxed at his words and reached for him, some deep part of her needing to touch his body. Placing her palms over his chest, she looked up at him. "If you turned this Kat, she must have been human before."

He nodded and she frowned.

"Shifters almost never turn humans." The survival rate was around one percent if she remembered correctly. "Why did you turn her?" What if he'd harbored feelings for the female? Just because they hadn't been lovers didn't mean Aiden had never wanted the female.

At her question, his expression darkened. "She was minutes, *seconds*, away from death. We didn't know if it would work, but she was dying so I had to try."

"You care for her." That shouldn't bother Larissa, but for some reason it did. Logic did not enter into her thoughts, only the strange new feelings of possessiveness that could drown her if she allowed them.

"Yes. But not in a romantic sense."

She believed him. It was the only thing that locked all those jagged emotions back into their cage. "What is an enforcer?"

His eyes slightly widened. "Right, you wouldn't know," he muttered. "When shifters and vamps came out to humans, my kind formed Councils all over the world. Each Council has one or more enforcers who basically investigate the more serious problems our people might have. They also mete out the kind of justice the humans won't. Up until recently North America only had one. Now we have two. A male and female. Both live with my pack and the male is mated to Kat."

"He is one of the fiercest of your kind?"

Aiden nodded.

"And you used to push his keys for fun by purposely calling his female 'honey'?" What was wrong with Aiden? She knew how territorial shifters were and he'd been trying to annoy a powerful one intentionally. It didn't make sense. She didn't like the thought of him putting himself in any amount of danger.

Aiden frowned for a moment, then grinned, his fingers digging tighter into her hips. "Push his buttons?"

She felt her face flush as she nodded. Stupid idioms. She'd found entire lists of common popular phrases on something called Google, but they'd been confusing and nonsensical. "Yes." She'd been thinking of keys on a keyboard. It made more sense than a button anyway. "Why did you?"

Aiden shrugged, his demeanor changing. It was slight, but his muscles tensed under her fingertips. "I thought he was a fool. His would-be mate was right in front of him, but he was too stupid to claim her. It served him right," he growled.

The meaning of what he *wasn't* saying hit her. "You were mourning me and were angry at the other male for not being with the woman he cared for?"

He nodded, all traces of humor gone from his expression now.

After sixty years of her being gone, of Aiden assuming she was dead, he *still* cared. Why couldn't she remember this male? Anger and frustration clawed at her. She cupped his face between her hands. "Aiden . . ." She didn't even know what to say. Emotions pummeled her insides like a battering ram. Possessiveness and desire for this male mixed with the need to take care of him. Because something told her that he'd been burying his emotions and covering his pain for a long damn time and that bothered her.

Maybe it was their link that told her, she wasn't sure. Last night before they'd gone to sleep she'd tried to mute the bond between them in an effort to regain more of herself, but maybe that was stupid. Maybe she *needed* to be foolish and just embrace this male and wipe away all the pain she saw in those dark eyes. Pushing up on her tiptoes, she went to give him a soft kiss, but he crushed his mouth over hers like a man starving.

Like he couldn't help himself.

God help her, she didn't want him to stop. As their tongues and lips clashed in a frenzied mating, he picked her up by the hips, giving her no choice but to wrap her legs around his waist. Grinding against him, she groaned at the feel of his thick length pressed against her lower abdomen through their clothes. Just the sensation of his arousal made her nipples tighten in awareness.

Thankfully he didn't have a shirt on so she could feel all that raw power humming beneath her fingertips. The male was truly beautiful, but something told her that wasn't what had drawn her to him originally. If anything, it might have repelled her. She'd never been one to be swayed by a handsome face or a hard body. Aiden was a little cocky but underneath that swagger he was so caring. She'd hardly spent any time with him, but what little she'd seen so far told her a lot about his character.

When she'd been slicing him up in the woods he'd done everything he could to deflect her blows but not cause her injury. He'd been mourning her for decades, and he hadn't even been able to cut her when she'd needed that tracking ink out of her skin. If for some reason she never regained her memories, she still didn't want to lose this male. Even the thought of that happening sent a shot of agony ricocheting through her.

Larissa tore her lips back from Aiden's. "I might never regain my memories," she blurted, needing to let him know.

"Then we'll make new ones." He didn't hesitate. As if it wasn't a question for him.

Her throat tightened as she watched him, as she felt the most beautiful warmth spreading across their bondmate link. This time she crushed her mouth to his. With impressive speed, he moved them until they fell onto the longer sofa, her underneath him. She loved the feel of his big body stretched out on hers.

As he started kissing his way along her jaw, then down to her throat, she slid her fingers through his blond hair and clutched onto his head. His hands moved under her T-shirt, shoving it upward as he teased the column of her throat with his tongue and teeth.

With him she felt absolutely no fear. Not even as she bared her neck. Even though she had to feed, she'd rarely fed others unless in dire circumstances. And only then had she offered her wrist. Never her neck. The sensation of baring herself to Aiden was freeing, exhilarating and she was getting so turned on she knew he must sense it. Her inner walls tightened as he blazed a path of kisses to her stomach.

"Off," he murmured against her skin as he shoved her T-shirt upward.

Without pause, she pulled it over her head. As she tossed it behind her, his fingers dipped into the waist of her pajama pants. Slowly, torturously, he tugged them down her legs. She knew it wouldn't be wise to have sex with him now because she would absolutely not stop at just one time—but she was pretty sure he had something else in mind as he lifted up one of her legs and started to kiss her ankle.

As he slowly made his way up her inner calf, her entire body tingled in awareness. She was completely naked whereas he still wore pants. She liked being laid out like this for him.

He met her gaze, his expression so damn needy she couldn't fight a shudder that rolled through her. Keeping his eyes pinned to hers, he continued kissing his way up her leg until he reached her upper inner thigh. When he swiped his tongue along the seam of her inner thigh, so close to her wet heat, yet not close enough, warmth flooded the juncture between her legs. She wanted to feel all of him invading her: his tongue, fingers, his hard length.

I wish I could fuck you right now, but since we shouldn't, I'm going to make you cry out my name. Aiden's voice was a dark promise in her mind.

The words he communicated telepathically set her on fire. She still wasn't used to communicating like that with anyone other than her family but it felt right on the deepest level to let Aiden in like that. She struggled to find the right response, but couldn't find any words at all as she let her head fall back on the couch.

Not seeming to need or expect a response, he pressed his hands between her thighs to spread them wider. She gladly obliged him. When he swiped his tongue up the length of her already wet slit she jerked against him. Unable to stop herself from touching him, she grabbed on to his head.

With some of his blond hair splayed on her thighs as he began the most delicious assault on her nerves, this looked so much like her dream that she wondered if she was *still* dreaming.

When he centered on her clitoris, swiping his tongue over it with the perfect amount of pressure to drive her insane, she forgot everything and just held on to him.

She wasn't sure how long he teased her, but it was driving her crazy. Her body was sensitized, as if he had a direct line to all her nerve endings. But he wasn't giving her enough stimulation and something told her that he knew exactly what he was doing. How much he was teasing her.

When he slid one, then two fingers into her sheath, her hips vaulted off the couch. He plunged deep, her slickness allowing him to move in and out of her as he finally increased his pressure against her sensitive nerves.

Say my name, he demanded.

"Aiden." His name tore from her lips even as she projected it to him. *Aiden.*

Groaning against her, he buried his fingers deep inside her and held them there, doing something positively wicked as he curved them against a spot that drove her crazy. Pleasure shot out to all her nerve endings as a wave built inside her.

Higher, higher it pushed as her nipples tightened, her back arched, and her inner walls clenched even harder around his thick fingers. She grabbed onto his shoulders as her fangs descended. God, she wanted to feed. Needed to taste Aiden again.

After savoring his blood earlier she'd realized just how quickly he could become an addiction in the best way possible. Her orgasm slammed into her, her inner walls squeezing around him as he showed her clitoris no mercy.

His tongue teased and stroked her until it almost bordered on pain. Her climax seemed to go on forever, stretching out impossibly long until finally he tore his head away from her. Feeling almost bereft, she was surprised when he crawled up her body and bared his neck to her.

"Feed." He used that same demanding tone as before. The one that should have annoyed her, but now turned her on more.

"I can't." She didn't think she'd taken too much before but she didn't want to risk it.

"I've recovered enough and I'm stronger than when we first met." Even if he was stronger, she wouldn't know.

But she didn't sense a lie and as he dipped his head to hers, angling his neck so that it was right in front of her mouth, she swallowed hard. Her fangs ached, but she told herself to show control.

"Take from me," he whispered, his big body tense above hers.

Her eyes grew heavy-lidded and focused on his vein as her control snapped. Sinking her fangs into his flesh, she slid her hands up his back as he groaned in pleasure. His fingers were still buried deep inside her as she began to suck. With each drag of his blood, he pulled his fingers out, then pushed back in. The rhythm was slow and erotic and the more she drank his sweet blood, the stronger she felt.

As they writhed against each other, he cupped one of her breasts with his free hand, strumming her already hardened nipple with his callused thumb. The gentle action sent her into overdrive as another orgasm rippled through her. This one was less intense, but just as wonderful as it ebbed out to her already frayed nerve endings.

Using hard-won control, she pulled her head back and withdrew from his neck. Though he would heal anyway, she licked the tiny wounds to instantly close them. Nuzzling against his neck, she tightened her grip around his waist as he finally withdrew his fingers from her and returned her embrace.

He buried his face against her neck and inhaled her in a way that told her exactly how much he wanted her. Needed her. She desperately wanted to feel his thick length inside her, but kept a tight rein on her baser wants.

She wasn't sure how much time passed but eventually Aiden's voice cut through her thoughts. *We need to leave soon.*

I know. She was definitely getting used to this telepathic thing with him.

He lifted his head then, his expression fierce. "We're going to find Magda and get answers. It might get ugly."

There was no maybe about it, and even though she

couldn't remember Aiden she wasn't surprised by his attitude. Shifters and vampires were very similar in the way they handled justice. That woman had lied to Larissa and set her up to kill Aiden. A man who she was now coming to understand had meant everything to her. That witch was going to pay.

She still worried about Aiden though. She'd seen him in action, but Larissa wasn't up to her normal fighting self and they had no clue what this witch had in her arsenal. The unknown was the scariest of all. The thought of something happening to Aiden sliced her up. She didn't care that she didn't remember him. She knew that if she lost him, she'd never get over it. If she had to choose vengeance against Magda and discovering the truth about her parents and past or Aiden's safety, Aiden would win.

Chapter 12

Larissa ran her finger along the edge of the chipped ceramic plate sitting under her now-lukewarm cup of coffee. She'd ordered something to be polite and even though she could imbibe liquids, after having Aiden's taste still lingering on her tongue she didn't want to dilute it.

She stared out the window of the small diner attached to the gas station where he was currently buying cell phones. The entire setup of the place was strange to her, but everyone here had been friendly. Possibly because they didn't know she and Aiden were supernatural beings. Aiden had told her that while they might have come out to humans twenty years ago, they didn't go around advertising what they were. Apparently there were many hate groups who would love to see them dead. Not that she was exactly surprised by that. People often feared what was different to them. Some things never changed. It wasn't as if she planned to show off her fangs, so unless Aiden shifted in front of everyone they should remain undetected.

A dark SUV pulled up right in front of the big window of the diner. The windows were tinted but she could see the passengers in the front seat clearly enough. Brianna O'Brien and an unknown male. Must be her shifter mate.

Larissa turned away from the window and leaned slightly out of the booth for a glimpse of Aiden in the attached gas station. There were no barriers between the two establishments, but with too many people in the way she couldn't see him. She could sense him though.

Your friends are here, she projected.

Paying now, will be over in just a sec.

She turned back to the window to see Brianna and a dark-haired, bronze-skinned, lean but muscular male step out. Both of them looked at her through the glass, as if they sensed her presence. Or Aiden had told them where they were sitting. She didn't like being so exposed by the front of the restaurant, but there had been no other seating and Aiden had needed to eat.

Brianna half smiled and nodded at her before the male looped an arm around her shoulders and they headed inside. The bell jingled over the door a moment later. Out of respect, Larissa slid out of her seat and stood. She might not know her in a friendly, intimate way, but she was acquainted with the fae female.

And as another royal, it was only proper that Larissa stand for Brianna. The young blond female seemed almost amused as they approached the booth. "Larissa

Danesti," she murmured, "it's good to see you alive. This is my mate, Angelo Medina."

Larissa nodded at the male with the piercing hazel eyes and murmured a polite greeting as she motioned to the booth. "It's nice to see you looking so well, Brianna. Respectfully, I can't believe your brothers didn't have a stroke when you mated," she said softly as they all slid into their seats. The humans from the two booths surrounding theirs had already paid and left dirty dishes behind, but she still didn't want anyone to inadvertently overhear.

She hoped Brianna and Angelo would take her statement the way it was intended. Larissa was curious about their relationship and how things worked with the female's royal family. Shifters and vamps had always been blunt and she hoped that hadn't changed in the last few decades she'd been in stasis.

The other female smiled and snuggled closer to her mate, her adoration for him clear. "Best decision I ever made, but yes, my family is still adjusting. *Especially* my brothers. My mother has been surprisingly okay with it. I can't believe that Aiden from Angelo's pack is 'The Aiden' who mated with Vlad's daughter," she whispered the last part before continuing. "It never occurred to me that he was the same male." She shook her head slightly.

Aiden chose that moment to return to the table. With his exceptional hearing he would have heard their conversation from the gas station. He slid into the booth and promptly slung an arm around Larissa's shoulders as he nodded at his friends. She loved his immediate possessive display. He was making it clear what she meant to him. It didn't matter that the others could scent her and Aiden's bond, even Brianna with her almost human senses, Larissa needed him to claim her publicly. Something she hadn't even realized she wanted until that very moment. "It's not something I advertise," he murmured before sticking his hand out to Angelo.

The two males did some sort of hand clasping/bump thing that wasn't exactly a shake, but more complex. She wondered if it was a shifter thing she'd never known about or a new human way of greeting. Or maybe it was a male thing because Aiden didn't do it with Brianna.

"You guys hungry?" Aiden asked.

They both shook their heads as a waitress with a stained apron approached their table with a warm smile and a pad of paper. "What can I get for you guys?"

The lack of formalness in people amazed Larissa. Her world had been so very different. She found she liked it, just as she was getting used to the jeans Aiden had given her. They were snug, warm, and surprisingly comfortable.

"Two coffees, black," Angelo murmured, obviously ordering to be polite. As he did, he laid a twenty-dollar bill on the table and slid it to her. "We're not hungry but this is for taking up one of your tables."

Surprise rolled off the waitress as she smiled. "Thanks, y'all. I'll bring your coffees in just two shakes and I'll refresh yours," she added to Larissa.

Larissa wondered if the "two shakes" was an idiom she'd missed in her reading and made a note to look it up.

"So what do you know about Larissa's coven?" Aiden asked quietly, his question directed at Brianna.

It appeared there would be no working their way into the conversation, something Larissa was grateful for.

Brianna gave her an almost apologetic look as she shrugged. "The Draculesti coven disappeared almost overnight. Obviously I don't mean literally, but in a matter of a year their property was sold off—most of it—and the coven just . . . ceased to exist for lack of a better description. I wish I knew more but you know how fae and vamps were and still are. We're a little more connected now because of technology, but back then I'd only heard rumors about the great Vlad's coven. Some said he decided to completely withdraw from the human world, which I always thought was a stupid theory because your kind need humans to survive. Some said they were killed by a rival coven, but no one ever stepped up and took responsibility for supposedly killing your family so I think that was a lie too. According to my mother the coven still owns a castle in Romania. It's owned under a shell corporation, but it's definitely linked to the Draculesti line. As a favor to me, she's sent investigators to the castle for in-person investigation, but other than that I don't know more. I apologize."

Larissa wasn't sure what a shell corporation was, but had a pretty good idea. "Please do not apologize. You've given me more information than anyone since my awakening. I would like to thank your mother personally at a later date."

"Of course." Brianna nodded. "I'll extend your regards for now."

Larissa could feel Aiden's amusement through their bond and turned to look at him, her eyebrows raised.

I love how almost formal you two are with each other, he said through their link. "Here," he said aloud, pulling out a cell phone and setting it on the table. "This is your new cell phone. It's got a couple thousand minutes on it and I've programmed my new number and Brianna and Angelo's number into it. I've also programmed my Alpha's number in it just in case."

Meaning in case something happened to him or all of them. Something Larissa refused to consider. Nothing would be harming Aiden. Not with her around. She might still be gaining her bearings in this new world, but that hadn't changed how deadly she was. "Thank you."

"If you guys are done, we should get out of here," Angelo said, watching the busy parking lot. He didn't seem stressed about anything, just observant of their surroundings. "I want to see if I can pick up that witch's trail at the hotel. The sooner the better."

When Larissa had told Aiden that she and the witch had checked into a hotel and reserved two rooms for a week he'd been thrilled. Larissa had just assumed if Magda was a liar she'd have already taken their things and left, but a call to the hotel had told them that the rooms were still theirs. Aiden wanted to track Magda using scent and the only place he might be able to pick it up was there. Larissa thought that was unlikely to happen, but they needed to start somewhere while Aiden's packmate Ryan did whatever investigations he was doing on the witch.

Larissa nodded, then nudged Aiden slightly in the side. *I'm going to find someone to feed. I'll be quick.* She wanted to drink a little more blood before they left in case they didn't have time once they reached Winston-Salem. Even though human blood was much weaker than supernatural blood and she didn't like the idea of drinking from anyone but Aiden, she had to. She couldn't depend on him too much and weaken him. Not when they would need their strength. The last thing she wanted to do was hurt him.

He frowned, those dark eyes of his going pure wolf for a moment. *I'll go with you.*

No. She wasn't a child. It was embarrassing enough that she didn't understand half the conversations going on around her or that she barely knew how to use a cell phone, she refused to have a babysitter while she fed.

His jaw tightened as he watched her. It was clear he wanted to argue, but eventually he relented, giving her a tight nod. *Find a female and take her into the bathroom. Then meet back here.*

She glared at him. *I don't need you to tell me what to do. I might be behind on some things, but I can feed without instructions. I'm over five hundred years old and have been hiding what I am and how I need to survive for longer than you've been alive.* He jerked back at her words, but slid out of the booth, allowing her to stand.

She didn't care if she surprised him. Refusing to

look at him again as she headed toward the gas station, she started looking for a human to mesmerize. It didn't matter that vamps had come out to the world, she wasn't asking someone for their blood. Right now she was going to *take* what she needed so they could get the hell out of there. Annoyance filtered through her as Aiden's order rang through her mind. She couldn't believe he'd felt the need to tell her to feed from a female or where to go. Like she was that infantile? She was embarrassed enough by her lack of modern knowledge—she wouldn't let her mate baby her, and definitely not in front of others.

"Brianna and Angelo have made contact," Connor murmured before sliding his cell phone back into his pocket.

Liam nodded, his expression tense as they headed across the yard to the parking structure. "Good."

"Jayce said that human female's friends from last night were a dead end. Apparently they showed up at her place and his vamp contact questioned them." At least it had saved Jayce a trip.

Liam grunted another affirmative as they continued. Their boots crunched over the icy ground. Even with the sun rising in a cloudless sky, the snow from the night before wouldn't be melting any time soon. He and Liam were meeting with two Brethren vampires in less than an hour on semi-neutral ground to discuss the male Natalia had killed.

Connor had already established a relationship with the Brethren a couple of weeks ago after a case Erin, one of his packmates and the newest enforcer in North

America, had handled in New Orleans. Shifters and vamps had needed to work together and his pack had learned about a sick fucking practice ancient vamps liked to engage in after pregnant shifters had started being kidnapped and eventually killed. Since it hadn't been condoned by the Brethren and the four ancient vampires had worked together with shifters to keep the peace among their kind, Connor was more than willing to meet with them about this issue. He knew Natalia had acted only in self-defense and he wasn't worried about her innocence, but he knew situations like this could get out of control. Especially when someone's relative was one of the deceased.

"Seriously, why did it have to be the brother of a Brethren member?" Liam muttered, mirroring his own thoughts.

Connor lips pulled into a thin line. "No shit."

"She's taking this pretty hard," Liam said, shooting him a quick glance as they reached his truck.

They'd decided to attend this meeting low-key, without a big show of numbers from the rest of the pack. He and Liam didn't need the backup anyway, but more than anything, he wanted the ranch protected. These were his people and he'd do anything to keep them safe. From the cubs to the strongest warriors. "Yeah, I know. Teresa told Ana and she told me." At the thought of his mate, he smiled despite everything on his plate.

Think about me while I'm gone, he projected to her.

A moment later, he heard Ana's voice in his head. *You're not even off the ranch yet.*

How do you know?

Because Vivian is making me wait by the gate to wave you and Liam off and I haven't seen you two leave yet.

Vivian is making you, huh?

A slight pause. *Maybe it was my idea.*

"You haven't even been separated from her for five minutes yet," Liam said good-naturedly.

"What?"

"I know you're talking to Ana. You get a goofy look on your face every time you two communicate."

Connor shrugged and palmed his key fob. After nearly fifty years separated from the one woman who had the ability to bring him to his knees, he didn't care what he looked like when he communicated with her. "Like you're any better." If anything, his brother was worse over his little human bondmate.

His brother grinned. "Just wait until Ana's pregnant. Then you'll be—"

They both froze almost simultaneously. His wolf clawed at his insides, the foreign scent drifting on the air making his hackles rise. Without having to say a word, both brothers stripped off their clothes and shoes in seconds and shifted to their wolf form.

A vampire was close by. Maybe more than one. There were too many heartbeats at the ranch to decipher who was who, but the new scent subtly teasing his nose was definitely foreign.

East? Liam asked through their familial telepathic link. Not all related shifters could communicate telepathically but he and Liam came from a strong line and could in both human and wolf form. They usually chose to talk aloud in human form, but when they were wolves, this was the only option.

Connor paused, inhaling again what he'd scented only hours before at that club. Definitely vampires. Their crisp scent was unmistakable, like freshly washed clothes in summertime. It wasn't bad, just different from his and other species. *Yes*, he said to his brother, running to the other end of the parking structure.

There was no way in hell he should be scenting vamps on his land. And not this close to the ranch. The drive to where everyone lived was at least a couple of miles from the highway and the rest of the surrounding land was hundreds of acres of untamed hills. Which meant these fuckers were close. *Ana, get Vivian and Lucas inside. We have a breach. Vampires. Contact everyone and be careful. Love you.*

She cursed, then said, *On it. You be careful too. I love you.*

His packmates would all know what to do and so did Ana. His mate was smart and tough and he didn't worry about second-guessing her decisions in a crisis. She would be securing the main house and calling everyone, ordering them what to do. Though he could never truly lock down the worry he felt for his bondmate, he compartmentalized it and focused on the task at hand.

December's on her way to the main house. She's calling Kat, Liam told him, the worry in his brother's voice potent. December had the healing capabilities of a shifter because of the baby she carried, but she couldn't

shift like them yet and she was weaker in her pregnant
state.

We've got a lot of protection here. Connor knew his
words didn't matter when Liam was worried about his
mate, but they would have to do.

As he and Liam neared the end of the parking structure that was the same size as the barn they had for
their horses, they both slowed at the open exit.

They're fucking close. Connor forced his growl down.
Right now was about stealth. In front of him he could
see one of the fences penning in their cows. It extended
around all the way to the line of thick woods. Beyond
that he couldn't see shit. Didn't matter what kind of
extrasensory abilities he had. He couldn't see through
trees. But something told him the vamps he scented
were closer. There was no wind right now. . . . He
looked up into the rafters.

Without needing to communicate, next to him Liam
did the same. Connor tensed, slowly creeping back inside, keeping his gaze upward. Scanning the dark
shadows, he saw three areas that didn't quite blend in
with the darkness. But the figures came damn close.
Which told him these weren't young vamps with no
experience. Hell, the fact that they'd breached his land
and they were here in the daylight told him all he
needed to know about the strength of the vamps. Daywalkers were fairly rare, created only if their makers
were.

I see three, Liam said.
Same here.

Connor howled now, letting loose the anger he'd been restraining. No need to remain quiet now, not when he'd spotted the intruders. Next to him Liam howled and in the distance the innumerable howls of his packmates rose up like the most beautiful symphony.

Almost instantly, three males dropped from the rafters, moving with rocket-like speed, their boots thudding against the hard earth. Dust whooshed out beneath them, making soft puffs in the air.

The three males looked similar. Dark hair, glowing amber eyes, all leather clothing. Like a fucking vampire cliché. One stepped forward, a short sword in his hand. The speaker of the group focused on Connor from thirty feet away, his expression full of rage. "We just want the female."

Fuck. Connor couldn't talk to the male like this and while he wanted nothing more than to simply kill these intruders, he knew he shouldn't. Not when his pack's well-being was at stake and he had to look at the big picture. Sometimes being Alpha sucked. *I'm changing,* he told Liam. Translation: cover me if these bastards try to attack while I'm mid-shift.

The heady rush of the change was almost instantaneous as he shifted back to his human form. "Give me one reason why I shouldn't slaughter all of you where you stand," he demanded, his voice more animal than man. Right now he was barely hanging on to his humanity.

These bastards were on his land. Where his beloved mate lived. Where his adopted cub lived. Where everyone who depended on him lived. Hell. No.

The leader spoke again, his voice low and angry. "I told you, we just want the female."

"You're going to need to be a little more specific than that." For all Connor knew this was about Larissa and not Natalia. Not that it mattered. Even if Aiden's mate was here and he had the ability to give her to these vamps, he *wouldn't*.

"That bitch who killed our maker."

"Again, be specific." Connor bit back a smile as all three snarled in rage.

"I know she's here. She killed Emil. We want her. It's our right to exact vengeance."

Ah, so this was about Natalia. Some of Connor's tension lessened. He'd expected some of the dead vamp's offspring—and that's how some viewed themselves in relation to their maker—to want retaliation, but he'd thought he could nix the problem by meeting with the Brethren.

Connor let the leash on his wolf slip intentionally, let his animal's need to strike bleed into his eyes. "She *is* here. She is my responsibility and more than that, she's my packmate. You trespassed on my land minutes before I'm about to meet with Juhani and Narek." Two of the Brethren members, including the dead vamp's brother, Juhani. Connor's wolf bared his teeth in glee when they all shifted their feet nervously. But he didn't pause. "You either have balls of fucking titanium or you're the dumbest vampires to walk the face of the earth."

"I'm gonna go with dumb motherfuckers," Jayce said. Connor could scent and feel his presence behind him, but didn't turn.

He also scented Erin with the male, and could only imagine the display the two of them made behind him and Liam. At the other entrance, a dozen of his pack-mates all in wolf form appeared. Growling low, they began to advance until Connor held up his hand. The vamps were completely caged in. To attempt to run or attack now would be stupid. "You have two options. Fight me now and die. Painfully. Or come with us to meet Juhani and Narek in chains." Because there was no way in hell Connor was letting these males leave. There were no second chances for this kind of trespass.

The lead vamp glanced over his shoulder and the two others did the same. When he turned back to Connor his expression was still defiant, but he nodded. "Fine. We go with you to meet Juhani. I can't imagine he lets the bitch survive for killing his brother." He sounded so damn smug Connor covered the distance between them in less than a second and slammed his fist into the male's nose.

A satisfying crunch rent the air as the vamp flew backward and landed with a grunt of pain. If he'd been human, the male would be dead from the impact of the blow. He wiped at his face, cursing as he shoved to his feet, but he didn't make a move to attack. Maybe he was smarter than Connor had originally thought.

To give them credit for not being completely stupid, the other two vamps also stood there and raised their hands in surrender.

Without him having to say a word, Jayce and Erin strode past him and took all three vamps to the ground, one after the other, cuffing them with silver restraints that had likely been blessed by the fae with some sort of binding spell. Connor's own mate had a sword blessed by the fae that ashed feral shifters and he knew that Jayce had two swords that could ash vamps or anyone with vamp blood in their system. Clearly, Natalia had used one of the enforcer's damn swords the night before. So he wasn't surprised that these two had something they used to restrain supernatural beings.

Go see your mate, then we're leaving, Connor projected to Liam as he made his way to his discarded clothes. He was going to see Ana too. The need to assure himself that she and Vivian were all right superseded everything else, including pack responsibility. And once he saw that they were okay, he was going to meet with the Brethren and deal with these trespassers before things escalated.

Chapter 13

*A*re you planning on talking to me again anytime this *century?* Aiden asked, his frustration at Larissa's silence building inside him each second that ticked by. It had been a little under two hours that she'd been giving him the cold shoulder and he was sick of it.

Larissa didn't look at him, just kept her jaw clenched tightly as they strode down the sidewalk toward the hotel where she'd been staying with Magda. *Now is not the time for a discussion of your idiocy.*

He growled at her frosty tone and spared a glance behind him. Brianna and Angelo were about twenty yards back, keeping a decent distance between them in case there were any more surprise vamp attacks. They were going to be the lookouts while he and Larissa infiltrated the hotel, then they planned to bring Angelo in to check the scent too. Now more than ever they needed backup.

Connor had contacted both him and Angelo about a vamp breach at the ranch. Aiden was just thankful that

no blood had been shed and that the breach had nothing to do with Larissa. His very frustrating mate. *My
idiocy? What the hell are you talking about?* he demanded
as they reached the first set of the spinning glass doors
of the hotel's multiple front entrances.

She looked at him and raised one dark, perfectly
arched eyebrow. "Perhaps you'd like to show me how
to use this fancy contraption?" she purred, her voice
dripping with ice as she motioned to the entry.

These types of entrances had been around when she
was alive. She was obviously trying to piss him off. "I
was just trying to help earlier." He couldn't understand
why she was so mad. It was like he'd accidentally
flipped some imaginary switch and he couldn't turn it
off. Ever since they'd left the diner she'd refused to
speak to him, only answering questions he asked aloud,
and he was positive she did that only because the others had been in the SUV with them. But if he'd dared
talk to her telepathically she'd completely ignored him.
And forget about touching her. He'd tried to put his
arm around her shoulders once but she'd shrugged his
hand away.

"If I need your help, I'll ask for it. But don't hold
your breath," she snapped out before turning on her
heel and stalking through the door. She moved quickly,
not giving him a chance to join her in her section of the
spinning door.

Scrubbing a hand over his face, he followed. His inner wolf clawed at him, demanding he make things
right between him and Larissa but he didn't know how.
They'd never argued when they'd been together. Not

truly and not once after they'd bonded. And he didn't know why they were now.

The hotel lobby was all plush marble floors and gold and white furniture that practically gleamed under the vintage-style chandeliers. He found it interesting that the witch had brought Larissa to such a nice establishment. Maybe it had all been part of her plan to keep Larissa happy before she put whatever her plan had been into motion. Larissa had been accustomed to only the best and this place was definitely that.

By the time he reached the front desk Larissa was already talking to one of the females there. Another human man was helping a man and woman who stood a few feet down and wasn't paying attention to them.

The human shook her head in answer to something Larissa had asked. "As far as the computer is showing, no one has been in either room even to clean. The instructions were very clear and we pride ourselves on catering to our guests' every need."

"Thank you so much for your help," Larissa said softly. "Have there been any calls to either room?"

Aiden leaned against the counter, blocking Larissa from the couple and employee at the other end of the long, white marble-topped reception desk. Even though they weren't paying attention, he didn't want anyone to inadvertently notice the soft glow coming from her eyes as Larissa slightly mesmerized the human woman. The gift that some vampires and some fae—like Brianna—had to persuade humans to be truthful was damn handy. Something Aiden wouldn't mind having.

The woman clacked away on her keyboard and eyed her computer screen. "Two were made to your friend's room. No messages were left."

"Thank you. I'd like to ask you for one more favor and it needs to stay between the two of us." Larissa's voice dropped, taking on a stronger tone. "You're going to give me a master key and not tell anyone about it and make sure no one sees what you're doing. I'll return it when I leave." Her demand was low enough that only Aiden and the human could hear.

"Okay, no problem." The woman's eyes slightly glazed over as she reached into a drawer and picked out a white card with a black magnetic stripe down the back and the gold emblem of the hotel stamped on the front. "This will get you anywhere you need to go." The woman slid it across the marble to Larissa in one smooth move.

"Thank you again. You've been most helpful," Larissa said as she palmed it. "I'm going to be leaving now and you're going to forget this entire conversation and that you even saw me here. Do you understand?"

"Yes, I'm going to forget I saw you here and what we talked about."

Larissa nodded once and stepped away, her low-heeled boots making a soft sound against the floor as she and Aiden headed toward the elevators. She still didn't glance at him when she pressed the button to go up. When she continued to ignore him as they stepped inside, he reached his limit on patience. He didn't care if he should give her space. That wasn't happening.

Not after being separated from her for so many years. She could be pissed at him all she wanted, but she wasn't going to ignore him.

Moving lightning fast, he pinned her against one of the shiny, mirrored walls of the interior. She gasped in surprise, her palms landing on his chest as he rolled his hips against her in a purely sexual move. Let her ignore *that*. Even pissed, she got him hot for her. Hell, when did he not want her.

"What are you doing?" she demanded, her voice an angry whisper even though they were alone.

"What does it feel like? I don't care if you're angry at me; just don't shut me out."

Her eyes narrowed to slits. "You treated me like a child in front of others. And not just anyone, but your packmate and another royal who's centuries *younger* than me." Her voice vibrated with her rage, her indigo eyes glowing that bright electric blue as she glared at him. "The fact that you treated me like an unequal makes me want to claw you up, not fucking talk about it." The elevator dinged at their floor and taking him by surprise, she shoved at his chest with incredible force. Moving with that beautiful, vampiric speed, she was out in the hall a moment later, her expression haughty as she glared at him.

Turning from him, she practically stomped away, her sweet ass swaying in a rhythmic motion that almost made him forget his damn name. As she strode down the hall, something slammed into him through their link before she put a lock on it again. It felt a lot like embarrassment.

That was when her words and actions registered. She was embarrassed, not angry. Okay, she was still freaking pissed at him. Of that, he had no doubt. But she was also embarrassed. He couldn't understand why. He'd just wanted to help in case she was nervous about feeding in a strange place, in a completely new world. And yeah, he'd been terrified to let her out of his sight for even a moment. He hadn't thought about things from her point of view. She was one of the oldest vamps of her race, definitely from one of the most powerful lines, and he hadn't treated her with the respect she demanded and deserved. But he wasn't ready to apologize for caring about her.

Still trying to come to terms with the Larissa he'd known and the Larissa currently walking away from him, he hurried after her with a burst of speed. Snatching the master key card from her back pocket, he danced back when she growled and tried to grab it from him.

"What game are you playing? We don't have time for this," she hissed.

Ignoring her, he knocked on the closest door. He couldn't scent anyone inside, but that didn't mean anything. After a few moments, he opened the door and said, "Housekeeping," just in case it was occupied. Luckily it wasn't.

Ignoring Larissa's muttered protests, he continued inside, pulling his cell phone out as he glanced around the pristine room that smelled of subtle cleaning supplies. Nothing harsh though. A place like this would use natural stuff. He fired off a text to Angelo telling him they'd had a slight delay but would be searching Larissa's room soon. Once his packmate responded that everything was clear downstairs, he shoved his phone in his pocket and turned to face his very sexy mate. It was time to talk.

At the sound of her phone buzzing across her night-stand, Magda rolled off the naked, sweaty body of the human male she'd been fucking. She didn't recognize the phone number on the caller ID but it was a local one. "Hello?" She stretched out against the soft sheets, letting the cool air rush over her bare body.

Next to her the male stretched out and flipped the television on, but at least he had the good sense to mute it. So many of these humans were idiots.

"Ms. Smith?" a man whispered, as if afraid to be overheard.

She instantly sat up. She'd given the obviously fake name to a few people at the hotel she'd checked Larissa into days ago. "Yes?"

"That woman you wanted me to keep tabs on showed up. And she's not alone."

Her heart sped up. "You're sure it's her?"

"Yes. I even took a picture with my cell phone. Long, black hair, really beautiful, kinda intense blue eyes."

Yes, that was Larissa Danesti. "Who was she with?"

"A man with blond hair. He's pretty tall and muscular, a little scary looking. I think . . . he might be one of those shifters." He whispered the last part. "It's hard to tell on sight, but he's huge."

Magda had no doubt who it was. "Did you get a picture of him?"

"No, just her. The man was watching everyone and I didn't want him to get suspicious if he saw me."

"When did they arrive and where did they go?" Magda wondered if they'd gone up to Larissa's room. Or Magda's supposed room. She'd just checked into the neighboring room so Larissa wouldn't know she had her own place in Winston-Salem.

"They got here just a few minutes ago, but I'm not sure where they went. I asked Jenna—that's the other concierge working with me today—and she acted as if I was stupid. She said she hadn't talked to anyone in the last couple minutes. It was like she couldn't remember helping them. I think they probably paid her off or something."

Of course this fool would think that. Magda could have easily spelled this guy, forcing him to contact her if he spotted Larissa, but she'd gone with the easier option. Cold, hard cash. The human probably took bribes all the time, and considering what she'd paid him, she knew he'd call her immediately. "Are they still there?"

"I saw them head toward the elevators, but I'm not sure where they went. Maybe to her room. I don't have access to the security room and besides, there aren't any video cameras on the individual floors." He was back to whispering.

Of course there wouldn't be any cameras. It was one of the reasons Magda had picked the high-priced hotel.

Guests there valued their privacy, so while the security was good, they didn't record all of their guests' comings and goings. "You've been very helpful. Like I promised, I'll owe you a tip when I see you again. For now, just keep an eye out. If she leaves, call me."

"I will."

Once they disconnected, Magda found her human lover watching her with curiosity. He was twenty-two, in fantastic shape, and could fuck for hours. Unlike her master, this human let her dominate him and she could come as much as she wanted. Which was a lot, with his stamina. Good sex fed her natural powers, something her bastard of a master knew, so she fucked these humans as much as possible to remain strong.

Excitement hummed through her at the thought of capturing Larissa. The female would have regained more of her strength by now, which was good and bad. Taking her captive would be harder, but definitely not impossible. "I have a task for you and Donovan. Go get him." At her demand, lust flared in his eyes as he raked a gaze over her naked body and she knew what he thought she meant. He quickly slid off the bed and left her bedroom in search of his friend, no doubt telling Donovan to get naked too.

But a threesome wasn't going to happen now. Not until the two humans completed their mission. Luckily she wouldn't have to waste the energy on spelling them. She fed their addiction to vamp blood and they were having what they considered fun playing with supernaturals. Idiots. Amazing fucks, but idiots nonetheless. She wasn't going to contact her master about the Larissa sighting just yet. Magda would send these two males to trail Larissa, and once they'd located her, Magda would then move in and spell the female. But if Aiden Nicholl was with Larissa—and she had no doubt the shifter was—she had a feeling they might have backup from his pack. Just in case they did, she wasn't going to take the chance of losing Larissa again and incurring her master's wrath. Her humans were disposable, and if they failed, the master would never need to know.

Besides, she had tracking ink on her two males also. If something happened to them, she could just track their bodies, dead or alive.

Chapter 14

"Think Juhani and Narek know we own this property?" Liam murmured as they drove down the long, winding dirt road to their meet-up place.

Connor shrugged. He'd had his brother buying up property all over the state in the past couple of weeks. None of it was under the pack name, but that didn't mean members of the Brethren couldn't figure out who the owner was if they did enough digging. "I'd say there's a fifty-fifty chance they know." He didn't give a shit if they did. Especially not after what had just happened at the ranch.

"I don't like this," Jayce muttered from the backseat where he sat next to his mate.

Connor glanced in the rearview mirror to see Kat roll her eyes. "You don't like it because I'm here."

Jayce grunted and linked his fingers through hers, holding her hand possessively.

As they drew closer to the dilapidated barn he

planned to demolish in the next couple of weeks, they all tensed. There were two SUVs already there. Connor glanced around the expansive property. The barn sat in the middle of the land with nothing but snow-covered grassy plain surrounding it for about eight acres. It would make an ambush damn near impossible. Unless the vamps had a sniper waiting somewhere. Good thing Connor had that possibility covered.

"West-side tree line, about twenty yards left from that gnarled-looking oak," Liam murmured. "Saw a flash. Could be nothing."

Connor tapped his earpiece to turn the volume up and repeated to Erin what Liam had said. Once she gave him an affirmative she went silent. They'd dropped Erin and Noah off at the main road and the two had trekked onto the property on foot. If these vamps thought to attack with snipers, they were going to get very dead.

"We knew they wouldn't come alone," Connor said in a small attempt to ease the tension he felt building in the vehicle.

But Kat was a witness to the killing. Though he hadn't planned to bring her originally, after the shit that went down at the ranch, he wanted her to give her firsthand account to the two Brethren members. They'd be able to sense if she was lying. Unfortunately her presence made Jayce slightly unpredictable. The enforcer might live at the ranch, but Connor wasn't his Alpha and the male didn't take orders from anyone. Except Kat. If it remotely seemed as if she was in danger, Connor was worried Jayce would kill first and ask

questions later. And that would cause a war. Killing
powerful vamps was one thing. Killing a Brethren member . . . hell no.

As they neared the other SUVs, Erin's voice streamed
through the earpiece. "Two vamps down, both had
sniper rifles. We've got them cuffed. They're not talking, but they're also not being aggressive. They didn't
fight back once I identified myself."

The lack of aggression was a good sign. "One of you,
secure the rest of the perimeter."

"Noah's already on it."

"We're going in. Keep your volume on." If anything
happened, he needed her to know immediately. She
could communicate with her mate telepathically and
the two of them could either back them up or get the
hell out of here if the situation demanded it. But Connor already knew neither Erin nor Noah would ever
bail.

"Will do."

Connor parked and the two SUVs carrying half a
dozen of his warriors parked next to him. After scanning the area again, he and his group exited the vehicle.
He motioned for everyone else to stay put, including
the group of warriors holding the three vamps from the
ranch. They'd bring them out when necessary. Only he,
Liam, Kat, and Jayce would attend the meeting.

Moving with stealth, they crossed the thirty yards to
the entrance in seconds, barely making a sound over
the snow-covered ground.

He and Liam went in first, with Jayce and Kat behind them. Upon entering they found Juhani, the tall

blond Finnish vamp lounging on a bale of hay with his hands behind his head as he leaned against one of the rickety-looking stable doors. He wore faded jeans, black boots, a black T-shirt, and a green bomber jacket that had seen better days. Narek on the other hand, stood next to him, arms crossed over his chest and a frown on his face. The man wore a three-piece suit complete with vest and pocket watch and looked as if he'd stepped off the cover of a magazine.

Seriously? Liam asked telepathically.

Connor's lips twitched but he didn't respond or look at his brother because he was afraid he'd laugh if he did.

"Is there a reason you insisted we meet in this hovel? And is there a reason you arrived with . . . backup?" Narek sneered in a cultured European accent as he flicked a disdainful glance Jayce's way.

Behind him Jayce growled so low in his throat Connor could barely hear it. All humor evaporated and he let his wolf show in his eyes. "Is there a reason three vampires breached my ranch an hour ago in an attempt to take Natalia?"

At the question Juhani straightened, unfolding his long legs and moving to stand next to Narek. "What? Who?"

"They're all daywalkers and supposedly of Emil's line."

Juhani's jaw tightened as he shot an angry look at Narek. The two stared at each other, their eyes glowing in an electric blue Connor had seen only in certain bloodborns. Most vamps' eyes glowed amber. He also knew some vamps could communicate telepathically and had no doubt that's what they were doing.

A few moments later they both turned back to the four of them, but all their focus was on Connor. "Where are they?"

"Here."

"We did not authorize anyone to infiltrate your ranch. We request that you let us speak to them, here, in full view of you, but you may do with them as you wish afterward. I want to know if they're working alone."

Relief that they hadn't been behind this surged through him as he nodded. "We'll bring them out after we're done here. How many snipers do you have in the woods?"

At the question Juhani grinned, the action making the ancient male look almost boyish. "Just two. And I'm guessing your people have disabled them because we can't reach them." He tapped his ear, indicating his own earpiece.

Connor found that interesting. Maybe they could communicate telepathically only with certain vamps. Maybe it was a power-level thing or a distance thing. Later he'd have to ask Aiden if he knew. Connor didn't respond to Juhani's statement because there was no need. "What are we going to do about your brother's death?"

Juhani lifted his shoulders. "I hated Emil and his death is no loss to our kind. However, if his death had been intentional, your packmate would be dead by now." His eyes flashed bright blue for a moment before reverting to their paler hue. "As it is, I saw a video feed that streamed live from the building. It was self-defense. There will be no vengeance from my family line or from Emil's line."

Behind him he heard Kat snort and resisted the urge to smile. She was still learning so much about their ways. Snorting at the words of a Brethren member wasn't done. But he didn't blame her reaction considering three of Emil's line had just trespassed on their ranch.

Juhani's eyes narrowed a fraction, but he didn't glance Kat's way. "After *today*, after we have spread the word to his entire coven, there will be no attempts on the female's life. I will make it clear that if anyone goes after her, they'll be punished by me. Keep her locked down for twenty-four hours while we spread the word."

Connor nodded, surprised by how easy the meeting had gone. Under other circumstances that might have made him suspicious but after working with these males, albeit via satellite and phone conferences just a few weeks ago, he had a better feel for them. No one wanted a supernatural war. They had enough of their own shit to deal with. "I'll trust you to keep your word." If he didn't, Juhani would find himself at war with Connor's pack. Something Connor didn't need to say aloud.

"Before I talk to those little bastards from Emil's line, what are your thoughts of the vampires and humans high on vamp blood the news has been showing recently?"

Connor flicked a glance at Liam. *How open do you think I should be?*

Liam shrugged. *Be honest. I think they're fishing for information because they're just as lost as us. Either way, it generates good will if we're open with them.*

Especially after what had happened with Natalia. Neither of them said it, but Connor knew his brother was thinking it.

Connor looked back at Juhani and Narek. Juhani was clearly the spokesman of the two, but he divided his attention between the two of them out of respect. These were two very powerful vampires. "We're not sure what's going on, but Kat"—he motioned behind him—"saw something interesting at the club last night. Kat?" He didn't take his eyes off the two vampires as he spoke. It didn't matter that the vibe in the barn was mellow, he wasn't turning his back on these males.

In his peripheral vision he watched her and Jayce step forward, Jayce a foot in front of Kat, blocking her with his body. She cleared her throat. "I've always been a seer, even before I was turned. I read auras, moods, and before you guys came out to the world, I've been able to see your true nature. Last night I saw something I've never seen before and it was freaky as shit. Your brother and the other vamps there looked as if they were like—I don't know how to describe it—but almost like they were puppets. They weren't in control of themselves, something dark was. Something . . . I don't know what it was. It was like this dark mass had invaded their bodies."

Connor watched as the two males exchanged an unreadable glance before looking back at them.

Juhani spoke. "Something strange is going on with some of our people. For once the news isn't wrong. We've never heard of vampires being controlled before, but anything is possible."

"Could it be a witch?" Connor asked, thinking of the female who had lied to Aiden's mate.

Juhani nodded slowly. "It is possible, but it would have to be a powerful one. But for the scale with which vamps and humans are being controlled, I don't see how a witch could do it without draining herself constantly. She would fry her brain trying to control so many individuals. We think it's something darker."

Connor's frown deepened. Darker? "You mean . . . demons."

The blond vamp shrugged in that casual way. "They can control humans on occasion—why not vampires?"

Connor didn't respond because he wasn't sure what he thought. "What do you know of the Draculesti coven?" he asked, changing the subject, taking everyone in the barn off guard if the sharp scent of surprise rolling off everyone was any indication.

Narek took a slight step forward. "Why do you want to know about them?"

"I'm curious."

Narek's amber eyes narrowed before they lit up blue. He watched Connor, assessing him, before they returned to his natural color. He was the first vamp Connor had met who had amber eyes in his natural state. "No one is just curious about the extinct line."

"So they're all dead?" he asked, unperturbed by the hostile statement.

"I didn't say that."

"Extinct implies it."

"They're not dead," Juhani interjected. "Well, we don't think they are. Vlad always did what he wanted, arrogant bastard. His coven could be living in Antarctica for all we know. Why are you asking about them?"

Connor glanced at Liam. *Go get the vamps.* Once his brother strode from the barn, Connor looked at Juhani and Narek. "We're bringing in the three males from Emil's line. As a show of good will, I'm giving them to you to do with as you see fit. They were upset because their maker was killed. I can forgive *that*. But they trespassed on my property. Cubs live there." And he wouldn't forgive that. Something he didn't need to tell them.

Juhani and Narek both nodded, but Juhani spoke. "I will personally take care of them."

Surprising him, Jayce took a step forward, everything about him menacing. "If that girl is harmed by anyone, I don't care if you aren't involved, I'll personally rain fucking hell down on all of you." The threat was low, more animal than man.

Connor gritted his teeth. Jayce wasn't his packmate and wasn't under his purview. Besides, Natalia and Kat had become very close friends recently. Connor had a feeling that was the real reason Jayce was threatening the two vamps. If something happened to Natalia, it would hurt Kat.

Juhani and Narek didn't respond, just glared daggers at Jayce. A moment later Liam and another member of his pack dragged the three vampires inside. Connor was glad to be rid of them. He wanted to get back to the ranch and check on his mate and cub.

"My pack is investigating vamp blood dealers in the area, among other things. If we find out anything of use, I'll contact you," Connor said to Juhani, wanting to leave on a good note. He never burned bridges if he could forge a contact instead.

Juhani nodded his appreciation while Narek continued to glare at Jayce. Just freaking great. The last thing Connor needed was for those two to get hostile with each other. Nodding at his packmates and Jayce, they all started to leave.

As they exited the barn, he received a text from Ryan. *911. Natalia ran away. Teresa panicking. Call me.*

"What the hell was she thinking?" Teresa slammed down the note Natalia had left on the counter next to one of Ryan's computers.

"She's young and scared," he murmured as he slid a SIG with a suppressor into a shoulder holster and zipped up his puffy winter jacket.

She shouldn't be surprised that he was carrying a weapon, but she'd never seen him armed before. It was sexy, even though that should be the last thing on her mind. Not when her younger sister had left a note telling her she was leaving the ranch because she didn't want to cause any more trouble for everyone. After the scare with the three vamps showing up a couple of hours ago, she'd apparently freaked out.

"It's insanely stupid." Okay, it was more of a selfless act, but Teresa wasn't thinking straight. Her young sister was out in the world on her own and she had no clue where Natalia had gone.

Ryan opened up the smaller of his laptops and glanced at her, his expression soft but determined. "It's not stupid. She's worried about the cubs and the pregnant females," he said before focusing all his attention on his computer screen.

With December pregnant and two new pregnant females who'd recently integrated into their pack, Teresa actually understood her sister's thought process. Fighting the full-blown panic clawing at her insides, Teresa started pacing behind Ryan as he clacked away on his computer. Her sister should have just waited for Connor to meet with those vampires.

Less than thirty seconds later, Ryan stood and snapped his razor-thin laptop shut before tucking it under his arm. "Let's go."

"What? Where?" Had he found her already? It seemed impossible, but the male worked magic on those computers.

"I tracked her using her cell phone."

"How?" she asked as she hurried outside with him. When Teresa had found that note, she hadn't even thought about going to anyone else. Not even her Alpha. She'd known Ryan would be able to help.

"She has an Android phone and it's synched with her Google account. With her password, I just logged in and tracked the phone using her Device Manager. I didn't even have to do anything illegal." He sounded almost disappointed as they raced across the yard to the parking structure.

"Is she far?"

"No, it looks like she's in one of the cabins at the Fontana ski lodge. Or at least that's where her phone is."

Hope surged through Teresa but she tried to temper it. She wouldn't relax until she held Natalia in her arms and knew she was safe. As she slid into the passenger seat of Ryan's truck, another thought struck her. "Hey, how do you know Natalia's password?"

He shot her a disbelieving look as he started the engine. "I can guess almost everyone's password here at the ranch. It's simple guesswork and I got hers in two tries."

"There's no way you could guess mine." Teresa didn't tell anyone that stuff or write it down anywhere.

His lips quirked up as he pulled up to the gate. "Hmm."

"Hmm, nothing. You can't know mine. I use different passwords for everything."

"I bet you a kiss I can guess your e-mail password. Maybe not exactly, but I can guess the letters and numbers in it," he said as he jumped from the idling vehicle. After opening the gate, he slid back in and didn't bother shutting it. When she saw one of the males waving them off and closing the gate behind them she realized why.

"I'm sure with a dozen guesses you could probably narrow it down." She wasn't letting this conversation drop. Partially because she wanted the distraction and talking about her runaway sister wasn't going to do her sanity any good. Thinking about kissing Ryan probably wasn't any better.

"Three guesses. If I get it by the third try, I get to kiss you anytime, anywhere. And if we kiss *before* I call in my chip, those kisses won't count. This will be a kiss I demand."

The thought of him getting to demand a kiss whenever he wanted was hotter than she wanted to admit.

"What happens if you don't guess?"

He paused for a moment as he contemplated. "Then you can demand a kiss from me anytime, anywhere."

Shaking her head, she didn't fight the small grin tugging at the corners of her mouth. "Deal. Now wow me with your amazing abilities."

"Your favorite fruit is the blueberry. You like it so much your kitchen has a blueberry theme. I remember you nearly biting the head off one of your cousins who wanted to make a blueberry surprise dessert for Christmas since you are the only one who makes blueberry desserts. And, though I haven't seen them personally, I heard Ana teasing you about your flannel pajamas with a blueberry pattern. I think it's safe to say you have an obsession with the tiny fruit." He shot her a quick glance for confirmation.

She gritted her teeth. Damn him. And damn her for being so stupid. "Yes," she muttered.

"And the last four numbers of your social security number are eight-six-three-one. I guess that you use those numbers along with the word blueberry. Probably a shortened version of the word so it doesn't actually spell out a known word in the dictionary. You probably have the numbers first and separate the numbers from your word with something like an @ symbol or a hyphen. Am I getting warm?" he purred, all smug and sexy.

She wasn't sure how he knew her social security number, but she wasn't surprised. This male knew way too much about everyone. But she liked seeing him so relaxed around her, liked that there wasn't that strange tension in the air between them. Instead of answering him, she gritted her teeth. She wasn't going to confirm that he was freaking right.

"So I *am* close. Okay, my official guess is 8631-blue."

"Nope."

"All right . . . 8631-blueb."

"I hate you," she said, no heat in her voice as she fought a building laugh. She still wasn't convinced he hadn't already known her password, but she didn't care if he had cheated. She wanted to kiss him again. Badly.

"Anytime, anywhere." There was such a note of raw hunger in his words that she squirmed in her seat.

As he pulled out onto the highway, he shot her a knowing look, no doubt scenting her own desire. But then a thought occurred to her and made her go cold. She was so damn insecure where this male was concerned and she hated it. After driving in silence for a few minutes, she asked, "Were you just trying to distract me back there with that talk about kissing?"

He snorted but didn't take his eyes off the road. "Will you open my laptop?" he asked, ignoring her question.

Though she wanted to continue her line of questioning she did as he said. A screen immediately popped up. A map with a red dot in the middle of what looked like an almost desolate area blinked insistently. There were a couple of buildings on the screen, but it wasn't a populated area. "Has she moved?"

"No, that's still the ski lodge."

Relief slid through her. They were just a few minutes away from the main lodge and there were plenty of side roads to the outlying cabins. Considering how good Ryan was with directions she knew they'd be there soon. Then she could bring her sister back to safety where she belonged.

"What do you want from me, Ryan?" she blurted, feeling as if her skin was too tight for her body. She was too old for games and she needed to know his intentions.

"I want to court you." His answer was immediate, which soothed the most primal part of her.

She paused a moment, digesting his bold statement. Courting was what shifters did when they were serious. What they did when they had long-term plans. The term was a little old school, but she and Ryan weren't from the newest generation. "You want to or you're going to?"

"I'm going to. I'm making my intentions clear, right here, right now, but . . . I need to talk to you about something. About *me*. We don't have enough time here, but once we get Natalia back to the ranch we will. Once we've talked, you can decide if you still want me."

His words and the potent, sharp punch of fear that

rolled off him surprised her. It wasn't acidic, but the sharpness stung her nostrils. "Still want you?"

He nodded, his jaw clenched tight, and he wouldn't even glance at her as he pulled off onto a nearly hidden road, driving them higher into the mountains.

She was quiet as she digested his words. She couldn't imagine there was anything Ryan could have done that would make her not want him. Not the Ryan she knew. "Does this have something to do with Lucas?"

Blinking in surprise, he looked at her then, his dark eyes glittering with something she couldn't define. "No, but Lucas and I are a package deal."

At that, she laughed. "No shit, cowboy. If you were the type of male to ditch a kid for a female, you wouldn't be the male for me." Realizing what she'd said, she blushed. "Not that I'm saying you *are* the male for me, just . . ." She trailed off and he got that smug look again as he steered them up the winding mountain road. "Do you have, like, a secret human family somewhere or something?" She knew that was unlikely but she was impatient to find out what he was hiding and anything was better than worrying about her sister.

"Seriously?"

"Okay, do you—"

"Teresa, no more fishing." There was an unexpected commanding note in his voice that she felt all the way to her toes. Even though Ryan was one of the biggest, sexiest males she'd ever met, she sometimes forgot he could be so dominating. He was usually quiet and reserved and always on one of his computers.

She clamped her mouth shut and stared out the window, watching the snow-covered trees move by at a glacial pace as Ryan slowed and turned off onto another small road. Surprising her, he stopped about twenty yards down from the main road and pulled into a cluster of bare, snow-topped pine trees.

"What are you doing?" she asked.

He plucked the laptop from her and slid it under his seat. "The signal is pinging about fifty yards north from here. I want to go in on foot."

Teresa sucked in a sharp breath. She hadn't realized they were so close, but she was ready to find her sister. "Has Connor got back to you?"

"Yeah, he's on his way to the ranch. He said if we can't handle things to call in for backup. But it's pretty clear she just ran away."

Teresa nodded and grasped the handle. "Let's go get my sister." As she slid from the vehicle, her boots crunching over the icy ground, she stilled and very quietly shut the door behind her.

Inhaling deeply, she took a few tentative steps toward the front of the vehicle. Full-blown panic settled in her bones as she realized what she was scenting nearby. Blood.

When she glanced at Ryan and saw the quick flash of fear in his dark gaze, she knew she wasn't imagining things.

A bolt of terror, jagged and angry, shot through her as she took off racing through the woods. If someone had hurt her sister, they were going to pay.

Chapter 15

Aiden watched Larissa carefully, his wolf in his gaze. It was unsettling the way he stared at her, but she didn't let her emotions show and tried to block their link as best she could. It was difficult when he was insistently pushing at it, sending all sorts of emotions her way. Lust being the main one.

"Why are we in this random hotel room?" she asked quietly, much of her earlier annoyance fading. She knew he'd just been trying to protect her, but she didn't want to be a female who needed protecting. And she didn't want him to view her that way.

"Before we take one more step out that door, I want to clear the air. This"—he motioned between them—"cold shoulder treatment is never going to work for me. Ever. I don't care if you're pissed at me, punch me in the fucking nuts, claw me to pieces, do whatever you need to do, but don't ignore me. Don't push me out. We're bonded and that means something." His tone was determined, but the anguish in his expression sliced her up.

She knew she'd hurt him and she hated that. Biting her bottom lip, she perched on the end of the plush king-size bed and wrapped her arms around herself. The heavy weight of guilt settled on her like a smothering blanket as she struggled to find the right words. "While I know we're bonded, intellectually, I don't remember getting to that point with you, which makes all these emotions I'm feeling that much more difficult. And I like you—so much that it's a little terrifying. When you tried to order me around, it struck a very wrong chord with me. It's embarrassing that there's so much I still don't know or understand about this world. I am used to being the strongest person in most rooms." She didn't mean it arrogantly and hoped he wouldn't take it that way. "And I know it's not an excuse, but it's why I reacted so badly. I'm feeling embarrassed and stupid and so unsure of everything, but the one thing I still know how to do right is feed without help. It felt as if you were trying to control me when I didn't need it."

He rubbed a hand over his face, and all the tension fled his big body as he sat next to her on the bed. Shoving his sweater sleeves up, he kept a solid foot of distance between them. For some reason she didn't like that, even though she was the one who'd been giving him the cold shoulder the past couple of hours. She had no clue if she'd ever done it with him before. In previous relationships things had never progressed far enough with any of her lovers for her to care enough to argue with them. It had felt wrong to do so with Aiden, but she hadn't been prepared for any of the feelings he evoked inside her. When the tendons and muscles in his arms flexed, showcasing all that strength, she fought to breathe for a moment. He was so sexy it was ridiculous.

"I'm always going to try to protect you, whether you need it or not. And I expect the same from you. You're the strongest female I've ever met, but you were gone for sixty years, presumably dead. So I'm probably going to act fucking insanely territorial more than once. I'll be possessive and jealous and yes, likely try to protect you from nothing because I can't stand the thought of you being out of my sight for even a moment. But it's not because I think you're weak. I'm going to apologize in advance for all the stupid shit I'm going to do over the next couple of months, or hell, years. I lost you once, Larissa. I can't go through that again."

The agony that punched through their bondmate link hit her almost like a physical blow, square in the middle of the chest. While she'd been worried about her silly pride and appearing weak, he was just terrified of losing her again.

The need to comfort this male welled up inside her like an out-of-control tsunami. She never wanted to be the cause of his pain. Before she could talk herself out of it, she launched herself at him, straddling him and wrapping her arms around his neck as she buried her face against him right where his shoulder and neck met. Inhaling, she savored his spicy, earthy scent. She was such an idiot, pushing this male away for no reason. "I'm so sorry, Aiden."

A sharp sense of relief surged through her when he returned her embrace. She wasn't sure what she'd been afraid of, maybe his rejection. When he buried his face against her neck too, she realized how stupid a fear that had been.

"I just want to take you somewhere far from here and forget all this mess," Aiden murmured, his breath hot against her neck.

"I know." The thought was appealing. They could hole up together and she could get to know her bond-mate again without the world as a distraction. Maybe even start to regain her memories. It was a hopeless wish though. Leaning back, she looked deep into his eyes. His wolf was gone, only the man was watching her now.

Intently.

Possessively.

Need built deep, heating her from the inside out. His hands slid down her back, moved over her hips and down her jean-clad thighs before gliding upward again to settle on her hips. "Are you hungry?"

The human she'd fed from hadn't had strong blood, but Larissa was still feeling light-years better than she had only twenty-four hours ago. And she wouldn't feed from Aiden again so soon. Not after she had twice in less than a twelve-hour period, no matter how powerful he was. "I'm fine."

Those sexy lips of his pulled together in a thin line as if he didn't believe her. "Bite me," he murmured.

Her nipples tightened at the soft command, but she shook her head, unsure what he was getting at.

"Not to feed, just nip my skin like you used to. I miss the feel of your teeth and mouth on me." His voice was guttural now, full of need as he rolled his hips upward, pushing the outline of his erection against the juncture between her thighs.

"I used to bite you?"

Grinning wickedly, he nodded. "Yes. You never broke the skin unless you were feeding, but you loved to nip my neck and all over my body."

He rolled his hips against her again, drawing a shudder from her at the feel of his thick length against her covered mound. She hated that there were clothes in the way. It would be so easy to throw away caution, to let him inside her, to forget about everything and everyone for just a little while.

Aiden slid a hand up under the back of her shirt, stroking along the length of her spine in a rhythmic motion that drove her crazy. He was just touching her back, but she felt as if he was touching her everywhere. Sparks of heat skittered across her skin.

Feeling her eyes grow heavy-lidded, she dipped her head to his neck again, her fangs aching just being this close to his artery. The male had such exquisite, perfect blood. She'd never tasted anything so wonderful. But she wasn't going to feed from him again. *She wasn't.* No matter how strong the urge was.

As she inhaled his familiar scent, something rattled loose in her memory.

"You are such a cheeky little male." She waved a hand at *the giant, Adonis-looking shifter, trying to make him back off as she attempted to glide by him. The meeting between her*

parents and the Nicholl pack leaders had been tedious and she was tired of the stupid politics. She was exhausted and needed to feed and didn't have time for this annoyingly sexy shifter who seemed to take pleasure needling her whenever they were alone. He had to know how powerful she was yet he thought he could keep poking at her.

"Little? Sweetheart, I'll lift my kilt and show you what I've got between my thighs and if you still think it's little—"

"Aiden!"

A long pause, and a slow, wicked grin spread across his devilishly handsome face. "That's the first time you've said my name."

"Well, it is your name, is it not?"

He made a humming sound, stalking closer to her. She wasn't sure why she liked it, but her nipples pebbled against the thick material of her full-length ball gown. She backed up, then immediately cursed the show of weakness, but it was too late. Her bare shoulders skimmed the cold stone wall of the hallway before she gained her senses and straightened.

"I like hearing you say my name. Say it again," he demanded, rough and unsteady as his dark eyes went pure wolf.

She swallowed hard, not feeling like herself as she looked up at this big male. She placed one palm on his chest, meaning to push him away, but instead clutched onto his shirt. He was so hot to the touch, so strong. "I will not."

"Say it, Larissa." His eyes grew heavy-lidded with raw hunger as he watched her.

"No," she whispered, though her heart pounded.

He leaned closer, his lips skimming her neck, and God help her, she actually let him get so close. The male was a predator, a lupine shifter. Yet she was letting him practically lick her throat. It was almost as if she was possessed, unable to move him away. "Would you say it if I kissed you?" *he murmured.* "Or maybe you'd scream it while you're coming against my mouth?"

A shiver rolled down her spine at the visual. *He was so damn arrogant.* "You're so sure you can make me come?" *No, that wasn't what she'd meant to say. She'd meant to simply shove him back for his impertinence.*

He didn't respond, just made that sexy humming sound as he flicked his tongue over the sensitive spot behind her ear. He wasn't touching her with his hands, which were placed firmly on either side of her head against the wall. Somehow that made whatever this was, even more intense. Her entire body cried out for his touch. She was practically ready to throw herself at him.

That sudden thought made her straighten and finally shove him away. He stepped back under the force of her push, something akin to hurt in those dark eyes, but she ignored it. "You are far too forward. And I do not need you to achieve climax; I have someone waiting for me right now." *A complete lie, but he didn't seem to scent it as he moved in the span of a heartbeat, caging her against the wall, using his hands and body to pin her there. Now he wasn't holding back from touching her and she found she liked it very much. Too much.*

"You don't have a lover," *he ground out.* "I would smell him if you did."

She rolled her eyes. "That is because I bathe."

"He's a dead man." *He let out a low growl, and something dark flickered in that gaze.*

Possessiveness had never turned her on before, but seeing Aiden get so worked up made heat flood between her thighs. She didn't like the way he made her feel so out of control, as if she didn't own her body. She needed to teach this wolf a lesson. One kiss and she would put him in his place. Before she could stop herself, she leaned up and put her mouth to his. Yes, she was absolutely possessed. The moment their lips touched, her entire body lit up with desire.

Larissa's eyes snapped open and she leaned back to see Aiden watching her hungrily. "I was an arrogant bitch," she whispered.

At her words he laughed, the sound so rich it filled her soul. She didn't know how she knew, but something in her subconscious told her she'd missed this laugh very much. "Why would you say that?"

"I thought you were arrogant, but the truth is . . . I was too." Now look at her. No coven, missing memories, no money, no way to support herself. She was completely dependent on a pack of shifters to help her find whoever had killed her parents and to help her figure out this daunting new world.

"You weren't arrogant. You were . . . very secure in who you were. As old as you were and as much of the world as you've seen, it would have been strange if you weren't so confident."

She let a smile touch her lips at his heartfelt words. "You're very wise for such a young pup."

He brushed his lips over hers, the light touch almost chaste. "I'm not so young anymore."

Savoring the quiet moment because she knew it would be fleeting, Larissa wrapped her arms tighter around him, pulling him close. Her breasts pressed against his chest as she laid her cheek against his. "I want to feel you inside me. I want you to completely possess me," she whispered. It was too soon and the wrong time and place, but she needed him to know.

He jerked under her and made a strained sound before he let out a low growl. Taking her by surprise, he stood and placed her on her feet. He pinned her with an intense gaze. "We need to leave now or I'm taking you against the wall, on the floor, and maybe the bed. I won't be gentle and we'll likely get kicked out of here for the noise we'll make."

The way his voice shook told her he meant every word. Unfortunately, it made her even hotter. She wanted nothing more than to make very good use of the bed. Now wasn't the time or place. But very soon she was going to get this male under her, on top of her, and every other way she could possibly imagine.

As if he read her thoughts—or more likely the scent she was throwing off—Aiden growled low in frustration and stalked from the room.

Ryan took off after Teresa, cursing her speed. Even in human form she was damn fast. They weren't far from Natalia's last known location and the scent of blood grew stronger the closer they got to their destination. As he reached Teresa, he wanted to tell her to slow down, but she did it anyway.

As the thick forest started to thin, they both slowed their pace. Through the trees he could see a two-story cabin. One of the ski lodge rental places. The sound of

grunts and angry shouts filled the air, somewhere beyond the cabin, but it couldn't be too far past. When
Ryan heard Natalia scream, he didn't even think, his
wolf just took over.

His clothes, SIG, and shoes scattered around him as
he shifted form and raced toward the cry. Under normal circumstances he would have used more stealth,
but he knew without a doubt that Teresa was going to
run right into danger no matter what he did. So he had
to beat her to it. There was no way in hell he was letting
her get hurt.

He could hear her behind him, but ignored her as he
raced toward the cabin. He slowed when he reached
the back of the place and crouched low as he raced
along the edge of the outer wall. Risking a quick glance
behind him he was surprised to see Teresa still in her
human form—holding his fallen weapon. He knew the
female could use it well, but he didn't want her getting
tangled up in whatever the hell was going on.

Forcing himself to drag his focus from her, Ryan
peered around the corner of the house. He assessed the
situation in seconds. There were two shifters in wolf
form, one he recognized as Natalia, battling with four
vampires. One vamp was on the ground, likely dead.
Three were taking on the unknown male wolf who was
ripping them to shreds, while one vamp grappled with
Natalia.

Ryan looked up at Teresa and growled low in his
throat. She seemed to understand him because she
nodded and stayed put. Without making a sound, he
crept across the snowy ground, barely feeling the chill

against his paws as he zeroed in on the blade-wielding vamp.

The male raised his knife out to the side as Natalia bit into his other forearm. Growling, she tore into him, making the male howl in pain. But he didn't drop the knife, poised to stab her through the side, possibly piercing her heart. The vamp's expression was filled with rage. He didn't even see Ryan until it was too late.

With a burst of speed, Ryan covered the final few feet between the vamp and Natalia. The vampire's glowing amber eyes went nuclear as Ryan launched himself through the air. The vamp dropped his blade and rolled off Natalia as Ryan slammed into his shoulder, throwing him off balance.

Adrenaline pumping through him, he landed on all fours, but swiveled back quickly to face the male. Though Ryan saw Natalia in his peripheral vision, he ignored her, focusing on the threat instead. Growling low in his throat, he flattened his ears against his head.

The vamp dove for the blade and Ryan struck hard and fast. He clamped his jaw around the male's throat, ripping and tearing until he reached the bone. He didn't savor killing any being, but this bastard had been trying to kill his packmate. A second after the male went limp, Ryan completely severed his head. Crimson stained the white ground in a macabre display.

Not dwelling on the gory sight, Ryan started to turn when a very distinctive puff of air filled the air. *His weapon.*

Moving lightning fast, he swiveled to find the three

vamps, who'd been attacking the unknown male, already dead. Two had been ripped to shreds, their heads severed. The third lay in a pool of blood, gasping for air. A red stain covered the front of his shirt, where Teresa had clearly shot him.

Depending upon his age and strength he might have been able to survive the injury. That wasn't happening. Before Ryan could move, the other male wrapped his jaws around the vamp's neck and ripped it off as if it were paper.

After he was done, silence reigned in the forest for a long moment. Ryan was aware of Natalia behind him and Teresa off to his right, weapon still in hand. The gray wolf stood near the headless vamp bodies, watching all of them carefully.

Using his hated gift, Ryan tried to sense the male's state of mind. The only feedback he got was a sense of satisfaction. No rage or anger directed their way. Taking a chance, Ryan shifted forms, letting the change come over him in a rush of energy until he stood in the snow. For how much adrenaline he had pumping through him, he barely felt the cold. He kept his gaze pinned to the greenish gray eyes of the male wolf.

"You okay, Teresa?" he asked.

She nodded and in his peripheral he could see her hand slightly shaking. "Yeah. That vamp was going after you. It's why I shot him," she whispered.

Shit. He wanted to reach out to her, to comfort her, but held off. He wasn't making a move until he knew who this other male was and what threat he posed. If any. "Natalia, you okay?" he asked without turning around.

He heard her making the change from shifter to human and a second later she said, "Yes. Thanks to him."

Ryan's gaze remained steady on the male. "Shift to human or I'm going to consider you a threat," he growled softly, his threat very clear. If this wolf didn't shift, Ryan was attacking.

A few moments later Aldric Kazan stood in front of them. Now that Ryan knew the male and Jayce were related, he could clearly see the family resemblance. This must be what Jayce had looked like before he got those awful scars. Wherever they'd come from. "Aldric Kazan," Ryan said clearly, wanting it known that he knew exactly who this male was.

Aldric's dark eyebrows raised. "That's right."

"What the fuck are you doing here? And who are— were—those vamps?"

"He saved me," Natalia said softly, coming to stand next to Ryan.

Ryan ignored her. "Answer me."

The male rubbed a hand over his dark, military-short buzz cut. "I followed the female from the club. She mentioned something about Jayce and I wanted to know if it was my brother so . . . I tracked you guys to that ranch last night. When I saw her sneaking out this morning I didn't think anything of it until I spotted those fuckers following her. So, I followed them. End of story." He shrugged, his expression so similar to Jayce's it was jarring.

"What the fuck were you doing at that club last night?" God, it seemed like an eternity ago, not the night before. So much shit had happened since then.

Ryan didn't know much about Aldric, something that pissed him off. Normally he could find out anything about most anyone. But this guy had no pack and appeared to live most of his life off the grid. Not completely, because almost everyone left a paper trail, but his was very thin.

The male's eyes hardened. "None of your fucking business. I talk to my brother and no one else."

Ryan's jaw tightened. He didn't like it, but he also didn't like having Teresa and Natalia out here so exposed. He wanted to get them out of the cold and back to safety. "We dispose of these bodies. Then you can follow us back to see Jayce." Of course Ryan would be alerting Connor as soon as he could get to his phone.

The male snorted obnoxiously before stalking to a small green duffel bag. When Aldric pulled out a blade, Ryan tensed, ready to attack. Teresa raised the SIG, no shaking hands now. Ryan inwardly smiled. That was his female. Or he hoped she would be soon.

Aldric looked between the two of them. "Untrusting bunch, aren't you?" he muttered before slamming the blade into the nearest vamp's chest.

Ryan watched in fascination as not only the body turned to ash, but the severed head as well. That was some serious magic. Like Jayce's blades. Moving quickly, Aldric finished off the rest of the fallen males before tucking his blade back into the bag and pulling out fresh clothes.

"Why were the vamps after Natalia?" Ryan asked.

"She killed their maker," Aldric said, as if it should be obvious.

Okay, that sounded on par with what Connor had relayed in his last couple of texts. "You parked nearby?"

"Yeah." The male flicked a glance Teresa's way, noting the weapon still in her hand.

"Look at her again and you're not going anywhere." The words were out before Ryan could stop himself. His canines and claws broke free at the thought of anyone remotely threatening Teresa. Aldric wasn't even doing that, but Ryan hated the entire situation and his inner wolf wanted to strike first and ask questions later. Teresa was his, and right now the urge to keep her safe and secure was very real.

"Jeez, jackass. Took you long enough to go all protector male on her," Natalia muttered next to him.

He ignored her, but the comment seemed to defuse the tense atmosphere. Teresa sheathed the weapon in the back of her pants and Aldric took a step away from them as he picked up his bag. "I know where the ranch is, but I can follow you there?" The last part was a question.

Ryan nodded. "We're parked not too far from here." He pointed in the direction they'd come from. They could get Natalia's vehicle later because he wasn't letting her out of his sight.

"The road leading from this cabin connects with the main one. I'll wait until you go by and follow."

"Fine." Ryan waited until Teresa and Natalia moved into action, not taking his eyes off the other male.

Aldric did the same, keeping his focus on Ryan as he picked up his bag and headed to wherever his vehicle was. Once they rounded the corner of the house, Ryan pulled Teresa into a tight embrace, running his hands up and down her arms and looking her over.

"You're okay?" he asked, inspecting her even though she hadn't sparred with anyone.

She looked at him incredulously, her dark eyes wide. "I should be asking you that." Before he could respond her gaze snapped to her sister who was hovering a couple of feet away. "And you! What the hell were you thinking running away like that? Connor's ironed everything out. You just need to stay at the ranch for a day until word spreads that you did nothing wrong."

To Ryan's surprise Natalia burst into tears. She looked impossibly young, maybe because she was naked. Even though nudity wasn't a big deal with shifters, he felt uncomfortable standing there while she was nude and her emotions so exposed. He turned away as Teresa rushed to her sister's side and pulled her into a tight hug.

He wanted to tell them to hurry and save the tears for later, but knew he couldn't. As it was, he was walking a tightrope with Teresa. Very soon he planned to lay himself bare to her in a way he'd never done to anyone. Once he did, she held all the cards. If she rejected him, he'd deal with it. Even though he was afraid to hope she'd accept him as he was, if she did, he was going to publicly claim her. Well, more publicly than he already had. Then he was going to win her heart.

Chapter 16

*H*er room is two down from this one. Larissa projected to him as they reached the next door in the long hallway. *And mine is the one after. In case there's an ambush we should go in through the neighboring room. Or I'll go in from the balcony.*

Agreed. He'd seen Larissa in action before and knew she could scale an outer wall by holding on with just her fingers. She moved more nimbly than a feline shifter. The outside of this hotel was all brick, so if necessary, she could infiltrate the room from the outside. But he hoped it didn't come down to that.

When they reached the door right before Magda's room, he handed the master key to Larissa. Her eyebrows rose, her indigo eyes flashing bright blue for a fraction of a moment before she took it. While every fiber inside him screamed to take over, to move in ahead of her to check for potential danger, he decided to make a small concession and treat her like the powerful vampire she was. Plus . . . he couldn't scent anyone inside. If he had, his wolf never would have allowed him to let her take the lead just yet.

Moving whisper quiet, Larissa slid the key card into the door so silently he didn't even hear it. With just as much precision, she opened the door, paused, then continued inside without glancing back.

No one's in here, she said, even though he scented they were alone.

He eased the door shut behind them. This room was just as big as the one they'd been in, but the floor-to-ceiling gold-and-white-striped curtains had been pulled back, letting sunlight filter inside. When Larissa stepped into a stream of light it illuminated her, reminding him of the first time he'd seen her. Before they'd even spoken.

She'd arrived with her coven members, and while the majority of their vehicles had been understated, she'd been driving a new Ferrari right off the line. A 1953 twelve-cylinder red thing of beauty—he still had it in storage. For some reason he'd never been able to part with it even though it was just a physical object. It had kept him connected to her. One of the few things of hers he still owned.

That car hadn't compared to her though. When she'd stepped out decked from head to toe in leather, with high-heeled boots, that thick dark hair shining under a rare sunny Highland day, it had been all his fantasies rolled into one tight little package. He'd been absolutely dumbstruck. And she'd looked right through him. Or so he'd thought. She'd admitted later that she'd been just as affected—but her attraction had angered her.

Things between them had been physical at first, but their time together, short as it was, had forged a bond between them nothing could have ever pierced if they'd had the chance to thrive as a couple. At least he believed that to be true. Even after all their years apart that fundamental link between them was still there, titanium strong.

What's wrong? Larissa's worried voice cut through his thoughts and he realized he'd been staring at her.

Shit. He was going to get himself killed. Or worse, lose focus and not be able to protect her. He gave a sharp shake of his head. *I'm good.*

She didn't look convinced, but lightly tapped a finger against the adjoining wall. *No one is in there. Should we use the door or the balcony?*

The balcony would give them the element of surprise if there was a trap waiting for them, but Aiden didn't think the witch wanted to hurt Larissa. Not yet at least. She'd kept her alive—albeit weak with crap bagged blood—for a reason. Aiden wanted to find out what it was. *The door will be the least conspicuous mode of entry.*

They both moved back toward the front of the room, stopping at the connecting door. When Larissa went to open it, Aiden snagged the key card from her fingers. Maybe he wasn't as evolved as he thought.

Her lips pulled into a thin line, but she stepped back, as if she'd expected his reaction. *Sorry,* he said.

No, you're not. A smile tugged at her very kissable lips.

Ignoring the way his body reacted to her, he slid the key card into the door with the same amount of stealth she'd used. Seconds later they were both inside the empty room. As he stepped inside he felt almost . . . dirty. He couldn't explain it. Inhaling, he wondered if it was something left behind by Magda.

I feel it too, Larissa said, as if she'd read his mind. Since he hadn't voiced his thoughts aloud or even telepathically, he realized that meant she was starting to be more in tune with him on a subconscious level, but didn't mention it. As a supernatural, he was superstitious by nature and he wasn't going to jinx anything. If she was starting to be more in tune with him without even realizing it, he was going to let it happen naturally. Larissa didn't look at him as she scanned the pristine room. *I was never in here before. She always came to my room. I wonder if she even slept here,* she projected, seemingly more to herself than to him.

Aiden inhaled, taking in all of the scents and memorizing them as he moved to the closet. Larissa moved to the bed and looked underneath it as he opened the closet door. Like the perfect team they'd once been, they scanned every possible inch of the room in less than a minute. As they moved with their supernatural speed, he still couldn't shake the strange feeling moving over him, like oily fingers skittering over his bare skin.

That bitch. Larissa's voice sounded loudly in his head. *Something rattled loose in my fucked-up memory—I know what we're feeling because I felt this centuries ago thanks to another witch. Magda spelled the room. I don't know what the purpose is for, maybe just an alert spell, but I don't like it. Let's move to my room. Stealth be damned, since she likely knows we're here.*

Aiden knew what an alert spell was. It was like a supernatural alarm system. And it made sense Magda had left one. "Let's go now," he ordered. Whatever this was, it wasn't an alert spell. He didn't know how he knew it. He just did. Whatever he was feeling was starting to weigh on him, making him feel sluggish. Right now of all times he couldn't afford to have his reflexes dulled.

They flew out the main door in seconds and hurried down to her room. Once he was sure no one was inside, he went in first. The room felt normal, but there were more scents that accosted him now.

"You smell that oakmoss scent?" she asked as she hurried to her closet.

"Yeah." It was sharp and woodsy.

"That's Magda. Memorize it," she muttered as she rifled through her clothes.

He would. It was the reason for their trip here. Aiden hated even being in this hotel, but he'd needed to get Magda's scent for himself. Larissa could have tried to describe it, but it wouldn't matter. His wolf needed to scent it to track it. Now no matter what, no matter how many years passed, if he ever ran into this female again, he'd know her scent. Closing his eyes, he inhaled deeply. Oh yes, he would never forget the scent of the female who had dared lie to Larissa about his existence. Aiden's phone buzzed in his pocket and when he saw Angelo's name he answered immediately. "Yeah?"

"Saw two human males entering the hotel. They both look like fucking underwear models," he muttered.

"That kind of thing interest you?"

"Fuck you," Angelo growled. "If you'd let me get to the point, I heard them talking and their convo was fucking weird. One of the males said something about 'following the female and reporting in with their findings.' They didn't say much more before they disappeared inside, but it was strange enough that I wanted to let you know."

"Thanks, man. Did you get a picture of them?"

"Yeah, texting as we speak."

"If we see them, we're going to tail them. Get the SUV ready."

"On it."

Once they disconnected Aiden found Larissa peeking out from the doorway of the bathroom watching him.

"Find anything interesting?" he asked.

She shook her head. "I heard what he said. We need to leave?"

"Yeah." If these human males were of interest, Aiden wanted to track them. "I think you should leave everything here. I want to burn it all just in case. We can use the tub."

Her expression grim, she nodded in agreement. Without a word, she grabbed the few clothes from the closet and he started taking anything that looked like it belonged to her or even smelled like Larissa from the drawers. Once everything was in the ceramic tub,

Aiden started to light one of the matches from the matchbook he'd grabbed from the desk when Larissa's hand sparkled that familiar fiery blue.

Relief surged through him at the same time she yelped. "What the hell?" she squeaked, the flames flickering out, but not completely dying. Her wide eyes met his and grew even wider. "You're not surprised. . . . You *knew* I could do this?"

He nodded. "Yeah. You didn't try to fry me yesterday so I figured you either hadn't regained your powers yet or didn't remember." This was one of her deepest secrets, the power passed on from her mother's line. He wondered if she understood that she possessed more than this simple ability to create a beautiful fire. Way more.

"How could I not remember," she whispered as her eyes glazed over for a long moment. "Oh my sweet Lord." She stared at him for a hard moment, a hundred questions in her eyes before she focused on the tub. Holding out one of her hands, she let loose a tiny stream of lightning-like blue flames. All her clothes and everything else they'd grabbed that wasn't nailed down burst into a kaleidoscope of shimmering colors before turning to ash. "Holy. Shit." After a long look at the ashes in the tub, she stared at him. "What else haven't you told me?"

There was even more to her gift, but he wouldn't tell her. Not when the gift could benefit him. This was something she'd need to remember on her own. And the last thing he would do was stunt her memories. So far everything she'd recalled had been on her own. He refused to tell her things if it could affect her recall. "We need to leave."

"You *will* tell me what you're holding back," she growled, sounding more shifter than vampire as they hurried from the room.

He snorted and motioned toward the opposite end of the hallway than they'd come from. "Let's wait by the stairs. If the humans come up the stairs we'll hear them. We'll tail them after they leave."

"What if they're not part of all . . . this?"

He shrugged. "Then we'll find another lead." Aiden knew his packmate Ryan was hard at work finding more about this Magda and he trusted the male and his entire pack. They would give Larissa her life and memories back. She was already starting to remember so much. The ability to start fire and not burst into flames herself was unique for a vampire. But what she could do with that fire was incredible. Like nothing he'd ever heard of before. Nothing he'd ever seen. "I'm not telling anyone about your gift." *And you shouldn't either,* he said as they reached the door to the stairs. *Absolutely no one.*

He could sense her apprehension as she nodded. Once they stepped into the stairwell, he left the door open a crack and watched the hallway with interest. If the humans Angelo had overheard were involved in this mess, there was nowhere they could escape to now.

"Something seems different about you," Brianna said from the front passenger seat of the SUV as she watched Larissa intently. The fae female had turned around in her seat as they waited outside the hotel to see if the two human males exited soon. Both Angelo and Aiden were inside keeping an eye out for the males.

Larissa half smiled and shrugged. "I'm just starting to feel more like my old self, that's all." That wasn't remotely it, but she couldn't tell this royal member of the fae that she'd just discovered her amazing power. Some part of her subconscious had simply triggered it in the hotel bathroom. They'd needed to burn her belongings and she'd created that fire or whatever it was. She hated that she couldn't remember this part of herself. It made her wonder what else she was forgetting. And she really wanted to try it again. It had filled her with the most amazing sense of power.

"Hmm, or more like you're starting to connect with Aiden." Brianna's blue eyes were kind and warm, so unlike the few fae Larissa had interacted with in decades past.

Larissa was still unsure who she could trust about pretty much anything, but talking about Aiden was a safe enough subject. "Yes."

"He's a good male. I watched him save a human who'd been on death's doorstep without pause. He had nothing to gain for his good deed. He always steps up if anyone in his—and now my—pack needs anything. And Connor, even though his parents were killed by fae, has never made me feel unwelcome. Not even before I mated with Angelo." The petite female snorted. "He was actually protective of me when I didn't need it."

Larissa nodded, trying to figure out why Brianna was telling her this. "Okay."

"I love the entire Armstrong-Cordona pack. They're my family now." Something dark glinted in the female's eyes. It was there so fast, then gone in the blink of an eye.

But Larissa knew she hadn't imagined it. And she knew exactly what Brianna wasn't saying aloud. If Larissa hurt anyone in the pack, Brianna would be her enemy. "I might not be able to remember him, but I once loved Aiden enough to defy my coven and leave behind everything I'd known to be with him. I would never hurt him or any of his packmates."

A faint smile ghosted across Brianna's lips at that. "You two rocked the supernatural world back then with rumors. I still can't believe this Aiden is the same one who mated with a Danesti vampire."

"Do you think my parents are really dead?" Larissa blurted. Aiden didn't know anything about their disappearance and she felt uncomfortable talking to him about them anyway. Not when they'd hated him enough to send assassins after him.

"I honestly don't know. Your father was very secretive when he wanted to be. Even with your own kind." Her voice was soft, apologetic.

Unfortunately it was true. Both her parents had been incredibly secretive, even with her. Sighing, Larissa shifted against the leather seat and looked out the tinted window. One of the human males she and Aiden had spotted from the stairwell going into her hotel room was exiting. He had something in his hand and was looking at it. A cell phone.

Angelo and I are coming out. One of the males is talking

to the front desk and the other just stepped outside. We're going to follow them, see where they go. Make sure the SUV is running. Aiden's instructions were rapid-fire.

When Brianna reached across to the driver's side and started the engine, Larissa asked, "Did Angelo just contact you?"

"Yes." Excitement hummed through the other female. "This might be the lead you need. Maybe they'll lead us back to Magda."

Larissa could only hope.

Moments later both Angelo and Aiden slid into the SUV. As they did, the other male she'd seen earlier from upstairs exited. He looked in all directions before joining his friend on the sidewalk. They talked a few seconds, then started walking briskly down the sidewalk.

"Did they say anything of use inside?" Larissa asked the men.

"Sort of. They seemed disappointed not to have found you, but they're excited about going back to, and I quote, 'tag-team her.' One wants to gain access to the back door this time, as he put it," Aiden said wryly as Angelo pulled away from the curb.

"It could be Magda they're referring to. When we first arrived here I caught her having sex with a vampire in a dark corner of the hotel bar. Some witches crave sex like vampires crave blood." As Larissa understood it, it was a power thing. Magda hadn't even tried to hide what she was doing from Larissa. If anything, it had almost seemed as if the female wanted her to join them.

They followed the two males a couple of blocks until they slid into a two-door sports car. Larissa wasn't familiar with the make or model, but guessed it was newer. Angelo used impressive driving skills to follow the humans without making it seem as if he was following them. They drove for over twenty minutes in the more commercial, downtown district until they reached a residential area.

The homes were large and beautiful and looked older than many of the modern type of architecture she'd seen. When she saw a sign that proclaimed this was a historic area it made sense.

"I'm getting out," Aiden murmured as Angelo pulled up to a stop sign.

"What?" Larissa asked, but he was already out the door.

I'm tracking them by scent. Tell Angelo to park somewhere close. If I need you guys, I'll let you know. We can't afford to be seen right now and it will be easier for me to track on foot. I want to see if I can pick up Magda's scent.

Though Larissa was frustrated he'd left so abruptly, she responded and then relayed the message to Angelo and Brianna. After that Aiden went silent and Angelo found a quiet place to park under a large oak tree in front of a two-story home that seemed to be unoccupied. The longer the silence stretched between her and Aiden, the more frayed her nerves became. She could still feel their bondmate link in place, but it didn't negate her worry for him. Since she didn't want to distract him she didn't reach out. If she inadvertently caused him harm she'd never forgive herself. But she feared this was all part of a larger plot. What if Magda wanted to hurt Aiden? What if—

Larissa nearly jumped out of her skin as Aiden slid into the backseat, a huge grin on his face. "I have an address and I think Magda lives there," he said as he held out a handful of mail.

All of the envelopes were addressed to Magda Petran.

Chapter 17

Magda resisted the urge to break her phone into pieces. That would make her even more agitated than she already was. Sending Perry and Donovan to track Larissa had been a long shot, but she'd needed humans going after the female, not vamps. They hadn't even gotten a glimpse of the vampire or her mate at the hotel. Just a hotel bathtub filled with ashes.

She wondered at that, but figured the female had destroyed all her belongings so Magda couldn't spell something of hers. Well, too late for that. Even without the tracking spell working, the other spell she'd cast on the beautiful vampire was still holding.

For the most part.

Closing her eyes, Magda leaned back against the rocking chair on her back porch and focused on the extra hex her master had demanded she cast. These types of things took so much blasted energy that it was beyond frustrating to do. When she concentrated like this she could almost see her spells in the physical sense as well as feel them.

Right now the memory loss spell she'd cast on Larissa had tiny fissures in it. Which meant Larissa was regaining some of the memories Magda had blocked. It had to be because of the shifter Aiden. He was an unfortunate snag in her master's plans. His presence seemed to have unlocked something inside Larissa.

Taking a deep breath, Magda focused on the biggest of the spiderweb-like fissures and chanted low in her throat as she tried to mend it, but it started to widen even more. Immediately she opened her eyes and pulled all her concentration from the fissures, not wanting to agitate them even more.

She would just have to leave it be for now. Because if it broke completely, there was no telling what her master would do. While she might not know why he'd wanted that spell on Larissa, she knew it was very important to him. There had to be something in her grimoire that would help her to mend the spell.

As she thought of her master, she decided to call him. He'd been gone almost all day with no word of when he might return. Her annoyance flared at that. She had to tell him everything she did, yet he told her absolutely nothing. He just made demands and didn't even give her good sex anymore. In the beginning things had been so different between them. She'd thought he cared about her. Now she wondered if she was just another tool for him to use. It was hard to believe considering how beautiful she was, but maybe he'd found someone else. Even the thought made her see red.

He picked up on the third ring. "What?" he asked impatiently.

His tone was like nails on a chalkboard. "Where are you?"

A long pause. "Why?"

She gritted her teeth. "I'm curious."

"Have you found Larissa?"

"No," she said quickly.

"Then you have no reason to contact me." His tone was annoyed more than cold.

"I want to know what you're doing." And who he was doing it with. Magda wondered if he'd found someone else to fuck. He didn't seem to care that she slept with humans, but she didn't like the thought of him fucking anyone else. Not when she wanted to be the female who ruled by his side. She was all that he would need.

"Turn on the news in an hour and you'll see what I'm up to." His voice had taken on that lower tone she recognized. The one she feared. He wasn't quite himself when he sounded like that.

It was clear he wasn't going to tell her anything else. "Fine," she snapped.

"I'll be back to your place in a few hours. Be ready for me." A soft demand.

"No." She sounded braver than she felt. She wasn't going to just wait around for him anymore.

"What did you say?" His words were a bare whisper.

"I'm not going to wait around for you to do with me as you please. You can return or stay away; I'm not going to be here regardless."

He went silent again, this pause seeming to stretch on forever. "You will be there for me, naked on the cellar floor, ready to please me."

"Why don't you find a whore to fuck?" she spat, letting her anger unleash. Without seeing him face-to-face she found it much easier to lash out. Besides, if he punished her it would likely just be rough sex.

Now he chuckled softly. "Is that what this is about? Are you jealous, sweet Magda? There's no one else for me but you. I allow you your human dalliances because it pleases you, but I will not take anyone else's body but yours. You belong to me."

Her nipples tightened at that. She belonged to no one, but she still liked the possessive note in his voice. "If that's true, you're doing a poor job of showing me lately."

He sighed, sounding more like the male she'd originally fallen for. "I will make it up to you tonight. Until then, no fucking your humans and no touching yourself either. Your next orgasm will come from me."

"Fine." She didn't care what he said though as she slipped her hand down the front of her pants. She wasn't wearing anything underneath and immediately stroked her pulsing clit.

"If you do, I'll know and you won't like the consequences." He sounded darker again, that tone sending a shiver snaking through her.

"I won't," she said before disconnecting. But she didn't stop pleasuring herself. She needed the release. A self-induced orgasm wouldn't give her the burst of power one from a lover would, but it still fed her. He wouldn't know and the truth was, she wasn't sure she cared if he did. She couldn't help but wonder if maybe it was time to cut her losses and run. He might be powerful but he wasn't omniscient and she was very good at hiding.

His annoyance faded as he ended the call with Magda. The little witch had just about outlived her usefulness. But not yet. Every time they fucked he siphoned power from her. She was just too stupid to realize it. That was the only reason he allowed her human lovers, not because he cared about what pleased her.

For a while he'd been able to fake his infatuation with her to gain the knowledge he needed, but she was growing tiresome. Still, he needed Larissa, and Magda could be useful in finding the vampire. Larissa was the key to what he needed, but the witch had that grimoire hidden and he needed that as well. Witches always kept their spell books well-guarded. Magda was the first witch he'd come across in centuries whom he'd been able to charm enough to give up some of her spells and knowledge. Her youth had a lot to do with it. She thought she was so special and powerful, but she wasn't using a tenth of what she could be.

Not like him.

Darkness rattled inside him, threatening to take over completely, but he shoved the growing blackness back down. He was in control of himself. Not . . . them.

The price of wielding so much power was a high one, but one he'd been willing to pay. Sacrifices to the darkness helped feed his power but he had to give them something truly worthy. He had to give them Larissa. They'd demanded it of him so many times. Once he drained all her blood and drank it himself, he would be unstoppable. If he'd been able, he'd have siphoned everything from her before she'd come out of stasis. But her blood had been virtually useless then. Like dead, rotten blood for someone like him. He needed Larissa at the height of her power, not weak and pathetic. Unfortunately that was a double-edged sword. She'd be much harder to kill once she regained her powers. But not unstoppable, especially if Magda's memory-loss spell held. That was the key. If the vamp couldn't remember what she could do, he could destroy her.

Those from the darkness had shown him the truth of what he could be once he killed the last Danesti and took the rare gift prevalent only in her line. Someone like Larissa had never appreciated what she'd had before she'd gone into stasis. She'd kept her gift a secret just like her mother. He'd killed her parents and he would kill her.

Taking Vlad and his wife's lives had been not only the biggest gamble of his existence, but the hardest thing he'd ever accomplished. But everyone underestimated him, looked right through him, thought he was a nobody. He'd relied on spells and poison to incapacitate them. After he'd poisoned them, killing them hadn't been exactly easy, but he'd pulled it off. Some still wondered if Vlad and his coven were actually alive. He snorted. Supernaturals and their rumor mill. Of course he'd been feeding the rumors for years, keeping everyone wondering. And he still owned the last castle belonging to the Danesti line. Technically it was Larissa's since it was linked to her family, but soon that wouldn't matter. Soon he would make everyone respect and fear him. The world would be his. No more pandering to these weak humans.

Placing his hands on the giant round stone in the middle of the dank, deep cave, he let their power flow through him. The stone was slick from the leftover blood of his many sacrifices. Those from the darkness tugged at his control, trying to wrest more of him away, but he yanked back.

Magda had taught him that he was the owner of his soul and no one could take it unless he allowed them. He fed the darkness blood, but his soul was his. As long as he retained it, he retained himself. It was one of the useful bits of knowledge the witch had given him.

His entire body hummed and vibrated as he concentrated on the three vampires he planned to control. He imagined their blood running through their veins, focused on it as if it were the only thing in the world.

Surrender more to us and you'll rule everything. You won't need the Danesti female. The voices from the dark rose up in unison inside him.

He shoved them back down and continued concentrating on the sweet, red blood flowing through his three targets' bodies. He didn't need the powers of the darkness to control these vampires. Grasping tight, he did as Magda had taught him and guided the vamps into action. He whispered thoughts in their minds, telling them exactly what they wanted to do.

Dusk had fallen, but because of the time of year it was still early enough for most businesses to be open. The bank would be open and these three, while not daywalkers, were still powerful in their own right.

All he needed was for them to rob two safe deposit boxes, then leave their spoils in a place he'd designated. Then he would have them kill themselves. Easy cleanup for him and he would get what he wanted.

Watching through their eyes, he found it almost impossible to distinguish which male was which as they parked in front of the bank. They moved in unison, not bothering with masks or disguises. He ordered them to release their fangs and claws.

On the sidewalk humans screamed and scattered in all directions. He looked up at one of the video cameras on the way in and ordered one of the males to flip it the bird.

The moment they entered, chaos ensued. All three pulled pistols from their waistbands and started firing randomly. He didn't give a shit about anyone who got in the way. The recon he'd done personally told him this little bank wouldn't react well to a robbery. Especially not one like this.

Screams filled the air and he smiled as he watched people falling left and right from their wounds. A fat human wearing a suit and tie attempted to cower behind a potted plant. With his big belly he was doing a piss-poor job of it.

Him. Grab the one with the key card hanging around his neck, he ordered one of the males while simultaneously ordering the other two to stand guard.

The shriek of the alarm bounced off the vaulted ceilings, the shrill sound cutting through his oversensitive hearing. Since he was controlling these males he heard and felt everything they did.

Shaking himself, he tried to ignore the distraction of the noise as he directed the lone vamp to the safety deposit boxes. He'd learned that a wealthy human kept two at this bank, both filled with uncut, untraceable diamonds.

Soon they would belong to him. He could use the money to fund so many things and this was child's play. He was sending a message to everyone, including the Brethren. This world was his playground.

Once his vampire had ripped the drawers from the wall and taken the contents, he ordered the male to kill the bank employee. Blood sprayed the wall of metal drawers as he raced from the room, his boots thudding loudly against the tiled floor as he met up with his friends.

He ordered both vamps to stop ravaging and feeding from two lifeless humans before they all ran out the door.

A thrill raced through him at the thought of all those glittery diamonds. And not long after that, a beautiful dark-haired vampire would die at his hands. Then nothing would stop him.

He guided his minions to the getaway car he'd planted blocks over. They flew down the sidewalk, not caring who they ran over. As they ran, he suddenly lost control of one. The link just snapped, completely severing his control.

No!

He saw nothing. Ordering the other males to stop, he told them to turn and jumped back in fear. A red-headed female with two blades and canines advanced on his vampires before he could order them to fight back.

His connection died instantly as she killed them. Blinking, he fell back from the stone slab and wavered once. As he tried to stand, he vomited up blood, the reaction so familiar to him now he didn't bother to stop it.

Weakened, he would need to feed and fuck soon. Rage bubbled up inside him that he'd lost all those diamonds at the hands of that bitch.

He knew exactly who she was too. Erin Flynn, member of the Armstrong pack. No doubt her Alpha had sent her since he'd been snooping around Winston-Salem, asking questions he had no business worrying about. Stupid shifter thought he could eliminate the blood dealing in the area. Soon the Alpha was about to find out that was the very least of his problems. Connor Armstrong was a thorn in his side, and one he planned to eliminate as soon as the time was right.

If the Flynn female was in Winston-Salem, he might have to change up his plans for the evening. Going back there might not be safe yet. Especially not when he was feeling so weak. He'd need to make another blood sacrifice if he wanted a quick shot of energy and power. At least finding a victim shouldn't be a problem.

Chapter 18

Fontana, North Carolina
Thirty minutes ago

"I've already texted Angelo and Aiden," Connor said into his cell to Erin, one of his most trusted warriors—and also the newest enforcer for the Council. "Help them secure the witch's house and the neighborhood. I've got a situation, but am leaving as soon as it's ironed out. How far out are you?"

"Maybe twenty minutes if the GPS is right. How's Jayce handling everything?" she asked quietly, the rest of her unspoken question crystal clear.

Ryan had contacted Connor about a serious cluster-fuck that included the appearance of Jayce's brother. Now this Aldric had helped kill five vampires to protect Natalia. *After* Connor had told the Brethren he'd keep his packmate locked down for twenty-four hours. This was another hassle he didn't need. Not when he was desperate to get to Winston-Salem and back up his packmates. They were going to end this vamp-blood-dealing shit soon. "Not sure yet."

"All right. We're headed through downtown right now. I'll call you as soon as Noah and I make contact."

As they disconnected, Connor's mate walked into the living room. Ana smiled softly at him and immediately pushed him back against the couch before curling up on his lap. "You look exhausted," she murmured, nuzzling his neck, kissing and raking her teeth against his skin.

Shuddering, he wrapped his arms around her and held her tight. He closed his eyes and for a long moment pretended the outside world didn't exist. Other than Liam, Ana was the one constant in his world. He would do anything to keep his pack safe, but Ana was the ultimate reason he drew breath every day. "Once all this shit is taken care of you and I are taking a vacation and—"

The front door slammed open, startling them both. Ana jumped from his lap and he immediately stood, ready for whatever issue was next. Vivian raced through the door and paused in the entryway, looking at them for a brief moment through the connecting archway. Tears glistened in her big eyes. Connor's heart ached at the pain he saw etched there. She might not be his by blood, but he considered her his cub.

"Honey—" Ana started, but the little girl raced up the stairs.

Before either of them could move Leila rushed in the house, her face stricken. The sixteen-year-old shifter

Jayce and Kat had adopted bit her bottom lip as she looked at them. "I'm so sorry," she muttered.

"What happened?" Ana asked carefully.

"I . . . sort of yelled at Vivian. I don't really mind if she goes through my stuff and I've never given her grief before, but I'm sort of seeing this human guy in town. We're not doing anything . . . yet." She cleared her throat, averting her gaze somewhere over Ana's shoulder. "But still, I want to be prepared and Vivian started going through some private stuff of mine . . ." Her face turned bright pink as she glanced at the floor.

Sudden understanding slammed into Connor as the girl trailed off. This was so not something Connor wanted to hear about. Ever. And he really hoped Jayce didn't hear about this human male. "I'll leave you two to talk," he muttered, hurrying from the room and heading in the direction of the kitchen. As he left he heard Leila say something about Vivian finding her condoms and, oh God, he did *not* want to know about that. She was only sixteen.

As he started a new pot of coffee, he scented Jayce and Kat entering the house. Seconds later they walked into the kitchen.

"What's going on with Leila? I saw her and Ana leaving and she looked like she was crying." Jayce's expression was more worried than angry.

Connor shot a quick glance at Kat, who didn't seem concerned. Maybe she knew what had happened. "Girl stuff, man."

"I told you she's fine. Some stuff you just don't need to worry about," Kat murmured, making a beeline for the brewing pot. She inhaled deeply before asking, "Have you talked to Erin? Have they met up with Aiden and his new mate yet? I can't wait to meet her. What's she like?"

"Okay, no more coffee for you," Jayce muttered, leaning against one of the counters.

Connor just shook his head as Kat practically bounced off the walls. He'd never seen her like this. She was vibrating with energy. "She's old and powerful and Aiden is beyond enthralled by her." That was all anyone needed to know at this point. He didn't want to discuss that now anyway. He wanted to talk about the fact that Jayce's brother was about to arrive at the ranch.

Jayce's gray eyes narrowed a fraction. "How old?"

Connor shrugged. "Older than you."

The enforcer watched Connor for a long moment and he saw the second that understanding hit Jayce. "Aiden . . . Holy shit. Tell me that's not why you were asking Narek and Juhani about the Draculesti line. Our Aiden is not the Aiden who . . . She's alive? I thought their whole coven was dead."

"You realize you just said 'our Aiden'?" Connor asked.

"If you ever tell him I said that . . ." Jayce trailed off as he gritted his teeth.

"If you don't tell me what's going on I'll tell him what you said." Kat bounced up and down on the balls of her feet, looking eager for gossip. "Come on, the Aiden who *what*? And what coven? What are you guys talking about?"

Jayce just looked at Kat, and Connor could tell they were communicating telepathically. He could also tell that Jayce didn't tell Kat everything she wanted to know because she glared at him.

The buzzing of Connor's cell dragged his attention away. One glance at the caller ID and he tensed. "They're pulling down the drive now. Your brother's behind Ryan and the others."

Jayce's jaw tightened, but he didn't respond. Not that Connor had expected him to. He'd already tried to talk about it with him after Ryan originally contacted him, but Jayce seemed pretty wary about his brother. Which didn't give Connor the most confidence about this guy's arrival at the ranch.

"Come on, let's meet them outside by the front gate." Because he wasn't letting the male inside his home. The fact that he was being allowed on the ranch was the only concession Connor would give and that was because he'd saved Natalia.

"Sweetheart," Jayce started, but Kat cut him off with a sharp look.

"Don't even think about telling me to wait inside like some docile female. I haven't got to run in three freaking days and I'm going insane. Don't push me over the edge because you won't like the consequences," she snapped. Before either Connor or Jayce could respond, she stalked from the kitchen.

"Is that why she's acting like she's all hopped-up on something?" Connor asked as they followed after her.

Expression dark, Jayce nodded. "Yeah. Her wolf is fucking moody if she doesn't get to stretch her legs.

Plus she misses Aiden. Bastard," Jayce muttered under his breath, only half joking.

Connor refrained from responding. Aiden and Kat would always be close because he'd turned her into a shifter. And Jayce was more territorial and possessive than most supernatural beings. He'd probably always be a little on edge around Aiden no matter how platonic his and Kat's relationship was.

Are you with Leila? Connor projected to Ana.

Yeah. We're at December's eating cookies. Vivian is here too. I think they've made up. Vivian just got her feelings hurt. She looks up to Leila so much and was surprised when Leila yelled. She has no clue what the condoms were so this is nothing that can't be fixed. We're just going to have to set some boundaries for Vivian. She needs to stop going through Leila's stuff anyway. It's not fair to Leila.

Connor sighed. *I agree. We'll talk about that later. Keep the girls inside for now. Jayce's brother has arrived. Spread the word to everyone else to remain inside until I've felt this male out.*

I will. Love you.

Love you too. As the three of them stepped outside, Connor spotted Liam heading over from his house.

The warriors are all in place. If this guy makes one wrong move, we'll take him down, Liam said through their telepathic link.

Connor nodded before they all strode toward the front gate. Connor reached it first and drew the big gate back. Two trucks rumbled down the long pathway winding toward their ranch. One he recognized. The other he didn't.

Ryan pulled through first, Teresa visible in the front seat and Natalia in the backseat. The other truck parked ten feet from the gate, not pulling through. Because of the tint it was impossible to make out more than a large male's outline.

Some of Connor's tension eased. At least this wolf seemed to respect boundaries so far. "You want to do the talking?" Connor murmured to Jayce, who'd stepped up next to him. He was aware of Kat and Liam hovering in the background but they hadn't made a move to step closer and for that he was grateful.

"This is your territory," Jayce said.

"That's not an answer."

Jayce cleared his throat and for the first time since he'd known the guy, Connor would swear he was nervous. Maybe it wasn't hostility Connor had sensed after all.

"I'll talk, but interject anytime," Connor said.

Next to him Jayce relaxed a fraction. "Thanks," he murmured as the driver's door opened.

Connor couldn't scent any emotions, because as powerful as Jayce was, the male could cover scents when he wanted to. Just like Connor could.

As the unfamiliar male stepped out Connor watched him carefully. He looked at his brother, his expression unreadable, before focusing on Connor. The files Ryan had pulled up on this guy weren't necessarily bad, but the guy was shady at best. Wearing cargo pants, a long-sleeved T-shirt, and a short military-style buzz, he looked very similar to Jayce—except for Jayce's scars.

"Aldric Kazan." Connor stepped forward. "Why

were you following Natalia and why are you in my territory?" He knew what Ryan had told him, but he wanted to hear it from this male himself.

"I followed the female from the club last night, then saw her leaving your ranch this morning. It looked like trouble was following her, so I tailed them. The reason I followed her in the first place is because I wanted to see my brother, which you must know." He flicked another look at Jayce. His words were blunt, honest, the scent of truth rolling off him in subtle waves. He nodded politely at Connor. "Thank you for allowing me on your land."

Connor nodded once, then glanced over his shoulder. "Ryan and Teresa?" He tilted his head at Natalia, who had her arms wrapped around her slender body. She was such a feisty thing sometimes he forgot how damn young and sheltered she was. Right now she looked terrified and in need of some pack time. He knew Ryan and Teresa and the rest of her sisters would give her the support she needed.

Without pause Ryan stepped in between the females and wrapped his arms around Natalia's and Teresa's shoulders and headed back to their place. Connor breathed a sigh of relief once he knew that was taken care of. He also needed Ryan to run the information on the name Magda Petran, but that could wait a few minutes. Aiden had sent him the name half an hour ago and Jayce was running it through some of his own programs, but Ryan had more resources.

But one thing at a time. Connor turned back to Aldric and was surprised to see him watching Natalia go.

For a fraction of a moment, there was a naked longing in his gaze before his hard mask fell back into place. "Why were you at the club last night?"

"Investigating vamp blood dealing for some clients."

"Who?"

The male's jaw clenched. "I'm not divulging that."

"Why were you investigating then?"

"Have you seen the fucking news? This shit is bad for all of us." Again, truth rolled off him, but the statement itself was a simple truth. It didn't mean anything.

"You're an investigator now?" Jayce asked, his tone devoid of emotion. The male looked like a statue as he stared at his brother. And Connor couldn't help but notice the way he'd blocked his mate's body with his, refusing to let her step up next to him for support.

Aldric nodded, suddenly looking just as nervous as Jayce had moments earlier. "Yeah. Independent stuff, mainly for vamps. They like that I'm objective."

"Why'd you want to see me?"

Aldric swallowed hard. "I . . . It's been a long time. The little wolf said something about you being mated and . . . I wanted to see if it was true. I wanted to see my brother."

"Now you've seen, and now you can fucking leave." Jayce's voice was ice-cold as he turned and stalked away. Kat hurried after him, but not before sending a withering glare toward Aldric.

Aldric scrubbed a hand over his face and for one moment Connor witnessed raw agony etched into his face as he watched his brother. Connor couldn't even imagine what could have happened to make the two brothers stop talking. Liam was a lifeline for Connor, the best friend he'd ever had. But he wasn't a fucking family counselor and it wasn't his business anyway.

"Do you know the identity of the vamps you killed for Natalia?" Connor asked, knowing he would likely need to smooth out the killings with Juhani and Narek.

"Yes, they're from Emil's line. I've already contacted Juhani. You won't need to worry about retribution. I told those vamps to stand down and they ignored me. They got what they deserved." There was no remorse in his hard voice. In that moment, the family resemblance between him and Jayce was hard to miss.

"You know Juhani?" That was interesting.

The male shrugged his broad shoulders. "I've done investigations for the Brethren before."

"Are you working for them now?" A direct question like this he couldn't ignore, even if he didn't want to divulge the information. Connor would likely scent his lie.

A short pause before he sighed and nodded. "Yes. But I didn't know about your meeting with him and Narek until after I just called Juhani. I simply wanted to inform him of the vamps' deaths and to clear the female's name. That's when he told me he'd met with you—and my brother. I'm sure you will call him for confirmation, but the female is still protected. She just needs to remain locked down for a while."

"Small world," Connor muttered. He glanced over his shoulder at Liam. *We could use him.*

Liam nodded.

It will anger Jayce, he said even though in the end, it
didn't matter. Figuring out who was behind this blood
dealing and keeping his pack safe was his number one
priority.

Liam just shrugged. *He'll get over it.*

Connor turned back to Aldric. "Would you be willing to share what you've learned in your investigation
so far?"

"Yes." The answer was so immediate it made Connor pause.

"Your employers won't mind?" His voice was a
deadly edge, warning this male to tread carefully.

Aldric's greenish gray eyes flared with anger. "They
don't own me. I'm investigating this shit because I
choose to. I will share information as long as you show
the same courtesy." When Connor didn't respond right
away, the male continued. "My strongest lead is a witch
with ties to many of the blood dealers. She's fucking
most of them, but I don't think she's their supplier."

His interest piqued, Connor asked, "What's her
name?"

"Magda."

"Petran?"

Faint surprise flickered across Aldric's face. "Yes."

Sighing, Connor pointed to the nearby parking
structure. "Park in there and join me in my home."

"Will Jayce be joining us?" The note of hope in the
male's voice took Connor by surprise.

"Not likely."

If he was disappointed, the male masked it well.
"Thank you for allowing me onto your property. Once

we're done here, I'll be heading back to Winston-Salem, but if I come to Fontana again I'll alert you of my presence."

"Thank you."

He stepped back and allowed the male to drive onto the property. Liam moved up next to Connor and they wordlessly headed toward the parking structure. Just because they were allowing him brief access didn't mean they were letting this male out of their sight.

Connor, get to December's now. Erin's on the news. Ana's voice rang loudly in his head.

What the hell? He started to tell Liam when his brother tensed next to him, likely hearing the same thing from his own mate.

"Did Ana contact you?" Liam asked.

"Yeah," he said as his cell phone buzzed. It was Erin. "Hey."

"Alpha, we have a huge fucking problem."

"She'll be okay," Ryan murmured, pulling Teresa close to his chest in a tight hug. To his utter relief, she melted against him, wrapping her arms around his waist and laying her head on his chest. He leaned against the kitchen counter, pulling her with him and spreading his legs wider so she fit more snugly against him.

Natalia had locked herself in her room and refused to talk to either of them. He could hear water running and guessed she was showering or taking a bath.

"I know," Teresa whispered, tightening her grip.

He could get used to this. Too easily. Holding her this way was heaven and hell. Her compact body fit perfectly against his, even with the difference in their sizes. Like most of the Cordona women, she was petite with the perfect amount of curves. Curves he'd been fantasizing about for too damn long.

"Once she gets some rest, tomorrow everything won't seem as bad to her. Trust me. Maybe you should take a bath too." He knew Teresa took baths when she needed to relax. He shoved that thought away, however, because imagining her in any state of undress wasn't smart right now. Not when he needed to keep a level head.

Teresa leaned back to look up at him. "You want to stay for a bit?"

Throat tight, he nodded because he didn't trust his voice. Almost against his will his gaze zeroed in on her full lips. Now that he knew what she tasted like, the urge to taste her again built up inside him with a ferocious hunger.

One he couldn't let off the leash. Not if he wanted to keep Teresa protected. He refused to fuck things up with her. "You feel like talking?"

"Not particularly," she murmured, her gaze tracking to his mouth as she licked her lips in a way he couldn't mistake for anything other than an invitation. "But we *should* because I want to know what's been holding you back from courting me." The note of determination in her voice made him smile.

He'd put this off long enough. It was time to stop being such a pussy and just tell her. If she rejected him . . . he'd deal. He'd have no choice.

Taking him by the hand, she led him to her living

room, which had a warm country feel to it. Every house on the ranch had a distinctive stamp on it from whichever females lived there, and Teresa and her sister's imprint was vivid. It reminded him of how he'd grown up; slow, country living. Without giving him a chance to decide, she tugged him down on the long leather couch nearest the unlit fireplace and sat right next to him.

"Talk," she demanded, still holding his hand.

Meeting her dark, intense gaze, he started, knowing he needed to get everything out at once or he never would. "You are my mate. I felt it from the moment we met."

Her eyebrows rose, but she didn't respond, just squeezed his hand tighter. The pure spring scent of hope rolled off her, but not one ounce of surprise. Which told him she'd felt the same magnetic pull he did.

"I . . ." He tried to just come out and say it, but couldn't find the right words so he tried a different angle. "When I'm in wolf form, I can communicate with others, regardless of who they are."

Her pretty lips pulled into a thin line. "That's impossible unless you're related and even then, not all family members can."

His jaw tightened. "I *can*. Ask Connor and Liam if you want confirmation." The brothers had never asked him about the root of his ability and for that he was grateful.

She paused a long moment. "Okay, so you can communicate with other shifters in animal form and I'm apparently your mate?" The emotions that bounced off her when she said the last part were too many for him to sift through.

"Not apparently." She was. No doubt in his mind. "The reason I can communicate with others is because I'm an empath. I sense emotions on a higher level than normal shifters do and it's not always linked to scent. I *feel* emotions. I try to lock down that side of myself as much as possible because I don't want to intrude, but it's not always possible. Especially with you. I know it must have seemed like I was a fucking asshole with you, but I could sense your lust and hunger for me and it was making my wolf insane. I wasn't trying to be all hot and cold with you. I was just trying to survive. But I know I hurt you more than once and I'm sorry. Words are lame—I know that—but I'm still so fucking sorry for ever causing you pain."

She swallowed hard, holding his gaze. "When you yelled at me about my dress you made me feel insecure. That has nothing to do with you being an empath."

Even as shame filled him, he loved that she called him on his shit. "Yeah, I was a dick. You looked hot and I didn't want any other males to see you."

She blinked once, as if she was surprised that he'd admitted it. "Okay. I've heard of vampires and even humans with that ability. You're saying it like it's a bad thing. Are my emotions too much or something?"

He scrubbed his free hand over his face. He wasn't explaining this well at all. "I mate differently than other shifters. I don't have to take you from behind, to sink my canines into your neck as I'm buried deep inside you under the full moon."

She blushed prettily at his words and his cock jumped to attention at the visual he'd just evoked. What he wouldn't give to be buried deep inside her right now. To see her eyes heavy-lidded with pleasure as he dragged climax after climax from her.

"How do you mate then?" she whispered.

Reaching out, he tucked strands of her dark hair behind her ear, letting his knuckles graze her cheek before his hand dropped. He wasn't sure if she'd want to let him touch her after this so he wanted to take advantage. "When my parents mated, it was not exactly my mother's choice."

Teresa gasped, horror on her face. "He took her by force?"

He shook his head sharply. "No. They'd been courting for a few short weeks and were having sex when his empath side took over and bonded them for life. There was no ritual, no biting, he bonded them with the force of his hunger for her. It wasn't intentional, but he took the choice from her and she never forgave him for it. They were linked and had never even discussed long-term plans. Their mating was not a happy one." That being an understatement.

Ryan had lived with the bitterness of his parents' unhappy union his entire childhood. Most days he'd felt as if his mother had hated him too. He'd been able to sense her emotions and she'd known it. Though she'd tried to cover her feelings, it had been impossible and he'd always known that he was unwanted. A by-product of her unhappy bonding.

Teresa's expression was thoughtful as she watched him, but she didn't drop his hand. That had to be a good thing. "So what does that mean for us?"

Us. Okay, that was definitely a good sign. "It means I'm going to court you very slowly, but we can't have sex until you're sure you want to be with me long-term—permanently. I won't risk taking the choice from you and I already know what I want. You. Not just as a mate, I want the whole package, Teresa."

"That's why you've been a jackass the past few months?" She sounded incredulous.

He nodded. "I see you, breathe you in, and I want to cover you in my scent. Everything about you makes me want to claim you on the most primal level." And some deep part of him had been terrified that he'd somehow bond them together even without having sex. Though he'd known that to be an impossibility, it hadn't stopped him from pushing her away. The misery of his parents' mating had been a horrible thing, something he never wished to force on someone else. Especially not someone as wonderful as Teresa.

Smiling, she placed her hands lightly on his shoulders and leaned forward until her lips barely brushed over his. "You should have told me," she whispered.

"I was scared." Words he would never say to anyone but her. But the thought of losing her or inadvertently hurting her sliced him up inside. He'd felt like he was between that proverbial rock and a hard place with nowhere to go. "When I thought I could have lost you in that club—"

She covered her mouth with his, softly at first, but the emotions he felt raging under the surface were like nothing he'd ever experienced. Her need and hunger were like a wildfire, hot and out of control. His inner wolf clawed at him, telling him to assert his dominance. They might not be able to take things as far as he wanted, but he could still taste her pleasure on his tongue.

Relief and joy that she still wanted him punched through him, eating up all his former doubt. Hunger for her overwhelmed him, her own emotions battering against his. This time he didn't fight it. He opened himself up, savoring the way her warm, loving feelings wrapped around him. She wanted him, yes, but she cared for him. He could feel it bone deep.

On a growl he feathered kisses along her jaw as he pressed her back against the couch, covering her body with his. "I want to taste you coming against my tongue, Teresa."

A shudder trembled through her as she wrapped her legs around his waist and rolled her hips against him. Even through their clothes he could feel her heat. Very soon he was going to taste everything she had to offer.

As he started to kiss his way down her throat, a loud bang at the front door cut through the air. Before he could move, Connor strode inside, stalking from the entryway to the living room with a grim expression. "I hate to do this, but pack a bag, Ryan. There's trouble in Winston-Salem and we're heading out now."

Chapter 19

Winston-Salem, North Carolina
Two hours later

Connor calmly pushed his chair back from the detective's desk, showing more control than he felt at the moment. Something told him this detective was trying to push his buttons. Maybe the asshole wanted him to lash out. As he stood, so did Erin, Noah, and his pack's attorney, Reginald Baynor. The man cost a fortune but was worth every penny. Connor still couldn't believe the man had beat him to Winston-Salem, and he wasn't about to ask how he'd done it.

Baynor adjusted his silver tie out of habit. The human had a thing for the color. Maybe because of his dark silver hair and grayish eyes. "My clients are here as a courtesy. They've done nothing wrong and in fact are being hailed as heroes for eliminating the monsters who attacked those in the bank. You know as well as I do that you have no jurisdiction over how supernatural problems are handled."

"I sure as hell do when it spills over into my town and affects humans," Detective Cranford snapped as he shoved up from his desk.

"Are you charging my clients with anything?"

Instead of answering Baynor, the detective looked at Connor, his expression pleading. "What were those vamps doing in that bank? Why did they attack so brazenly? This type of thing has happened more than once in the past few weeks and it's only getting worse."

Baynor loudly cleared his throat. "If you're not charging—"

Connor held up a hand. "Detective, we have no clue why those vampires did what they did. My packmates were just here for pleasure and saw what was happening. As any good citizens, they did what was necessary to stop any more bloodshed. The wrongdoers are no longer a threat. What more do you want from us?"

The detective started to respond when his boss, a trim man with lightly graying hair Connor guessed to be in his sixties, stepped into the room, his expression grim but polite as he nodded at Connor, then focused on Erin. "You're free to go, ma'am. Thank you for assisting our town with the vampire problem. If we have any more questions, I'll follow up personally with a phone call, but you won't be dragged down here again."

The room went silent at the police chief's unexpected declaration.

Connor wasn't one to question good fortune, but he

glanced at his attorney and raised his eyebrows in a silent question.

Baynor eyed the chief curiously. "Why the sudden change of heart?"

The older man cleared his throat, appearing almost nervous. "I just got off the phone with a member of the Council and . . . the governor, who wanted to convey how appreciative he is of your selfless help with keeping our streets safe."

The governor? Nice. Jayce had told Connor that the Council would take care of this if his attorney couldn't, but damn. The Council had strong political relationships all over the country, including with the president of the United States, so it wasn't a surprise they had enough pull to contact the governor.

Connor shook the police chief's hand and nodded at his packmates and Baynor. "I'll meet you guys outside in just a sec. I'd like a word with Detective Cranford alone."

The chief of police hesitated but nodded. Unsurprisingly his attorney started to argue, but Connor gave a sharp shake of his head. The older man sighed and left with the others.

Connor turned to face the detective, who showed no fear as he faced him down. He got points for that because Connor knew his wolf was in his eyes. Because of this setback, Aiden, Larissa, Angelo, and Brianna were all waiting for the rest of them to infiltrate Magda Petran's residence. "I wasn't lying when I said I don't know what's going on. But whatever it is, it won't be a problem for long. We don't like this shit any more than you do." Such blatant violence for the world to see was not good for their image and the blood dealing just plain pissed Connor off. No one did that shit in his territory or anywhere close to it. No way in hell.

Gritting his teeth, the detective finally nodded. "Just make sure this type of thing doesn't happen here again."

Yeah, like he had any fucking control over what vamps did. He was doing his best to control the situation. Without responding, Connor stalked from the room. Outside he found Erin, Noah, and Baynor standing on the sidewalk in front of a group of reporters. Just fucking great. Someone had caught Erin's impressive kills of the vamps on their cell phone video and in less than two hours it had already gone viral. The news stations had picked it up and she was being hailed as some sort of superhero badass who protected humans. It was better than her being vilified, but still, they did not need this kind of attention. Connor had a feeling *that* was the only reason the freaking governor had called.

As he watched Baynor deflect all the reporter's comments, Connor made the kind of executive decision he hated making. Pulling out his cell, he texted Aiden and told the four of them to make their move on Petran's house now.

He hated sending his people into any situation where he wasn't there as backup, but he knew if any of them left now they'd be tailed by reporters. It was likely they'd be able to lose them, but if for some reason they didn't and shit got even crazier, they couldn't risk anyone catching the infiltration of Petran's house on video.

Right now shifters were being held up as heroes because of Erin. But that could change in the span of a heartbeat. Humans were so damn fickle and he wouldn't risk his pack or anyone else's safety. Plus they couldn't wait any damn longer. They'd been sitting on the residence for two hours and that was long enough. The longer they waited, the greater chance they'd lose a solid lead.

Going in now. Going dark. Will contact u as soon as we can. Aiden's reply was short and not surprising.

Connor didn't like that they'd all be going dark, but he understood it. They couldn't have cell phones on during an infiltration op for a multitude of reasons. He reminded himself that all four of them were well trained. While he may not know much about Larissa, she came from a powerful line, one that was feared and respected. And he trusted Aiden's judgment. So he figured she'd be able to take care of herself too.

Bypassing where Erin, Noah, and Baynor stood off to the side, he made his way to the SUV where Jayce, Kat, and Liam were waiting inside. Ryan and Aldric were in another SUV on the opposite side of the parking lot. Jayce had made it clear he didn't want to ride with Aldric, and Connor hadn't wanted to let the guy out of his sight until they exchanged intel—and leaving him at the ranch wasn't an option. A couple of reporters had looked at Connor and snapped his picture, but everyone was more focused on Erin at the moment.

"I told Aiden and the others to move in," he said as he slid into his seat.

Jayce cursed, but nodded. "Smart move. We'll have to drive around forever to lose these fuckers."

"I can't believe how crazed everyone is over Erin right now," Kat said from the backseat, awe in her voice as she watched a video on her cell phone. "Okay, I totally can. Her moves are amazing and she looks so sexy while killing those bastards. Which seems weird to say, but she really does. I bet she gets her own line of action figure dolls or something."

"They're action *figures*. There's no doll in there." Liam shook his head as he stared out the window. "It is pretty cool how well people are taking this."

Jayce snorted. "The Council is eating it up."

Connor met his gaze in the rearview mirror, sharing a hard, knowing look. They were both old enough and had enough experience that they knew how fucking quickly the tides of public opinion could change. Connor just hoped it lasted. Erin was good at what she did and her actions had been completely justified. But he had no doubt there'd be some asshole groups out there who managed to twist her actions around into something to be feared.

He couldn't worry about the future though. He had time for only the present. When Erin and Noah broke away from the crowd, he started the engine and glanced at Liam. "Call Ryan, tell him we've had a change of plans and aren't going to Petran's house."

"Where are we going?"

He shrugged and fought his irritation. "We're going

to drive around until we're sure we're not being followed." And he planned to switch vehicles. First he
had to call Ana and have her and another packmate
meet them with different SUVs. Then they had to make
the switch without being seen.

Larissa glanced at Aiden, who seemed edgier than normal. The sun had set and they'd been watching this
place for two hours. Aiden's Alpha finally gave them
the go-ahead. She'd been ready to move in a while ago
but had respected Aiden's desire to wait for his leader.

They were in the farthest corner of the expansive
backyard of Magda's house. The place sat on a little
over one acre of land and, according to Aiden's packmate Ryan, was over five thousand square feet. On Ryan's way to Winston-Salem he'd somehow managed to
find house plans and e-mailed the layout to Aiden, Brianna, and Angelo. He'd said that if she had an e-mail
address, he'd have sent it to her too. That made her
smile, though she wasn't sure what she'd do with an
e-mail address if she had one.

She didn't have a lot of experience to go on, but
everything about Aiden screamed that he was worried.
Crouched down next to one of the bare oak trees, he
kept unsheathing his claws then retracting them.

What's wrong? As she communicated telepathically
she realized just how quickly she'd gotten used to
talking to him like that in such a short period.

He didn't look at her as he continued to scan the
back of the house. Two rocking chairs were on the back
of the wide-open wraparound porch. The place seemed

so warm and inviting, not like the home of a conniving, deceitful witch. *Nothing*.

She nearly snorted. She might not remember Aiden well enough to be able to pick up on little cues, but when his claws unsheathed again, tearing into the bark, she gently touched his forearm. *Tell me.*

He finally looked at her, his dark eyes almost midnight black under the moon and stars. *I don't like going into the unknown, especially with you not at full capacity.*

I'll be fine. More than fine. While they'd been waiting for his Alpha to arrive she'd found two humans to feed from. The blood may be weaker than supernatural, but the back-to-back feedings had gone a long way in helping her. She felt amazing and while she wasn't sure if it was because of the blood or because of her newfound powers—which she still wanted to test out—there hadn't been any new activity at the house since they'd been watching it. The two human males they'd followed back to the house had gone in and never come out.

Aiden simply nodded before pulling his cell phone from his pocket. She'd watched him do something to the settings earlier so that the screen didn't light up and inadvertently alert someone to their presence. With it angled away from her she couldn't read it.

But after he did, he turned his cell completely off. *It's Angelo. They're moving in now. Time to go. On the count of two. One, two.*

With a burst of speed, they crossed the backyard to the porch in seconds. She'd secured her hair back in a long braid so it wouldn't get in her way, but a few loose strands whipped around her face with the rapid movements.

Once they reached the back porch both she and Aiden paused and listened carefully. She could hear at least a couple of heartbeats inside and there were lights on throughout the house. Her palms burned and tingled, taking her by surprise. When she looked down, her eyes widened. Her hands were glowing a soft blue mixed with white sparkles. Like tiny stars across a sky. She ordered whatever it was to stop and again, to her shock, it did. Okay then. Maybe she was more in control than she realized.

Aiden motioned with his hand that he was going to open one of the two French doors. The good thing about sneaking up on a witch was that they didn't have extrasensory abilities like vamps or shifters. The bad thing was, they often spelled their homes and a break-in would alert Magda anyway.

They were about to find out.

With an unsheathed claw, Aiden cut a hole in one of the glass panes. It made a soft slicing sound that was unavoidable. Instead of pushing it through, he tapped one edge so that it twisted inward, like a pinwheel. Before it could fall he snagged the whole piece and pulled it out. After setting it down beside him, he reached through the hole, unlocked the door, and opened it.

He peered in first. *Clear.*

Some primal part of her she didn't understand was rankled that he was going first, but she fought her annoyance. He wanted to protect her. She could deal with it. She had the strongest urge to protect him too so she couldn't fault him for wanting to do the same for her.

Following Aiden inside, she was struck by how normal the residence looked. According to the layout Ryan had sent them, she knew they were in one of the living rooms. From her limited knowledge and Google research of modern times, Magda's home appeared to have expensive but normal things most humans would. Art on the wall, leather couches, and a very large flat-screen television over a fireplace. The one thing that struck Larissa as they moved through the living room into a dimly lit kitchen was that the female didn't have any photographs. Nothing personal to indicate this home belonged to Magda.

But Larissa could scent the female. Her oakmoss scent seemed to permeate the very foundation of this place it was so strong. It was different from when Larissa had first met her. The witch's scent had been almost muted, but now it was suffocating and making Larissa nauseous.

Just as in that hotel room, she was starting to feel strange. Almost like something oily was skittering over her skin, leaving a trail of grimy fingerprints all over her. Shit. This place was definitely spelled.

On a muffled cry, Aiden shifted forms, his clothes and boots shredding before a pure white wolf stood next to her, breathing rapidly. *Sorry my wolf took over. Something about this place is off and it wanted to protect me. I feel in control now.* He looked up at her as he communicated and if it had been possible she'd have said there was surprise in those lupine eyes.

She frowned at him. *What?*

You're glowing.

Larissa looked down at herself and realized that *all* of her skin was putting off that blue glow now. She shoved up the sleeves of her long T-shirt and stared at herself. Little tendrils of blue fire licked against her skin, but she wasn't burning. Neither were her clothes. Everything about this felt familiar, as if she'd done it before, but she simply couldn't remember. Her head ached as she struggled to grasp those elusive memories. She was about to try to tone it down when Aiden shook his head.

You're protecting yourself from Magda. If Angelo and Brianna see you, we'll deal with that later. But I trust them not to say anything.

She still wasn't sure *what* was going on with herself or why she was actually glowing, but she trusted Aiden. *Okay. Where to now?* she asked as she bent to retrieve his fallen cell phone. It was the only personal object he'd brought in with him. Before they left she'd be sure to gather his clothes as well.

He cocked his head to the side then turned toward a door on the other side of the big kitchen. From the house layout she'd looked at, she was pretty sure it went to the basement.

Inhaling, she caught the faintest hint of blood. And something else lingered in the air. Something putrid . . . like death. Or dark magic. It was coming from behind that door.

At a soft sound, like a footfall, they both turned. Brianna and Angelo—also in wolf form—stepped cautiously into the kitchen. Brianna's eyes widened as she looked at Larissa, but she didn't say anything. Just pointed upstairs and mouthed *"All clear."*

Larissa pointed to the door and indicated they were going to find out what was on the other side. Brianna nodded and for the first time Larissa noticed the fae female's hand was glowing blue. Nothing like Larissa's own full-body thing, but a ball of energy like . . . something rested in Brianna's hands. Okay then. Looked like the fae could take care of herself.

Letting her claws on one hand extend, Larissa twisted the door handle with the other. It was hot to the touch, enough so that she was pretty sure she'd have been burned if she wasn't already a walking lighter.

Don't touch the handle. It's hot. I think it's spelled, she told Aiden, who simply nodded. She turned back to Brianna and indicated the same thing to her before slowly easing it open to reveal a walled-in set of stairs that descended. A soft flickering glow emanated from the opening at the end. Candlelight.

Instead of using her natural speed, she crept down the steps carefully with Aiden right next to her, paying attention to potential physical traps. Larissa was sure the witch already knew they were there, but that didn't mean they could rush in like fools.

Next to her Aiden was impossibly silent. She'd always been fascinated by how quiet he was for such a huge wolf. It abruptly registered what she'd just thought. *She'd always been fascinated.* Random memories of him sneaking up on her in the woods as they'd played with each other raced through her mind, one after the other.

Played.

They'd had fun together. So much fun. Something she'd never had much of until Aiden. Her throat tightened but she locked all those memories down, putting a pin in them until later, when she could savor each and every one of them. Talk about the worst timing ever to get some of her memories back. She was filled with a sudden rush of rage at whoever had taken her memories from her.

Aiden nudged her with his nose before veering in front of her and covering the last few stairs.

Damn it, Aiden.

He ignored her as he slowly peered around the corner. The moment he did, a gunshot blasted through the silence. Fear choked her as Aiden reared back, making a rough growling sound.

Chapter 20

Aiden jumped back from the open entryway, the wall behind him splintering as the bullet slammed into it.

Larissa's fangs descended, joining her already unsheathed claws. A volcano of rage erupted inside her that Aiden could have been injured. She knew he was old enough to possess the strength to withstand a hell of a lot of injuries, but that didn't matter. A head shot was still potentially lethal.

She shot a quick glance over her shoulder to find Angelo and Brianna tense on the stairs, Brianna's ball of energy hovering quietly in her hand.

"I've got this," she growled before turning and jumping over Aiden.

Larissa, no!

She ignored him. Using her vampiric speed, she dove into the entry, avoiding a barrage of shots as she twisted midair before landing safely on her feet on a cold stone floor. She didn't pause long though as she ducked down behind a giant barrel filled with—she didn't want to know.

In a matter of milliseconds she took in the room. A dead male lay on an altar surrounded by dozens of candles. His heart was missing from his chest. Another male was chained to a wall, welts covering most of his naked body as he slumped forward, unconscious. She could hear his faint breathing and heartbeat, so she knew he wasn't dead.

But all of Larissa's focus was on Magda, crouching behind the stone altar. Larissa heard but couldn't see the gun clatter to the stone floor. Probably out of bullets.

Larissa stepped out from behind the barrel and narrowed her gaze on Magda. At the sight of the dark-haired female, rage like Larissa had never known rose up inside her. As it grew, she was vaguely aware of a thin blue coating of flames moving out from her body, covering the floor, walls, ceiling, and altar. It snuffed out the small flames from the candles, but didn't touch the males as it moved closer to Magda.

The witch jumped up and stumbled back, her pretty face twisted into an expression of horror as she tried to escape. But there was nowhere to go. The female wore a blood-covered skimpy piece of lingerie that seemed obscene with the wet crimson stains on it. And the room smelled like sex, which told Larissa all she needed to know about this monster. The female had probably screwed her victims before torturing them.

Larissa's flames created a circle around Magda,

tightening smaller and smaller around the witch the angrier Larissa got.

"You shot at my mate," she snarled.

"I'm sorry. I didn't know it was you." She held up her hands in surrender.

Larissa's eyes narrowed as she closed the circle of fire even tighter. She tried, but couldn't scent a lie and wasn't sure why. "Why don't I believe you?"

"Someone broke into my home, I was just defending myself," she whispered, the fear rolling off her very real.

But her words were bullshit. "Your home in lovely Winston-Salem. The same city where you got a hotel room with me and pretended to be my friend, told me you wanted to help me find my parents' killers, and told me that a shifter named Aiden tried to kill them."

Big fat tears rolled down the female's cheeks, giving her an innocent, annoying quality. "He made me do it," she whispered.

Larissa didn't believe a word out of the female's mouth but held her anger in check—though not her fire. "Who?" she asked as she felt something tickle against the bare skin of her forearms.

Without looking down she knew it was Magda attempting to use a spell against her. It wasn't a surprising attempt, but it was weak. Larissa ignored it, not letting on that she knew what Magda was doing. When the witch didn't answer right away, she tightened the circle of fire within an inch of the female's feet. Flames danced up, licking against her bare calves. Larissa's eyes narrowed on the witch's left leg as she directed a few sparks to attack.

When they did, a surge of power raced through Larissa. Magda yelped and jumped up, trying to slap at her leg. As she did, the sleeve of her shirt caught the flames. Before it could move or singe the skin on her arm, Larissa put it out. "Answer," she ordered. "And don't lie or my fire will eat you up one inch at a time. I'll keep you alive for a decade of torture." Larissa wouldn't actually do that, but she hoped the reputation of vampires savoring their torture would resonate with the witch.

She also hoped Aiden didn't think she was capable of torturing someone like that. He was quiet along their link, but she could feel his solid presence directly behind her.

Magda shivered in fear as she wrapped her arms around her slender frame. Larissa could still feel the invisible fingers skittering across her skin and knew that Magda was attempting to buy time. Fine with Larissa as long as the female talked. "My master made me. Once he found out you were still alive, he . . . he ordered me to bring you back to Winston-Salem."

"And how did he even know about me?"

"There's a reference to your stasis in my grimoire. I wasn't lying about my line being connected to your coven. My grandmother was the one who assisted with the spell that put you under."

Yes, Larissa had guessed that was the truth already. Magda looked eerily like one of the witches from the Moldoveanu line that her own coven had worked hand in hand with. "Why'd you change your name to Petran?" She kept her voice soft, her question seemingly benign. The more truth she could get from this witch, the easier it would be to discern lies. It still bothered Larissa that she hadn't been able to tell the female was lying to her before, but she was watching for facial and body cues now. Maybe it was because she had been so weak after stasis that she couldn't scent them. Now she felt as if she could take on an entire army and hoped she'd be able to pick out lies from truths. Aware of the others close behind her, she reminded her fire that Brianna and Angelo were friends, not enemies. She didn't need to remind the fire about Aiden. The most fundamental part of her would never hurt him.

Magda shrugged. "Who the fuck can pronounce Moldoveanu?"

A truth. She could see it in Magda's tiny facial expressions. Now Larissa wanted to know more. "Who is your master?"

Raw fear sparked in Magda's brown eyes. "I can't tell you. He's a monster."

Her master was likely a monster. But so was Magda. "You cut out that man's heart and likely ate it," she said, tilting her head a fraction in the direction of the dead human. Not the actions of an innocent or sane woman. "Now tell me about your master. What does he want with me; what the hell did you or he do to my memories; and how is he able to control vampires?"

When she hesitated, Larissa engulfed the female's entire right leg in flames. Magda screamed, falling to her hands and knees. Larissa moved the fire back so it wouldn't completely engulf her. She was aware of Aiden moving up beside her. So far he'd been silent in her head and for that she was appreciative. She had a good control of this fire but feared she wouldn't be able to hold it. Even though it felt familiar to guide the flames, her power and energy were waning. She just needed to hold on to them for a little bit longer. Something told her Magda would be easy to break.

Suddenly she withdrew the flames from Magda's leg. The female's skin was unmarred, but she still rolled around, slapping at her leg as she shrieked in pain. It didn't matter that she hadn't actually been burned physically, she'd feel the phantom pains for a while. Larissa wondered how she even knew that, but didn't have time to dwell on the unexpected knowledge about her gift.

"Enough!" Larissa finally shouted.

Whimpering, Magda pushed up onto her knees to face Larissa. Once again she felt the whisper of fingers over her skin. Foolish woman. Kneeling so that she was at eye level, Larissa pinned the female with her stare. "You think I can't feel what you're trying to do? That I can't feel your pathetic attempts whispering against my power? You are a child with much untapped power, but you clearly don't know how to use it." If the witch did she wouldn't be resorting to the dark arts. True witches could call on power from within. "You have two options. Tell me what I want to know and I'll make sure your death is painless. Resist and you've just barely tasted what I can do. Understand?"

Larissa let the flames dance higher in a bright circle. Next to her Aiden growled at Magda, the sound low, deadly. The female nodded and collapsed against the floor. She pulled her knees up to her chest, looking young and terrified. But Larissa wouldn't be swayed by appearances. The female was pure evil.

"Who put me in stasis?" Larissa demanded.

"Your parents."

"Why?"

"They didn't want you mated with a shifter. They thought if they killed him while you were in stasis, you'd get over it once you awoke. You are virtually immortal. Maybe they figured you couldn't stay angry forever."

Larissa balled her hands into fists, furious at her parents. "What does your master want with me?"

"I'm . . . not totally sure. I swear it!" She held up her hands when Larissa's jaw tightened. "He wants your blood, but he doesn't tell me everything."

Shock rippled through her. Her blood was naturally powerful because she was a pure, bloodborn vamp, but why would anyone want it? She didn't think it could do anything for anyone long-term. "Why didn't you just kill me instead of waking me from stasis and take my blood that way?"

Magda's expression darkened and Larissa could tell that she wished she'd done just that. "Because he needs your blood fresh and he couldn't travel to Romania. Plus . . . he needed you to gain back some of your strength for you to be of use. Now I think I understand why," she muttered, looking around at the burning blue flames coating everything.

"How is he controlling vampires?" Because if he could, that meant none of her kind was safe. Larissa wondered if it was a distance thing. Maybe he had to be within a certain range.

Magda swallowed, fear rolling off her in waves so potent, Larissa nearly gagged on the foul scent. Like weeks-old garbage that had been left rotting under a hot sun. It masked everything else in the room, even the stench of death.

"Tell me," she demanded.

Magda shook her head, and moving with shocking speed, withdrew an ancient-looking dagger from behind her back. The jagged blade glinted for only a moment in the firelight before she raised it high. Larissa moved to cover Aiden, but he knocked her out of the way, lunging for the female. But instead of striking at either of them, she sunk the blade deep into her chest before either of them could stop her.

Cursing, Larissa frantically knelt down next to her as Aiden shifted back to his human form. Her flames immediately died. Behind them she could hear Angelo shifting too. With the witch dying, most of her spells would weaken, giving them more control over their wolves. But Magda couldn't die. Not until they knew everything.

Larissa didn't attempt to pull the blade out, not wanting her to lose even more blood. But she tried to stanch the bleeding, pressing her hands to Magda's chest around the entry point. The witch dragged in a gurgled breath and Larissa knew she had to be in pain, but Magda looked almost smug. Probably because she was dying on her own terms.

For a brief moment Larissa thought about giving her

blood to Magda to help save her, but quickly dismissed that idea. There was no way in hell she could share a part of herself with someone this evil, no matter how desperate she was. "Who is your master? Where is he?"

"Stupid bitch . . . your mate . . . killed . . . parents." She laughed maniacally before her dark eyes dilated and her body went completely still. Her hands fell away from her body as her facial muscles sagged, her jaw falling open as if in shock. Larissa knew from seeing more than her fair share of dead bodies, this was normal in the first stages after death. There was no more tension in her muscles because she was truly gone.

"Damn it," Aiden cursed as he looked up from the body. "You okay?"

"Yeah." She started to stand, but a wave of exhaustion swept through her and she stumbled. Aiden caught her, wrapping his arms around her waist and pulling her close to his naked body. "You need to feed," he murmured, his deep voice soothing.

"I'll be okay." She placed her hands on his chest and steadied herself, but it didn't help much. She had a lot of questions, like what was the deal with this fire-wielding ability.

Holding on to Aiden for support, she glanced around the room, everything coming into sharp focus again now that she wasn't intent on Magda. Brianna stood next to the chained male, her hands glowing a soft green as they hovered over his chest. Larissa knew some fae had a similar healing ability so it wasn't shocking.

"We need to get him to a hospital," Brianna said,

looking up at all of them. Angelo was in human form and moving around the room, seemingly inspecting everything. He just made a grunting sound and Larissa figured they were communicating telepathically.

Larissa and Aiden needed to be searching this place too. If they could find the witch's grimoire it might give them the answers they needed. If not that, something that could lead them to the nameless vampire. For all they knew, the vampire might show up and find them here. And it worried her that he wanted her blood. The only possible reason Larissa could fathom would be for a blood ritual and those were only for dark purposes.

She pushed lightly at Aiden's chest, and even that was a strain she felt all the way to her bones. "I'll be fine, I promise. We need to search this place for clues to find out who her 'master' is. What if he shows up and finds us all here?" Considering how weak she was, she was afraid she wouldn't be any help to anyone.

Aiden's expression tensed as he watched her. "We will. But take a break first. You just expended a hell of a lot of energy." He tilted his head to the side, his dark eyes going pure wolf. "Feed."

Swallowing hard, she looked at his chest. Her fangs ached, the urge to strike his vein and assuage her hunger was strong. But she wouldn't, even if it offended him. She'd already taken too much from him recently and she wouldn't risk feeding and weakening him. "No."

He growled softly, drawing her gaze up to his as his hands flexed on her hips. "Do you believe what she said?"

She frowned at him and clutched tighter. The edges

of darkness pushed in on her vision and a spark of fear skittered through her. She worried she'd pushed herself too hard. Without knowing the specifics of her gift, she didn't know what this could mean for her. "It was hard to decipher truth from lies, but I believe some of it was real. What did you scent?" His ability to pick out lies from truth was stronger than hers.

I mean about me killing your parents.

No. There had been a very small part of her that had reacted to the witch's words, but it had been borne out of fear, not because she didn't trust him.

Don't lie to me.

I'm not. Now is not the time for this, Aiden. We need . . . She swallowed hard and gripped him tighter. A wave of dizziness rushed through her as something wet dripped down over her lips. Blood? But that didn't make sense. Confusion intermixed with that darkness creeping in on her. What the hell was happening?

Aiden's eyes widened, all annoyance replaced by pure fear. *Shit, Larissa, talk to me.*

"Wh—" She tried to find her voice as it registered that her nose was bleeding. That had never happened before. Not that she remembered. It felt as if something was weighing on her eyes, tugging them down. She tried to hold them open, to grasp onto that link with Aiden, but she couldn't even do that as blackness consumed her.

Chapter 21

Sixty years ago

What was that sneaky male up to? Larissa lifted up on her toes to peer over the long stone wall in the local town. What she'd seen of the Isle of Skye was beautiful, but her coven had remained centralized to the Nicholl pack's castles and extensive land. They'd had no need to look for food as they brought their own humans with them—who they paid handsomely—as donors. Tonight Aiden had told her that he had something to do while his pack put on a big festive Christmas party, but that he would meet up with her later.

A dark, jealous part of her had decided to follow him. She knew it was crazy and something she'd never done before with a male. The truth was, no male would dare stray from her while they were lovers. Partially because of her father, but more likely because they feared her own wrath. But Aiden was maddening and even though he seemed completely taken *with her, she couldn't help the strange irrational urges he brought out of her. She knew the emotion was jealousy and she did not care for it. She was not a jealous female. Or she hadn't been.*

Larissa found herself feeling possessive when a pretty female from Aiden's pack entered the room or gave Aiden a lingering look. She knew he'd likely slept with many of them, and it shouldn't bother her. But it did. For all she knew he had a human lover he was coming to see in this nearest town. At that thought her claws dug into the stone. As pieces crumbled off and fell onto her new coat, she barely reined in her curse as she swiped them off her and took a step back. Her heels sunk into the grassy earth.

Despite the cold weather, she was wearing a knee-length blue ribbon-trimmed gingham cocktail dress. She'd seen a lot of fashion over the centuries and she loved this era with its fun, flirty dresses. To blend in with any humans she might stumble across, she'd worn a thick, ankle-length fur coat.

After hoisting herself back up, she glanced around and when she was sure there were no humans lingering about, she jumped over the wall in one quick move. Her heels barely made a sound on the cobblestone street.

Using her gift of speed, she walked lightly over the street down to the one she'd seen Aiden turn on moments earlier. He'd been carrying a big sack of something with him. Maybe presents for a human lover. As she looked around the corner she saw that the street was devoid of humans or other life. A long row of brick town houses lined the quiet area. They were set close together, as seemed to be common in this little town. Most of the homes had candles in the windows or wreaths on the doors to celebrate the holidays.

As she contemplated her next move and the insanity of her actions, a door three homes down opened. She slid back into the shadows and watched as Aiden walked out with a smile on his face. A pretty, wholesome-looking blonde walked out with him and gave him a big hug, profusely thanking him. Larissa's claws descended, wanting to swipe the smile right off her face. And definitely off his.

Her anger faltered when two young children appeared beside the female, clutching on to her legs and staring up at Aiden in awe. When they shyly thanked him, she frowned, confused. And when a young, handsome male about the same age as the female appeared in the doorway, her confusion grew greater. She noticed immediately that the man had a cane. Smiling, he shook Aiden's hand with his free one before he wrapped it around the female and pulled her close. He also thanked Aiden, true appreciation rolling off him, and if she wasn't mistaken, there were tears in his eyes.

Moments later they went inside and shut their door as Aiden descended the short set of stairs to the street. Standing there, he looked up at the full moon, his profile one of true beauty. Despite the cold, he hadn't bothered with a coat. His shirt was pushed up to the sleeves, showing off all those taut muscles she could make out even from her hidden position. And she knew under his kilt he likely wore nothing. Something she couldn't dwell on without getting flustered. Feeling incredibly foolish, she started to turn and leave when he spoke. "You can come out now."

Since she was the only person skulking around like some thief, she had no doubt he was talking to her. She figured she should be embarrassed—and perhaps she was a little—but she wouldn't show it.

Squaring her shoulders, she stepped from around the corner and strode toward him. He looked at her then, his wolf in his eyes as he took her in from head to toe. He watched her with unconcealed hunger and a shiver spiked through her.

"You spying on me, lass?"

She lifted her shoulders casually as she came to stand in front of him under one of the dim, whining bulbs of the streetlight. With her extrasensory abilities she could hear the buzz of the light. It seemed overpronounced in the quiet evening air. "Just curious."

"You could have asked to come with me," he murmured, his big hands settling on her hips as he pulled her close to him.

She didn't bother not to be affected by his simple touch as she slid her hands up his chest and linked her fingers behind his neck. "You didn't ask. What are you doing?"

"It's not important." He dropped a soft kiss on her lips, the light touch igniting a spark of desire in her that not even her gift could match with its beautiful flames.

She pulled back. "It is to me. I . . . found myself wondering if perhaps you had a human lover." She didn't form it as a question but it clearly was.

"Are you jealous, little lass?" he murmured, his head dipping to her neck where he nuzzled her gently.

She moved her hands down his shoulders to his arms and dug her fingers into his biceps. "Maybe I am." The confession cost her a big chunk of pride, but she didn't want to play games with this male.

Now he pulled back, surprise etched on his face. "Why would you be jealous? You are the only female for me. I never believed in mates until I met you."

The seriousness of his statement slammed into her. She felt the same way, but had been terrified she was just a challenge to him. She knew she was the first vampire he'd been with. And she wanted to be the last—and only—female for him. But admitting that was something else entirely. She wasn't used to showing weakness, and if she admitted to a shifter that she was willing to give up everything for him . . .
"Mates?"

His jaw twitched. "You think this is a game for me?"

She bit her bottom lip. The past couple of weeks they'd spent every second possible together and made love more times than she could count. But he was a shifter and she was a vampire. Their species did not generally mate. Or even sleep together for fun. They were both from strong lines and she knew neither of their parents would ever accept their mating. "I wasn't sure."

Anger darkened his expression for a moment before he sighed and scrubbed a hand over his face. He wrapped an arm around her shoulders and led them back the way they'd come. "How did you get here?"

"I drove, but parked near the outskirts of town and just followed your scent. I wanted to rip your face off when I saw that female hugging you."

He chuckled. "Didn't realize you were so bloodthirsty."

"I didn't either." *It was the truth.*

He motioned to the left once they reached the end of the street. It was a different direction from which she'd followed him.

"So what were you doing tonight?"

Aiden was silent for a long moment and she wondered if he'd even answer her. Finally he did. "Most of the humans *here know about our pack. It's not a huge secret. The High-landers have always believed in more than one can see."*

She nodded. "It's the same for our coven."

"I've known Donnan Brodie—that's the human's house where I was—since he was a babe. We've been friends a long time and I was bringing presents to his family for Christmas."

Smiling, she nuzzled her face against his chest as they strolled down the street. "That was very sweet."

"Aye, it was. And if you want to show me just how impressed ye are by my actions, I'll let ye take advantage of me in the next dark alley we come across," he murmured seductively.

Laughing, something she seemed to do a lot of these past couple of weeks, she playfully pinched his side. "You are hopeless."

"I also wanted to say good-bye to Brodie in case I'd be leaving soon," he said softly.

It took a moment for his words to register. But she wasn't sure she understood him. "Leaving?"

Slowing, he nodded and pushed her back up against a brick wall. She could vaguely hear the sounds of music and laughter a block or so over, but she tuned it out as he rolled his hips against hers. He spread open her coat and ground himself against her. Through his kilt and her dress, his erection was unmistakable and insistent.

When he didn't say anything else, she swallowed hard. She'd never put herself out there for any male, but Aiden was worth fighting for. Worth taking a risk for. If he didn't mean what she thought, she'd survive the rejection. Or try to. "Our parents have come to an understanding over the shield and protection of your people near our region. My coven is leaving in a few days."

He nodded. "Aye, I know."

"Do you want to come with me?" They would have so many obstacles to face that she wondered how they would make their relationship work. Even though it would be hard she wanted to try.

He shook his head and it was like he'd pierced her with a silver dagger straight through the heart. She struggled to suck in a breath at the unexpected agony. But his next words changed everything.

"I want to start over somewhere new with you. We'll never be accepted by our families. At least not right away. Let's go to America, start a life together. Once our families get used to the idea, we can go from there."

A cacophony of emotions exploded inside her. Pure joy at his declaration, but it was tempered by sadness because he was right about their families. She didn't want to admit it was the truth, but knew it was. Her mother had mentioned something about leaving this disgusting shifter den and Larissa had felt as if her mother had been watching her for a reaction. Throat tight, she nodded. "Yes."

His dark eyes seemed to glow under the moonlight. "I want to be more than just mates. I want to bond with you, Larissa. You're mine."

Bonding would unite them until death. They'd never be able to leave each other. And she knew she wouldn't want to leave this male. No sane woman would walk away from him. "And you're mine, Aiden."

She crushed her mouth to his, savoring his groan of appreciation as he gave back just as hard. As he ground his hips

*against hers it took all her restraint not to shove up her dress
and coat, wrap her legs around him and let him push deep
inside her. But she had more decorum than that. Maybe not.*

"Wake up, Larissa. You have to wake up." A vaguely
familiar female voice invaded her head. Larissa pulled
back from Aiden as her surroundings started to fade
and morph.

*Fear slammed into Larissa as Aiden's face started to grow
fainter. What the hell was happening?* "No," *she yelled at the
unseen female. Mentally shoving away the voice, she grasped
onto Aiden's shoulders and continued kissing him until her
surroundings came back into focus. She didn't want to leave
Aiden. She wouldn't.*

Chapter 22

Aiden held Larissa in his lap in the backseat of Angelo's SUV, his grip tight but not suffocating. Her head lay on his shoulder, her petite body lax, but not as if she was unconscious. Almost as if she was in a deep sleep. He tried to temper his fear, but he was losing that battle.

"Come on, Larissa. You need to wake up. I know you're in there." Brianna's voice was soothing as she worked her healing magic on Larissa. Her hands glowed that soft green as she held Larissa's hands in her own. She'd been trying wake Larissa for the past hour since leaving Magda's house and Aiden was starting to get worried the female fae was draining too much of her power. But he was more worried for Larissa. After her nose had started bleeding, she'd passed out. He'd caught her before she'd hit the floor, but she'd lost so much blood. He'd sliced open his arm and fed her.

That was when he'd guessed she wasn't exactly unconscious so much as asleep because she'd actually taken from him. It hadn't been much, but she'd drunk and had stopped bleeding.

Sighing, Brianna pulled her hands back and leaned against the seat. Her face was paler than normal. "I'm sorry, Aiden. There's nothing more I can do for her. She's not in pain or even injured. I would be able to sense it. She's just . . . sleeping for lack of a better word. She'll wake up when she wants. Whatever she did in that basement expended a lot of energy and sleeping is likely the only way for her to recuperate. I'm not asking about her gift because I can tell you want to keep it private, but have you ever seen her do that fire thing before?"

He nodded. She'd shown it to him right after they'd bonded and it had been . . . magical. He could still envision that night, watching the way she let her flames run all the way around the lake he'd taken her to. The fire hadn't burned anything in its path, just lit up the area like the best fireworks show ever.

Brianna seemed to relax at that. "Good. Have you ever seen her overextend herself?"

Feeling sick, he shook his head. "No. But she never had a reason to overdo it front of me. It was always about having fun with her gift when we were together." And she'd been full of rage in that basement.

They both turned as Angelo slid into the front seat. The vehicle was still running so he quickly pulled out of their parking spot at the hospital. "Dropped the human off in the ER and hurried out. Made sure to avoid the cameras," he said. "Baby, how are you feeling?" he asked Brianna without turning around.

"Good, just a little tired."

"How's your female, Aiden?" Angelo flicked him a quick glance in the rearview mirror, his packmate's expression worried.

"Okay." He knew what Brianna had told him, but he still wasn't convinced Larissa was okay. Nothing could convince him of that until her eyes opened. His throat tightened and he couldn't force himself to continue. Right now he was barely hanging on to his sanity. The only thing keeping him in control was the fact that their bondmate link was the strongest it had been since he'd found her again. It seemed like each second that passed, the link was tightening and strengthening to where it had been back when they'd first bonded. Though he wasn't sure how that was even possible.

"You should let one of us take you back to the ranch," Angelo murmured as he turned down a side street.

Aiden glanced out the window and watched as cars and homes passed by in a blur. He tightened his hold, resting his chin on the top of her head. "No one has time to make an extra trip right now." And they couldn't afford to lose even more warriors guarding the ranch. Whether he was there with Larissa or here, it wouldn't change her condition.

Angelo grunted as he turned down another residential street, taking them closer and closer to their meeting point with Connor. After Larissa had passed out they'd turned their cell phones back on and Angelo had gotten in contact with Connor. Connor and the rest of the packmates who'd come to Winston-Salem had managed to lose the reporters attempting to follow them.

Thankfully Ana and one of the warriors had brought different vehicles and traded out with Connor and the others, so it would be damn near impossible for anyone to track them. Now his Alpha and packmates were meeting up with the four of them back at Magda's. They needed to start cleaning up the mess, including disposing of the witch's body and locking down the house in case Magda's vamp "master" showed up. Aiden also planned to give Ryan all the cell phones they'd found at Magda's house in the hopes he could work his magic with them. Ryan had said he could do something with the GPS, but Aiden didn't really care about the specifics.

As they turned onto Magda's street, Aiden grew even more tense. The homes in the historic neighborhood were far enough apart that everyone had a lot of privacy. Not to mention the hedges or walls surrounding each house. He wasn't worried about being seen by humans, he was worried about his bondmate. All the reassurances in the world wouldn't help him right now.

Wake up, Larissa. Please. Closing his eyes, he buried his face against the top of her head, inhaling her sweet familiar scent. *I can't survive without you again, sweetheart. Come back to me.*

"I had no idea you could dance so well." Larissa linked her arm through Aiden's as they left the local pub.

A few drunk men stumbled out behind them, singing off-key as they headed in the opposite direction.

"You shouldn't be so surprised considering how well I dance between the sheets," he murmured, his seductive voice wrapping around her like a warm caress.

"Is that what you call it?" Grinning, she looked up at him. The night had turned out nothing like she'd expected. Larissa had been so worried that he'd been going off to meet a human lover but had found him giving presents to friends instead. Then he'd taken her to a local pub and sang and danced with such abandon. Watching him so relaxed, so happy, made her feel freer than she ever had before. She knew that life with him would be the greatest adventure and though she was worried about both their families' reactions, there was no turning back for her. Without a doubt she knew he was the male she wanted to be with forever.

He hummed a familiar Christmas melody as they made their way down the quiet streets. By now most humans would be asleep. In a few hours the sun would be up and everyone would be celebrating Christmas. But she was celebrating something else entirely. The start of a new life with the male she loved.

"This way," he murmured, reaching into his sporran and pulling out keys as he turned them down another side street. She spotted his car immediately, one of the few parked along the curb.

She snagged the keys from his hand and was thankful when he didn't protest. It took a lot to get a shifter drunk, and while he wasn't, he was definitely tipsy.

Once he'd settled in, she started the drive back to his pack's land. But they'd made it only ten minutes outside of *town when he pointed down a beaten pathway she'd have missed if not for his direction. "Turn here, I want to show you something."*

Curious, she slowed the car and turned off the main road. The road wasn't paved and was bumpier than she'd expected as they drove through a thicket of trees. Eventually the trees started to thin and the dirt road grew even more uneven.

"You can stop here," he murmured in a tone she might mistake for sleepy if she didn't know him by now. There was something wicked in his voice that sent a pleasurable shiver down her spine.

Before she'd pulled the key from the ignition he'd gotten out of his seat and was opening her door. Taking her hand in his, he plucked a bag from the backseat before he led her down the rest of the pathway until it opened up into a lush valley. Even at night she could see how beautiful the place was.

A wide lake glistened under the moonlight, surrounded on all sides by sloping hills that couldn't quite be called mountains. She could imagine how beautiful it would be in the daylight hours with the sun shining down on all the greenery. A pale mist seemed to cover most of the surrounding grass and sloping land, giving it a magical quality.

"What is this place?" she whispered though she wasn't sure why she did.

"My favorite place to run as a wolf. Most of the pack runs near the castles, but I love it here. It's peaceful."

She was touched that he'd brought her somewhere so special to him. She'd already seen him in his wolf form and he was a magnificent animal. So beautiful and fierce. "Thank you for showing it to me."

He just nodded and continued walking until they reached a

grassy patch in front of a cluster of rocks that lined the lake. Releasing her hand, he unzipped his bag and pulled out a folded blanket. "Take the other side," he said as he let it fall open.

She did and they worked to open it up and lay it flat on the grass. As she sat on it, she frowned. "Why did you have this bag in your car?"

He chuckled as he wrapped his arm around her shoulders. "I'd planned to bring you here tomorrow morning, but tonight is better."

She leaned into his embrace, soaking up his warmth. Though she wasn't affected by the cold like humans, Aiden put off the best kind of heat.

He nuzzled the top of her head, his warm breath teasing her. "You know why tonight is better?" he asked.

"Why?" She buried her face against his chest as she wrapped her arm around him. The male smelled like pure heaven. She wanted to bottle his scent.

"It's a full moon." His quietly spoken words left no doubt what he meant.

Vampires didn't undergo any rituals when they mated for life. Not in the way shifters did. For an instant, she went still before she looked up to meet his dark gaze. His eyes glittered with so many emotions. Love, lust, and just a hint of fear. That one nearly knocked her back. But she planned to make sure he never felt fear again where she was concerned.

When she stood, she saw his fists clench at his sides, as if he had to restrain himself from tugging her back down to him. Her thick coat pooled around her feet seconds after she slipped it off.

Aiden sucked in a sharp breath, his wolf in his eyes as he watched her slowly reach around and unzip the back of her *dress. After it joined her coat on the blanket, she stepped out of it and straddled him.*

He shuddered, his big arms coming around her in a tight grip. "You're sure?"

"More sure than I've been about anything in my five hundred years." She'd lived long enough to be secure in her decisions. And she knew there was nothing about tonight that she'd ever regret. She wanted Aiden to claim her, to mark her under the full moon with his canines so that everyone would know they belonged to each other. Afterward he would be marked with a tattoolike symbol so the world would know he was hers and she'd carry small scars from his canine piercing. He'd been so damn careful about not marking her so far because he could have mated her without bonding. But she knew it had been a lesson in restraint for him. Now they didn't have to show any restraint. And in a few hours, the world would know what they'd done.

"Larissa, come back to me." Once again Larissa's surroundings blurred as Aiden faded away. She wanted to shove the voice away again, but this time it was Aiden speaking.

Aiden begging her to come back. She'd do anything for him. Confusion slammed through her until she opened her eyes and found herself sitting on Aiden's lap in the backseat of a vehicle. His head was tilted back against the seat, his breathing steady, as if he was sleeping or dozing.

Larissa barely moved her head as she took in her surroundings, not wanting anyone to realize she was awake. A female shifter she didn't recognize was sitting in the driver's seat muttering under her breath about some male's pigheadedness and a male with a computer in his lap sat in the passenger seat talking to himself. The vehicle wasn't moving or even idling, but where were they? And how had she gotten here?

Aiden? she shouted through their telepathic link.

His eyes popped open as his head snapped up. Relief flooded his expression before he pulled her into a crushing hug. She let out a yelp of surprise as he buried his face against her neck, inhaling her scent in that shifter way she loved. Eventually he pulled back, his dark eyes warm as he locked with hers. *How are you?*

Okay, I think. Who are the people in the front seat? Are they safe? What happened to me? Where are Angelo and Brianna?

Yeah, they're my packmates and Angelo and Brianna are at Magda's. He cleared his throat. "Kat, Ryan, this is Larissa, my mate."

Larissa half turned to find two sets of curious eyes on her. The beautiful female gave her a warm smile. "It's so nice to meet you. I'm glad you're finally awake."

"Nice to meet you too." She nodded at both of them before turning all her focus on Aiden. *Where are we? What happened at Magda's?* She remembered the female stabbing herself, then Aiden trying to get her to feed, then feeling weak. *Did I pass out?*

More or less. Brianna said it's more like you've been in a deep sleep. And you've been out a couple of hours. I got you to feed a little, but you need a lot more. You expended a lot of energy using your gift. We took that human male to the hospital, but now we're back at Magda's. He nodded once and she turned to look out the windshield.

That was when she realized they were at the end of the long driveway at the front of the dead witch's house. They'd come in the back before but she recognized it from the recon they'd done.

My Alpha and a few other packmates are inside right now sweeping for clues and Ryan is running scans of the phone records from the cell phones we found at Magda's. They're all disposable phones. He thinks he might be able to find something useful.

She nodded slightly and shifted against Aiden's lap. His hold tightened, soothing the disorientation she felt pushing up inside her. Coming out of that sleep where she'd relived some of her memories was jarring, even if the memories had been good ones. It had felt real, as if she'd been there. Not like a dream at all. *I remember more between us. I remember falling for you and Christmas Eve.*

His dark eyes went molten. *Do you remember bonding?*

She shook her head. *I woke up right before that.*

Disappointment flared in his eyes for a brief moment before he said, *You need to feed. It's the only way you'll gain back your strength.*

She nodded because he was right, but still protested what she knew he wanted. *I've already taken too much from you in the past couple of days, so please don't insist I take now. We'll find someone else.*

His jaw tightened and she knew he wanted to argue. Instead, he looked around her. "Kat, we need to take a trip into town and find a semi-populated area where Larissa can find someone to feed from."

Before Kat responded, the other male spoke without looking up from his computer. "Why not just take her to a vamp club? There will be plenty of willing donors." He shot her a quick glance. "You can even pick blood type."

Larissa's eyes widened. "There are places like that? That humans know about?" The place Magda had sent her to days ago had been only for supernaturals and she hadn't been there long enough to discover much about it. Even though Larissa knew that vampires and shifters were out to humans, it would still take some getting used to this new world.

Ryan nodded. "Yeah. I can look up some places and we'll go to the closest one."

"Or she can just feed from some of us," Kat said. The female shifter's casual offer left Larissa speechless. Shifters didn't just willingly offer up their blood to vampires. "You drink from Aiden, so you can drink from us, right?"

"Yes, but . . ." She glanced back at Aiden questioningly. *Is this female serious?*

"You can take my wrist right now," Kat said before Aiden could answer.

"That's very generous, but . . ." Larissa felt as if she was under a microscope as the pretty shifter watched her expectantly. "Why are you offering?"

Kat shrugged. "You're Aiden's mate and he's not only my maker, but my friend." All she saw was sincerity in the woman's expression.

"Kat, you don't have to do this," Aiden murmured.

She rolled her eyes as she held out an arm and

pushed her sleeve up. "I know that, but I want to. Take it or leave it."

Feeling insecure and still out of sorts, she glanced back at Aiden. *Are you okay with this?*

He nodded. *Of course. And I didn't ask her to do this, in case you're wondering.*

Larissa had wondered and she was glad he hadn't. It made the female's offer more significant. And it said a lot about Aiden's packmates, or at least this one in particular. Larissa turned back and gently grasped the female's wrist. "This is very kind. Thank you. I won't take much, but if I drink too long or you feel weak, please tell me."

"Okay." She shrugged as if what she was offering was no big deal. In that moment Larissa could see how very human this female had once been. Because a shifter offering blood to a vampire was just not done. At least not in Larissa's world. Or the world she'd come from. Her parents and coven had hated being under Aiden's pack's roof all those years ago and had done it only because they'd wanted something. Shifters and vamps hadn't intermixed much in general and definitely not from such strong lines. It humbled her that a shifter was being so kind to her when she had no reason to be, when Larissa could find one of those clubs the shifter male had mentioned. Something told Larissa she was going to like this new world very much.

Larissa struck as gently as she could into the slender wrist. The female's blood was sweet, strong, and as it coated Larissa's tongue, almost immediately she felt her strength returning. With her new strength, another barrage of memories assaulted her at once, as if they were all fighting for dominance.

Sucking in a sharp breath, she pulled back from Kat's wrist. Quickly she licked the tiny wounds even though they would heal on their own. No one else seemed aware of the emotions running through her, but she wanted to tell Aiden what she'd remembered.

Before she could speak, Ryan let out a whoop of joy. "I am a fucking genius!"

Aiden snorted, his grip around Larissa's waist tightening. "That's up for debate."

The other male gave him a good-natured grin. "I might know where to find that witch's master."

Chapter 23

"**I** don't understand how he located this place," Larissa murmured to Aiden as they drove down the winding road deeper and higher into the mountains. They'd been driving for almost an hour and a half and, according to Ryan's recent mumbled announcement, should be there soon. Ryan had given a brief explanation of why they should check out this place, but she hadn't understood much of his terminology.

"No one knows how he does this stuff." Kat snorted and glanced at them in the rearview mirror from the driver's seat. "He's magic on a computer. It's very cool and a little scary, what he can do."

On the other side of Aiden in the backseat, the male named Jayce grunted, as if he wasn't impressed.

"You got something to say?" Ryan asked without turning around from the passenger seat where he stared at that small computer screen.

It seemed to be a source of contention that the bald

shifter with the scars on his face and the blades strapped across his chest wasn't sitting with his mate. Or maybe he was angry he wasn't the one driving. Larissa had watched in fascination earlier as Kat had teased her mate about the females driving tonight. Because Erin, the redheaded female, had been driving another SUV.

"It's not *that* impressive," Jayce said, annoyance in his deep voice.

Aiden buried his face in Larissa's hair and she could feel his chest shake as he smothered a chuckle. *He's in a mood tonight.*

Why?

I think because Kat offered her vein to you without telling him. He's very proprietary and gets nervous about pretty much anything that could potentially put Kat in danger. Since he'd never take his anger out on her, he's going to take it out on any available male.

After Larissa had fed from Kat they'd joined the rest of the pack inside Magda's house and it had been impossible not to notice the way the male had gone still at Kat's announcement that they should all feed Larissa a little so she could regain her strength. Kat had told her pack-mates that she'd already done it and that Jayce should go next. He hadn't. Not that Larissa had expected any of the mated males to feed her. Or any of the shifters at all. She didn't care how many decades had passed. Shifters offering their veins, making themselves essentially vulnerable to a vampire—it would take some getting used to for Larissa. Kat hadn't seemed to understand what a big deal it was, which only showed her youth and human origins.

And you're not? she asked wryly. Aiden had flat-out refused to let any of the males feed her, baring his teeth at them like the wolf he was.

Fair enough.

It was very kind of Erin to feed me. I feel balanced again. Maybe not at complete strength, but even better than I did before I used my gift. That in itself wasn't very surprising though. The two females she'd fed from clearly had strong blood, especially Erin. Drinking from her had been like receiving a shot of pure adrenaline. And to feed so much at once was invigorating.

Good. If you want to feed from . . . anyone else, I won't fight you. Even in her head his voice was strained as he sent the words to her.

She chuckled under her breath. *Yeah right.* Aiden had been fine with Erin feeding her, but when the male named Aldric had offered, Aiden had looked as if he might rip off the other male's head. Literally. She guessed it was part of the reason he was riding in the other SUV behind them.

Larissa was pretty good at reading people and his offer had seemed sincere, but of all the people with them tonight, Aldric was the only one she couldn't figure out how he fit in. He was Jayce's brother but they hadn't seen each other in decades, according to Aiden. He was there only because Connor didn't want the male out of his sight and had refused to leave him at their ranch. That was more drama than she cared to

think about when she was struggling to keep everyone's names and relationships straight. All Larissa was
really concerned about was finding out who Magda's
master was and why he wanted her blood.

"Don't be jealous," Ryan continued. "All I did was
ping the locations of all the incoming and outgoing
calls to the nearest cell towers at the time of each call—
from all of Magda's cell phones. Then I just used the
timeline Larissa gave me from her time with Magda to
cross-reference when the witch might have received
calls from her so-called master. And then *all* I did was
hack into a couple of satellites—one currently being
manned by the government, I might add—and create a
detailed map of all the places anyone using one of the
phones has been in the last month. From there—"

"Are you done?" Jayce growled.

Ryan continued as if the intimidating-looking shifter
hadn't spoken. "I managed to pinpoint—within a mile—
where two of the calls Magda placed were answered,
one right before that crazy bank robbery. Since it's a
rural, out-of-the-way cabin I also found satellite footage
of multiple vehicles—"

"All right, you're a fucking genius. Is that good
enough?" Larissa was certain she heard laughter in
Jayce's voice as he turned to look out the window.

"It'll do for now. All right . . . pull in anywhere over
there." Ryan straightened and pointed out his window
into a small opening of trees.

Larissa glanced behind them to see the other vehicle
pulling off too. Connor, Liam, Aldric, Erin, and Noah
were in there. Angelo and Brianna had stayed behind to

dispose of Magda's body—she was pretty sure Brianna was going to burn it—and keep watch over the house in case anyone showed up. That left ten of them to infiltrate the place Ryan had found using his computer.

Larissa didn't care what anyone said—seeing the image of that cabin from a satellite in space with such clarity was very impressive. The technology today had grown so much from before she'd gone into stasis.

After they parked and filed out into the snow, Larissa felt more at ease. On a primal level, it didn't matter how nice Aiden's pack had been so far, being surrounded by so many shifters—deadly ones at that— had all of her instincts going on alert. It was definitely a vampire thing.

"How far are we?" Connor asked, his attention on Ryan.

"Five miles on foot. Haven't seen any movement in or out of the place in the past couple of hours and that's all live."

The Alpha nodded, then looked at Erin and her mate, Noah. "You two know what to do. Leave your earpieces on."

They both nodded and disappeared into the woods. To Larissa's surprise, Connor nodded at Kat. "You're coming with me and Liam."

She'd assumed the female would go with her mate, and could tell Kat wanted to argue, but she snapped her mouth shut when Jayce shot her a sharp look. It was clear he was communicating telepathically and that he wanted her with Connor and Liam too. Or maybe not there at all.

"You're coming with me," Jayce said to Aldric, not seeming too happy about it.

That was probably why Jayce didn't want his mate with him. Clearly he didn't trust his own brother. Interesting. As Aldric cautiously moved to stand next to his brother, Ryan passed out earpieces to everyone, including Larissa.

As Ryan, Aldric, and Jayce started to leave, Connor came up to her and Aiden. Aiden instinctively stepped forward, half blocking her body with his. Connor didn't seem surprised by it. She inwardly smiled at the display of possessive behavior. After feeding from Kat and Erin, Larissa remembered so much more about her past with Aiden and wanted to tell him. But she needed to do it when they were alone.

"You sure she's okay?" Connor asked quietly.

Larissa gritted her teeth. No matter how well meaning the Alpha was, she wasn't a child. "*She* is right here and I'm fine. If this vampire is even here, I want to know why the hell he wants my blood." And she was going to make this bastard pay for dragging her into this shit, and more important, for dragging Aiden into it. She didn't care how powerful this vamp was, she was too.

Connor had the decency to look chastised but she didn't believe it for a second. "I just need to know my packmate has the backup he needs."

Her fangs descended on instinct and Aiden snagged an arm around her waist as if he thought she'd strike. No, she wasn't that angry, just annoyed. "Your packmate is my fucking bondmate. I wouldn't do anything to put him in danger. If I thought I wasn't strong enough, I'd say so."

To her utter surprise, the Alpha smiled, a real one. "That's what I wanted to hear." He turned to Liam and Kat. "Let's go."

As the others disappeared into the woods, Aiden looked at her, eyebrows raised. *Ready?*

She nodded and they headed east for about fifty yards before moving inland toward their final destination. They'd already gone over what everyone should do in the vehicles so they didn't need to discuss it again.

I like it when you get all feisty. Aiden's voice was light.

Despite the situation they were in she smiled. *I probably shouldn't have snapped at your Alpha.*

Aiden shrugged. *He'd better get used to it.*

She blinked in surprise, but didn't stop scanning their surroundings as she and Aiden silently crept through the woods. *Why do you say that?* she asked as she swept her gaze over a thick cluster of rustling bushes. When a rabbit the same color as the snow peeked its head out, some of her tension eased.

I don't expect you'll be changing who you are, ever. And if you live at the ranch . . . He trailed off and she looked at him.

You want me to live there?

His expression darkened. *Where the hell do you think I want you to live?*

I didn't mean it like that. I just meant . . . I haven't even thought that far ahead, that's all. The truth was, she was just living one moment to the next. She knew without a doubt she wanted to be in Aiden's life permanently, but actual details about the future hadn't even entered her mind.

You still never answered my question. He looked away, his gaze vigilant as he took in the quiet forest. A wolf howled in the distance, but when he didn't react she figured it was an actual wolf, not one of his packmates. She knew shifters could tell the difference.

What question?

Do you believe what Magda said before she killed herself? That I killed your parents? Now that you're not about to pass out I want to know.

His question could have knocked her over for how out of the blue it was. Clearly it wasn't to him though. He must have been sitting on it since Winston-Salem. She gritted her teeth. *First of all, I did answer. I told you no. Twice. Do you really think I'd be here with you if I believed her?*

He turned to look at her then, his dark eyes vulnerable. That was when it hit her that he *had* been sitting on this since before she'd passed out. Reaching out, she took his hand in hers and linked their fingers together.

Truthfully, Aiden, even if you had killed them . . . I'd still be here. That knowledge scared the holy hell out of her. She'd been very close to her parents. As a bloodborn vampire, they'd spoiled her from the time she was born—and slightly smothered her. She'd been everything to them. Both her parents had been typical of what one might expect of a vampire in terms of brutality, but they'd been fair and had treated their coven with respect. Much of her father's reputation had been embellished, though not all of it. Even with how much she'd loved them, after everything she'd recently remembered she knew she'd never walk away from Aiden. He was hers and if he had killed them, it would have been because he didn't have a choice.

The sharp sensation of shock rippled through their link, but he didn't respond. Just tightened his fingers around hers and continued their trek. They moved at a pace slightly faster than a human would, gliding over the snowy ground with their supernatural grace and speed, but they were still wary of potential traps. For all they knew, this lead wouldn't pan out. But Ryan had seemed very sure that something was going on here.

"We're on the north side of the property. Something is very wrong about this cabin. Six vehicles visible, the scent of vampires, humans, blood and . . . something else is here. It's very faint, but we can smell it," Erin whispered, her distinctive voice streaming through their earpieces.

The female and her mate hadn't left long before they had, so Larissa guessed she and Aiden would reach the cabin soon . . . *Oh. Shit.* Larissa scented true darkness as they reached the edge of the trees that opened into a clearing where a seemingly innocuous cabin sat. There was no smoke coming from the chimney and there was no movement from any of the windows.

Is that death? Aiden slowed, tugging her closer to him, his canines descending as a low, almost imperceptible growl built in his throat.

Yes, but . . . "What you're scenting is dark magic. A lot of it," she said to the group as quietly as possible.

There was no wind so her voice shouldn't carry far. "I could be wrong, but I think the reason it's so faint is because it's coming from underground." She knew because she'd scented it before in one of her father's castle dungeons. She really wished she hadn't but at well over five hundred years old she'd seen a lot of shit. Especially with a father like hers. With all the violent deaths her father had caused, it only made sense that the souls of the dead would eventually call forth darkness. It was inevitable. Whether someone had intentionally or unintentionally called the dead, a darkness was pushing at that unseen veil between this side and the next. It was the only explanation for the sulfuric, putrid scent just barely trickling out. This wasn't just the scent of death, it was the scent of the dead.

And it wouldn't be satisfied until it was released. Until it devoured all the innocent blood it could find.

Chapter 24

"**Y**ou're positive it's the dead, not demons?" Connor asked Larissa quietly. Liam and Kat were nearby, listening via their earpieces, but hidden in the trees.

Aiden watched as Larissa shook her head. He hated that she was being thrust into potential danger again so soon after her fainting spell. More than anything he wanted to take her away from here, keep her safe. "I'm not sure of anything. I just know that scent. I guess it could be demons. Why?"

Connor shared a grim look with Liam before glancing back at them. "A vampire named Juhani mentioned demons in a conversation we had in regards to"—he spread his hands out—"all the crazy shit going on with vampires acting possessed."

Larissa looked at Aiden. *I know a vampire named Juhani. Is he from Finland?*

Yes. He's one of the Brethren. When Larissa raised her

eyebrows, he realized she didn't know what that meant. *They're four ancient vamps who semi-rule the vampire race now that supernaturals have come out to the world. They're not like shifters with our Councils. They don't have a very good pulse on their people.* He nearly snorted. *Clearly.*

Who are the others? she asked.

Their names are Narek, Andrei, and Luca. You know them?

Possibly. I know ancient vampires with those names. They were all leaders of powerful covens when my father ruled ours. They are likely the same vampires as only a few would be strong enough to lead all vampires. She looked back at Connor. "Your vampire contact might be correct. Either way, it does not matter. Something, whether demons or the dead, wants out and we need to stop it. I don't care if the vampire we're hunting is behind this, we have to do something now. Whatever that wretched scent is, we can't allow it to gain even a little purchase into our world. It will feed on anything innocent it can find."

Connor and Liam nodded simultaneously, their expressions grim. "You wouldn't happen to know how to stop this, would you?"

Before answering she looked at Aiden and he knew he wasn't going to like what she had to say. *My mother and I helped cleanse one of my father's dungeons when something similar happened. Because of all the people my father killed one year, their blood acted like a sacrifice of sorts even though that wasn't his intent. . . . None of that matters. I will need to use my gift. Depending on how far into our world this darkness has moved, I will need to be at top strength. For that to happen, I will need to feed.*

She didn't continue and Aiden realized what she wasn't saying. Before answering Connor, Larissa was letting Aiden decide if he was okay with her feeding from his packmates. He was pretty sure she could feed from him and he'd be fine, but now wasn't the time to test his strength. The first time she'd drunk from him she'd taken a lot.

Though he hated the thought of her lips on any other male, for any reason, he shoved his possessive, protective wolf back down and turned to his Alpha. "Larissa can do it but she needs to feed from everyone. Not a lot, but enough that she has the strength to do what's necessary." Because he would not lose her and if that meant she had to drink from other males, so be it.

Connor looked thoughtful for a moment before he focused on Larissa. Then he held out his arm and shoved his long sleeve back. "Take what you need."

Shock rolled off Larissa as she stared at Connor. She looked at Aiden and it took all his strength to nod that he was okay with this. This wasn't sexual, he reminded himself. If anything, it was an honor that his Alpha was doing this so freely.

"Thank you," she murmured to Connor before barely touching his wrist and gently striking his vein.

Everyone took turns standing guard while she fed. Ten minutes later she'd drunk from everyone—except Jayce, who'd flat-out refused, much to Kat's annoyance, though it didn't surprise Aiden—and was already glowing.

"Give us a couple of minutes," Aiden murmured to Connor, who nodded before stalking off with Liam.

"I feel like I could fly," Larissa said, awe in her voice. "I've never had so much supernatural blood at once. So much strong blood. Your pack is incredible."

"*You* are incredible." She hadn't balked at wanting to stop the evil nearby. Had just told everyone what needed to be done and was willing to jump into the fray, no questions asked. That bravery was one of the reasons he loved her.

She blinked, her indigo eyes turning that electric blue. Before she could respond, he bared his neck to her. *I know you don't want to feed from me and I understand—though I feel fine. Just take a little. I want my blood to be the last you drink right now. It's making me insane that you touched other males. I want my taste to be on your tongue when we go in there.*

Instead of telling him that she'd just been feeding and none of it had been sexual or making a half dozen other statements to attempt to soothe him, she clutched his shoulders, bared her fangs and struck. Not with the gentle politeness she'd used with the others, but with a rawness she reserved only for him.

He shuddered and groaned at the feel of her teeth sinking into his neck, at the erotic sensation each time she sucked on him. Pushing her back up against a tree, he pinned her there with his hips, rolling them against her and hating that they had clothes in the way.

Much too soon, she pulled her head back and licked his small wounds. When she met his gaze, her eyes were glowing as she licked the blood from her lips and teeth.

"As soon as we're done here, I'm fucking you for

days," he snarled, the harsh words ripping from him. He knew everyone could hear them through the earpieces and the most primal part of him needed every single male to know his intent. It didn't matter that most were happily mated. His wolf was not rational right now.

"Good." Her voice was just as harsh as his. *I like it when you lose that charming veneer,* she added as he took a small step away from her.

He took a steadying breath, exhaled. "Ready?" he asked.

She looked down and held her palms up. A bright blue flame shot from both of them, more brilliant than he'd ever seen it. Her eyes were still electric as she met his gaze again. "Oh yeah."

"Erin, Noah, Jayce, and I are converging on the cabin first," Connor said via their earpieces. "Once we've secured it, everyone else move in."

After the rest of them answered in the affirmative, they all went silent. Aiden and Larissa crouched in the shadows of two tall trees, their boots making small indentations in the snow. Around them everything was silent as they watched the house. And waited.

If he hadn't been watching so intently he may not have seen the multiple blurs of movement from the woods to the cabin. Still in human form, Connor and Erin were the only ones visible from his and Larissa's position. Moving lightning quick, they invaded the house, Erin using a window and Connor going in through the front door. He guessed the others were using windows on the other side of the quiet cabin.

"Everyone can come in," Connor said fewer than thirty seconds later.

Using caution, Aiden and Larissa sprinted to the front porch, reaching it at the same time as Kat and Liam. Aiden entered first, using his body to block Larissa's as he stepped inside. He could feel Larissa's annoyance through their link at his protectiveness, but it didn't bother him.

Once inside he saw Connor and the three others standing next to a kitchen table that they'd clearly moved to the side. A dingy rug had been pulled back to reveal a door cut into the floor. It lined up with the seams of the floor, but the hinges and small door were clearly visible. The rest of the cabin was definitely un-lived in. There were a few pieces of dusty wooden fur-niture that looked as if they had never been sat on and the fireplace had a nest of something living in it. He nodded at the unopened trapdoor as Larissa, Liam, and Kat came to stand next to him. Aiden also scented the remaining three males entering. The growing pu-trid stench of the dead was stronger inside, wafting over them.

Connor let his claws out before he looked at Liam. Aiden guessed they were communicating telepathi-cally. A moment later Liam crouched next to the door. Connor motioned that he was going to go first. As he did, Erin and Jayce pulled out blades. Both enforcers immediately handed a blade to their mates. Aiden let his claws free, as did the other males. Larissa's fangs and claws released, but she didn't let her flames loose yet.

Liam tugged back the door. It barely made a sound. From his position a few feet away Aiden could see a metal ladder, but the drop to whatever was down there, was dark. Connor started to move in, but Liam grabbed his upper arm in a tight grip. They had one of their telepathic conversations until Liam finally let go, but he looked pissed as his brother went first.

Aiden understood that as Connor's second-in-command, and his only brother, Liam wanted to protect Connor. It was his right and duty, but as Alpha, Connor had to go first in situations like this. He had to show everyone what he was willing to do. Otherwise how could he expect them to? It was the shifter way and why Connor was a respected Alpha.

Erin and Noah went next, then everyone else followed with Ryan closing the trapdoor behind them. The descending tunnel was dark, but with his supernatural vision Aiden could make out everything well enough. And there was definitely a light coming from somewhere below. No noise though. Which was surprising since they'd seen multiple individuals converging on the house from the satellite feeds. According to Ryan, no one had left since. That told Aiden that either everyone who'd entered was incredibly quiet, or whatever was below them was expansive enough that they simply couldn't hear where the others had gone—or the vampires were lying in wait to attack. That was definitely a possibility.

As Aiden dropped out of the tunnel onto solid stone ground, he immediately scanned his surroundings, taking in everything in one visual sweep. There were a dozen burning torches hooked on the stone walls around the circular cavernous space. A torch for each carved archway leading down twelve different tunnels. That putrid stench was much stronger down here. Not so overwhelming that he wanted to hurl, but they were getting closer to whatever darkness lurked down here. He rolled his shoulders once, trying to shake off his tension. Having Larissa in any sort of danger, no matter how capable she was, was wreaking havoc on his senses.

Larissa looked at Aiden, her expression grim. There were twelve tunnels and ten of them. Since there was no way in hell he'd be leaving Larissa—and he knew neither Jayce nor Noah would leave their respective mates—it could take a while to search them all.

Connor motioned that they should all bunch together like a football team huddling. Once they were close, he looked at all of them. "We'll split into twos and cover ground that way. Liam's with me, the rest of you pick your partners," he said, clearly out of courtesy because it was pretty damn certain who would pair off with whom. "That one," he pointed to the archway nearest to the overhead tunnel drop, "I'm designating as tunnel number one. The next is number two," he pointed in a clockwise motion. "And so on. We'll take the first five tunnels at once. Keep your earpieces on, and if you get into trouble, call for backup. Use your tunnel number so we know which one you're in. Fight if you have no choice, but wait for backup until we know more about what the hell is down here." His voice was whisper soft and serious as he gave them orders.

Even so there was still a chance they'd been over-heard if vampires were nearby. It was a chance they had to take.

When everyone nodded, they all split up, with Aiden and Larissa taking the third tunnel. He watched as everyone entered one of the tunnels before stepping inside with Larissa. They walked in silence, quick but conscious of possible traps or explosives. Right now he wasn't about to underestimate any possibilities. He couldn't measure for sure, but about one hundred yards in he heard a low chanting.

Next to him Larissa immediately slowed. Her heart rate didn't increase and she didn't put off any scents, but shot him a glance. *I hear it.*

What language is that? The chanting was almost non-sensical. He wondered if it was because he didn't know the language.

Latin.

Pausing, he strained to listen and realized she was right. It was Latin and the chanting male was saying only four or five words over and over. They all blended together, sounding like gibberish.

As they neared the entrance, the hair on the back of Aiden's neck stood straight up. Tingles raced down his spine and he had the most ominous feeling, as if he was walking straight into a mouth of hell. The sulfuric smell was incredibly strong now and the chanting sounded like something out of a bad horror movie.

Moving slowly they crept near the entrance. He had to force himself to continue and not grab Larissa and whisk her away to safety. His wolf clawed at his surface, ready to be unleashed and protect Larissa. Shadows moved and shifted against one of the high arching walls. From candles. Next to him Larissa was tense, her body rigid even as blue flames licked up from her hands, covering her arms like body armor.

Ready? he asked.

Larissa's jaw tightened. *Let's do it.*

They moved the last couple of feet toward the edge of the archway in silence. It took only seconds to take everything in. Shock punched through him as he saw a vampire wearing a dark hood kneeling in front of a blood-stained altar with three dead human females on it. Their blood spilled everywhere as the male's hands plunged into the chests of two of them and pulled their hearts out.

That wasn't what shocked Aiden. It was the dark aura almost hovering around the male like a thick cloud. He could see gaunt faces peering through the haze, their eyes an eerie red as they watched what the vampire was doing. As if they were hungry for . . . Oh, nasty. The vamp lifted one of the hearts and took a bite of it. Only the bottom half of his face was showing so it was impossible to see who it was.

Move back, he commanded Larissa. They needed backup and he wasn't risking this male overhearing him calling Connor and everyone else. The male probably couldn't scent them over all the stench of death.

Before they'd taken one step, the male's head whipped up. He dropped the hearts and shoved the hood back with his blood-covered hands. His eyes glowed red and he smiled evilly, his fangs shiny with blood as he stared at Larissa, lust and rage in his eyes. Oh yeah, this fucker was going to die.

"Kill the male, the female is mine!" he shouted and before Aiden realized what the male meant, nearly a hundred vampires dropped from seemingly out of nowhere. There was a lip of stone above them in the high arched cavern.

He couldn't believe he and Larissa hadn't scented them, but it was possible they were being protected by a spell.

Larissa let out a growl of rage, her blue flames spreading out on the ground around her. His wolf took over. As he underwent the change from man to animal everything around him funneled out for a moment. This was his weakest moment, in between the change, but he had no choice. His wolf was taking over whether he wanted it or not.

His bones broke and realigned and as he landed on all fours, everything came into focus in a rush. The vampire closest to him let out a shriek as he hurled something at Aiden like a javelin thrower. A short sword glinted in the firelight.

Aiden jumped, attempting to move out of the way when Larissa's body slammed into him. She cried out, her flames dying as they landed with a thud on the cold dirt floor of the cavern.

A wrenching agony like he'd ever experienced only once before sliced through him as he saw the blade embedded in her back, the tip coming out through her chest. Her eyes were a bright blue as she stared at him, her body covering his lupine form. It was as if time stood still.

"No!" the leader screamed as he jumped over the altar, sending the other vampires scrambling away from Aiden and Larissa.

Larissa stared up at him, that gaze so full of grief it felt as though his own heart had been pierced. She reached for him, put a shaking hand over his front paw.

On instinct he shifted back to his human form to hold her. He was aware of the vampire moving toward them but all he could focus on was Larissa, his mate, the only woman he would ever love. *Don't you dare fucking die on me.*

"Pull it out," she whispered, her brilliant eyes going glassy.

As they did, he felt the strangest tingle in his body and he knew exactly what she was doing. What she was gifting to him. *No!* he screamed to her, understanding her intent.

When her eyes closed and she didn't respond he screamed, the sound ricocheting off the cavern so loudly the advancing vampire stumbled in his tracks.

Chapter 25

Sixty years ago, Christmas Day

*L*arissa stood shoulder to shoulder with Aiden, her back ramrod straight as they waited in the great room of Aiden's parents' castle. Her parents were at the front of the room with his, looking just as furious. Perhaps more so. She'd never seen her mother or father so irate.

History had gotten many things about her father wrong—mainly because he wanted it that way—and while it was true his first wife had committed suicide, his second wife, Oana Danesti, was the true love of his life. They'd been together for centuries and while Larissa had been spoiled and a favorite among her coven, she knew in that moment, things would never be the same. Her father might be the one with the dark reputation, but her mother basically ruled him. He did what his mate wanted because he loved her more than anything. Whatever Oana decided, Vlad would agree to it, even if it meant casting his own daughter out. Deep down it pierced *her that her own parents could be so irate because she'd fallen in love with a shifter.*

It wasn't a choice. It had happened and she wasn't sorry for it.

"You're such a little fool," her mother spat, her eyes brilliant blue. Her hands fisted into balls as she clearly restrained herself from attacking Aiden. "He's just using you."

Aiden growled softly next to her before he wrapped his arm around Larissa's shoulders. "Watch how you speak to my mate."

At that, her father stepped forward. Then Aiden's moved toward Vlad. Both powerful males turned on each other, glaring as if they wanted to kill the other, but at least they weren't making any other hostile gestures.

"We love each other and we've made our choice. Either live with it or don't, but we've done nothing wrong. If anyone is being foolish, it's you. You have a chance to unite a shifter and vampire line, bridging the divide between our races. Think about all the good we could do with our example." Larissa stared her mother square in the eye, refusing to back down. Bridging the divide had nothing to do with why she and Aiden had bonded, but they had an opportunity to make a difference with their bonding. Supernaturals were always battling one another, but if two powerful lines accepted this mating, it could drastically change the way their races treated one another for all future generations. If her mother could take her stupid emotional reaction out of the equation she would see Larissa was right. But the second their parents had entered the great room, they'd flipped out, recognizing the bonding scent on both of them.

"Clearly we've sheltered you for too long if you think this

animal loves you. He's going to take your gift and discard you." Her mother's hands burst into blue flames and everyone in the room went still as they stared. Even her father seemed shocked at her mother's display.

Larissa's eyes widened at her mother's lack of control. Their family secret was a closely guarded one; only a select few in their coven even knew of it. She'd showed Aiden what she could do only last night after they bonded. Even then she hadn't told him everything because she hadn't wanted to overwhelm him. Her mother's words set something off inside her.

Do you trust me? *she asked Aiden.*

Disbelief shot along their newly formed link. You don't even have to ask.

Even though she knew it, she'd needed to hear it. Brace yourself. Turning toward Aiden she grabbed both his hands and released her flames. The beautiful blue licked up his arms, over his chest and head until it covered his entire body. Ignoring her mother's cry of outrage and his parents' growls of anger, she focused on the man she loved and funneled all her energy into Aiden.

She'd never attempted this before, but her mother had explained how it worked. How she could give her gift of fire to anyone she chose, not just her mate. Larissa had never thought she'd want to, but she trusted Aiden to give it back. It was the ultimate act of trust. Once she released it fully, he could keep it or return it.

It's yours until you decide to give it back to me, *she projected to him as she stepped back and released his hands.*

His dark eyes were wide as he looked at her, then everyone else in the room. I don't have to give it back to you, do I?

You just gave up your most powerful gift to prove to your parents that I can be trusted.

She nodded as he watched her, his dark eyes unreadable. Closing the distance between them, he grasped her hands in his and pulled them to his chest. I'm beyond humbled, Larissa. I didn't think it was possible I could love you more, but I do. Their reaction is worse than I thought, so let's leave tonight. We'll head to America. *As he spoke, she felt her power returning, the invigorating sensation flooding her veins as the blue flames transferred to her with such fluidity, it surprised her. To be able to control her gift so easily spoke volumes about his untapped power and their bond.*

As she absorbed her gift, she wrapped her arms around his waist, laying her head on his chest as she turned to her parents. Her mother looked even angrier than before, which told Larissa all she needed to know. "Your reaction is beyond disappointing and we're not going to stand around and argue about something that I couldn't change even if I wanted to. Aiden and I are leaving. I'll contact you in a month to see if you've decided to act rational."

Her mother's entire body burst into blue flames. "You will do no such thing!"

Larissa turned fully on her mother, shoving out her fire to shield Aiden and his parents in its protective bubble in case her mother had any stupid ideas. She wasn't acting as if she meant to harm them but right now she seemed unstable.

No matter how terrible their reaction to her and Aiden's mating had been, she wouldn't let her mother kill the people he loved and start a war. "I will, and you will do well to remember that I am just as powerful as you." *Larissa may not have flaunted it, but she had no problem reminding her* mother now. Before her mother could say anything, she took a threatening step forward. "If you attempt to hurt my mate or any of his pack I will return home and burn all your castles to the ground. I will fucking destroy everything you hold dear. You will absolutely honor the pact you made with his pack and act like the honorable vampires I know you to be. If you don't . . ." Her teeth clenched together as she tried to contain her building rage. She wasn't sure if she was speaking the truth or not because the thought of anyone hurting Aiden tugged at her basic instincts. She would destroy anyone who dared hurt him or cause him pain. Anyone.

"Larissa—"

She turned on her father, who'd been relatively silent up until now. "Don't even start. You taught me everything I know, so don't pretend to be shocked."

His mouth pulled into a thin line as he quieted. He didn't look angry so much as resigned as he turned to Larissa's mother. "Oana, let's step back and discuss this situation. Our daughter has made a foolish choice, but she's right about bridging the gap between our species."

Larissa nearly snorted at his words. "This situation." As if her being newly bonded to a shifter was a crisis to solve.

Her mother's flames disappeared as she straightened, her body going rigid and her expression turning cold. "There's nothing to discuss. We have no daughter anymore."

The words punched into Larissa's chest and for the first time in centuries she had the urge to cry. Before she could react, Aiden scooped her up, taking her completely by surprise. She knew what he was doing, saving her from becoming emotional in front of them. She appreciated it more than she could put into words. He didn't say a word to anyone as *he strode from the room, but she sensed his anger, aggression, and sadness intermixed as he hurried out of the castle to his car. She guessed he'd be driving them to his castle so they could pack some things.*

"I can walk," she eventually murmured, still struggling to comprehend what had just happened.

He didn't respond, but once they reached his car, he leaned against the driver's door and buried his face against her neck. "I'm so sorry to tear you away from your family." His voice was ragged and a new wave of guilt rolled through their link.

Pulling back, she cupped his cheeks with her hands. The grief etched on his face tore at her. "You have nothing to be sorry for. Fuck all of them. If they can't accept us, that's not unconditional love. That's not what parents are supposed to do." Her words didn't lessen her own grief much, but it felt good to say them.

He brushed his lips over hers and despite everything they'd just left behind, she knew mating with him had been the best decision she'd ever made.

The sword had fucking impaled her.

Panic swirled inside him, but he shoved it down. He had to trust Larissa's instincts on this.

Grabbing the blade, Aiden pulled it out of Larissa's back—even though it was one of the hardest things he'd ever done. She was still breathing, her heart still beating and he could sense their link, though it was faint. Too damn faint.

Though he wanted to feed her so she'd start healing, he knew these vampires would never let him get that far. But the vamps were all going to die. He'd lost his earpiece during his first shift, so he prayed Connor or one of his packmates had heard him.

Embracing the gift Larissa had given him, he held out his arms and let out another shout as her incredible fire surged through him. It shot from his hands like lightning, slamming into random vampires. Screams filled the underground cave as vampires burst into flames. Dozens started to run away from him, yet others ran at him like they were on a suicide mission.

Their leader raced toward the altar, jumping over it and away from Aiden, but he ignored the male for now. First he had to save Larissa.

Channeling the energy the way she'd taught him so long ago, he imagined the fire pushing out from every single inch of his body, covering the ground and walls and burning anyone who was his enemy.

As the flames grew, lapping at everything, it started to cover the room in a brilliant coat of blue. His heart nearly stopped when he felt Larissa's energy fading. Another wave of pain rippled through him and he shoved out again, this time with a blast of pure fire, incinerating everything in its path.

Horrible screams filled the air as the remaining vampires burst into flames. A few vamps managed to dive into the exit, escaping his fire. He started to direct the flames that way when he heard Jayce grunt and curse. Moments later, his packmates spilled into the cave, but they all jerked to a halt, staring at him and the cave in shock and a little horror.

He knew what he looked like and didn't care. Aiden pinned Jayce with a glare. "She's dying. Save her!" He didn't need to explain shit. The enforcer could help her with his blood and he knew it. If he didn't, Aiden couldn't even think about what he'd do.

"Behind you!" Jayce tossed him one of his blades.

Aiden didn't have time to be surprised as he jumped and snagged it from midair. Grasping it, he turned and rolled to the side, missing what could have been a debilitating blow to his neck.

The vampire held a sword deftly in his hands. He jumped out of the way as Aiden went to strike him with Jayce's blade. The weapon was light in his hands, but Aiden could practically feel the power humming through the thing. Holy shit. He knew it could ash vampires and that's exactly what he planned to do to this bastard.

Out of the corner of his eye Aiden saw Jayce scoring his wrist and putting it to Larissa's mouth. Then he saw Connor take an aggressive step forward. Keeping his eye on his adversary, Aiden shouted again, unable to even speak normally for all the adrenaline pumping through him. "Stay back! This is a *nex pugna*!" A death fight. Usually for Alphas but everyone would understand his meaning. This was his fight and no one else's. Because of this fucker, Larissa was pale, unconscious, and possibly dying.

He shoved that thought away and held on to their link, focused on the fact that she was still alive.

Channeling the power of the fire raging through him, he sent a blast out at the vampire as he dodged what would have been another deadly strike. The flames flowed around the male in a huge arch, as if he had a protective ball around him.

He was spelled. Clearly he knew of Larissa's powers and he'd made sure her flames couldn't penetrate him.

Aiden shot another blast at him as a test. This time a couple of thin streams of energy seemed to cut through. Pieces of the male's hooded robe fell away in singed chunks.

The vamp let out an ear-piercing scream, his eyes dark and tinged with utter madness. But the red tint wasn't there anymore. Neither were the hovering faces of the dead from beyond the veil. It was just Aiden and this madman.

Aiden's body lit up in blue flames, but he didn't feel their heat. "Is this what you wanted?" Aiden taunted as he struck out with the blade in a fast, jabbing action. He quickly jumped out of the way as the vamp attempted to strike him with his own sword. The male's arm sizzled from Jayce's blade. So the vamp was spelled but only from Larissa's fire.

"You fucking animal!" the vamp shouted.

"You'll never get it now," Aiden continued, walking in a slow circular arc around the male.

"I will if I kill you," he snarled, spit flying from his mouth.

Oh yeah, this guy was fucking crazy. There may be some truth to his words, Aiden didn't know. "I'll kill myself before I let you take it."

At that the vampire screamed again in that maniacal way before lunging at him with his sword. Despite his lack of control and clear rage, the vamp was skilled and nimble. Letting go of his control over the fire, Aiden used all the strength in his legs to jump high into the cavern.

Twisting midair, he came back down, slicing at the vampire's back with his blade. The vamp turned sideways at the last moment, coming up with his own blade. It slammed into Aiden's shoulder as Aiden pierced the male's chest.

It wasn't his heart though. Too far to the right and the guy didn't turn to ash. The wound just sizzled and burned from the blade's magic. Grunting in pain, the vamp started to pull his blade from Aiden's body as Aiden released his claws and punched all the way through the male's chest. Ribs broke as the male screamed in raw agony.

Grabbing the heart, Aiden let the fire loose again. The male's dark eyes widened as his heart incinerated. But Aiden wasn't done. Focusing on the energy, he blasted the blue flames through the male's entire body. In a brilliant explosion of light, the powdery remains exploded over him and the floor of the cave.

Unable to savor his victory, he dropped the blade and raced to Larissa's side. He was aware of his packmates and Jayce's brother hovering near the entrance, watching as Jayce continued to feed Larissa from his wrist. Though her eyes were closed, she was sucking hard, pulling in long gulps of blood. Relief didn't begin to describe what he felt as he looked at the woman he loved.

The enforcer's jaw was clenched tight, his piercing gray eyes locked on Aiden's. "That was some freaky shit you just did."

"Get ready to see some more." Kneeling next to his bondmate, he grasped both her hands in his and slowly, but purposefully, directed her powers back into her. Every second that passed, every second the energy drained from his body, he felt their link growing stronger and stronger.

As the last ounce of power left him, Larissa's eyes flew open with a start. She glanced between the two of them before lunging at Aiden, wrapping her arms around his neck.

The most potent relief surged through him, overwhelming emotion nearly knocking him on his ass as his throat tightened. "It's over. He's dead," he managed to rasp out. *Whoever* the hell that vamp had been. Aiden wanted answers, but right now all he cared about was that Larissa was alive in his arms. Everything else was just details.

"I thought I was dead. I can't believe that blade struck perfectly in the middle of my heart. It basically shredded it," she said with a tinge of awe.

If you hadn't been amped up on supernatural blood, I don't think you would have made it, he projected, unable to say the words out loud. As he buried his face in her neck, tears burned his eyes. He didn't give a shit who saw him. He'd sobbed like a fucking baby when he thought he'd lost her once. To almost lose her again . . . Hell yeah, he was crying.

I know. Through their link her voice was ragged and tired. The feel of her arms around him reassured him. *Thank you for saving me.*

He snorted. *Don't ever thank me for that. I'm just . . . I don't want to move yet. Maybe never.*

She squeezed him back.

He wasn't sure how much time passed, but eventually she pulled back, her blue eyes glittering with unshed tears. Reaching out, he brushed his thumbs over her soft cheeks when a few spilled over.

"We need to clean this mess up and block this cave," she said quietly.

"Already on it," Connor murmured from the entry.

Aiden looked up then, taking in everyone. First he focused on Jayce, who'd moved to stand next to Kat, his arm slung protectively around her. "Thank you."

Jayce shrugged, as if the words made him uncomfortable. "I owed you."

Aiden simply nodded, knowing that was all he'd get out of the male. He looked at his Alpha next. "I'm sure you have a lot of questions, but—"

"Let's get your mate out of here and start cleaning this shit up. Everything else can wait."

Hell yeah, it could. Standing, Aiden pulled Larissa up with him before scooping her into his arms. She let out a halfhearted protest before laying her head against his chest. His inner wolf was soothed immensely at the feel of her head resting against his heart.

"Maybe we could get Aiden some pants because I'm tired of looking at his junk," Jayce muttered.

Bursts of surprised laughter erupted from everyone,

echoing off the walls of a place that had seen too much evil and death. He pulled in a deep breath and released it slowly, his inner wolf quieting. For the first time in decades Aiden felt as if he were whole again.

The battle was over but his and Larissa's new life together had just begun.

Chapter 26

Four days later

Larissa turned the page of the crazed vampire Cornelius's journal/manifesto/tirade against the human race, wondering what insanity she'd read next. Everything in that cave had happened so fast she hadn't had a chance to see his face before she almost died and Aiden vaporized him. *That,* she wished she'd seen. But she knew who he was after reading the journal they'd retrieved among his other belongings. It had been hidden inside that wretched altar, the stone enclosure the only thing that had saved it from being incinerated by the fire.

He'd been a member of her parents' coven and while she'd never been friends with him, they'd been acquaintances. He'd even been with the group that went to Aiden's parents' castle. The male had been one of their scholars, a record keeper, and he'd been utterly brilliant. Well, mad and brilliant. He'd been witness to her mother's little light-show display the day Aiden and Larissa had left both their families. As a record keeper, he'd been aware of the Danesti line gift, but he hadn't realized it had been transferable.

Once he'd discovered that, he'd become obsessed with stealing the gift for himself. He'd even been the one who killed her parents, poisoning them and many of the coven members using knowledge he'd learned from the dark arts. She was still trying to come to terms with her parents' deaths, but figured that would be a long time coming. Unfortunately for Cornelius—but fortunately for her—it had taken him a long damn time to figure out where her parents had entombed Larissa. It was the first time she found herself thankful for their need for secrecy.

She'd finally regained all her memories, though she wished she didn't have them all. True to her word, Larissa had contacted her parents a month after she and Aiden had left. They'd apologized and invited both of them to stay in Romania. Larissa had been unsure about their motives—her mother had not been known to apologize for anything—and had convinced Aiden to let her go alone. They were her parents after all. It wasn't as if they'd kill her. She'd thought she could deal with them much easier without Aiden under their roof and would be better able to gauge their sincerity.

It had been a trap. They'd worked with a powerful witch to put her into stasis, then had planned to kill Aiden while she was under. Nothing had gone their way after that. So caught up in their own scheming they hadn't realized they'd gained a new enemy under their roof. After they'd been murdered, Cornelius started picking off more and more vampires until only those he trusted were left alive. Then he'd sold off almost everything, but had kept one castle and had made sure the rumors of Vlad and Oana remained alive for decades.

The man had truly been brilliant in an evil sort of way. He'd wanted to rule humans, to keep them "in their place on the food chain," as he put it in more than one of his rants. Using the dark arts he'd figured out he could possess Larissa's gift by taking all of her blood. Stupid fool. Her gift could only be given freely.

Sighing, she rubbed her eyes as she closed the journal. She wasn't even halfway through, but she needed another break. His ramblings were confusing and often hard to understand. As she laid her head back against the couch in the males' cabin at the Armstrong ranch, she half smiled.

About ten minutes ago she'd sensed two individuals sneak into the room. They were terrible at hiding, but as cubs she didn't expect them to be stealth predators. "You can come out now, little spies."

Seconds later, a little girl and boy jumped over the back of the couch, landing on either side of her. The girl was a jaguar shifter who would most definitely be a heartbreaker one day. Though something told Larissa that the lupine shifter next to her wasn't letting any male near Vivian. Ever. For a ten-year-old he'd shown surprising territorial instincts in the short time she'd interacted with them.

"What are you two doing? Aren't you supposed to be in school?"

Vivian beamed at her and gave her that wide-eyed look Larissa guessed was supposed to be innocent. "We don't have school today."

Lucas snorted. "She can tell when you're lying, Vivian."

"Oh, right." Vivian bit her bottom lip before grinning again. "It's our lunch so we have a break. Will you show us some more tricks?"

Ever since the story of Larissa's gift had spread around the ranch the kids had been hounding her for "one more trick." Grinning, Larissa reached out and touched both their heads. She coated just their hair in blue flames.

Squealing in delight, Vivian jumped off the couch and held her braids out to inspect. Then she released her hair from its ties and squealed some more. "This is so cool! Isn't this cool, Lucas?"

Lucas wasn't quite as energetic as the girl, but he grinned and ran to a mirror on one of the walls and inspected himself. "Yeah, it's pretty cool."

At the sound of the front door opening, both kids froze. Larissa scented the female before the door fully opened and withdrew the fire from their hair.

Ana Cordona walked in, a half smile on her face as she nodded at Larissa. "Are they bothering you again?"

"They're not a bother." Being around such innocent children was refreshing. Hell, being around this pack was beyond refreshing. They'd accepted her so quickly; this was just as stunning as all the changes going on in this new world. Yes, there was still prejudice against shifter-vampire matings, but things had come so far. It probably didn't seem that way to some, but for her things had literally changed overnight. She loved living in a place where all species were accepted.

The female's lips pulled into a thin line as she glanced first at Vivian, then Lucas. "Vivian is a little hooligan, but I expect more from you, Lucas," she said, laughter in her voice.

"Hey!" Vivian ran over to her adoptive mother and threw herself into her arms. "He's a hooligan too."

Ana laughed, the sound throaty and loud as she motioned for Lucas to come with her. "You two are in a world of trouble with Esperanze." As she directed them to the door, she gave Larissa a warm smile. "Your mate is on his way back. I just saw him and Connor wrapping things up."

"Thanks." Before the word was out of her mouth, Aiden strode into the room, passing Ana and the kids with a smile.

As always he looked fierce and sexy. And he was all hers. Larissa stood and before she'd taken one step, he crossed the distance between them. Gathering her close to him, he wrapped his arms around her waist and crushed his mouth over hers. His tongue played with hers as he rolled his hips against hers in an erotic, primal dance.

Breathing hard, he eventually pulled back, his dark eyes filled with hunger. "Tonight."

She knew what he meant with that one word. Her toes curled against the hardwood floor in anticipation of finally feeling him deep inside her. "Hmm, I don't know if I'm ready yet."

He let out a soft growl. "You've been ready for days."

"So you admit you've been overprotective and crazy to make me wait?"

Aiden opened his mouth once, then let out another sexy little growl. "Don't turn my words around."

She grinned and buried her face against his chest. "Just on principle I should make you wait four days, but I'm too needy right now." Aiden had been absolutely ridiculous about his "no sex" policy once they'd returned to the ranch. He thought she needed more time to rest and heal, but in reality she was perfectly fine physically.

The pack, including Brianna and Angelo, had spent almost two days cleaning up those caves and making sure no one else was down there. In addition to Larissa's fire, Brianna had used some of her healing magic to cleanse the place. But the female had also called in a favor to some of her fae brethren to help. Once all the evil remnants had been removed from that place, they'd filled in that first tunnel from the cabin with cement, completely blocking it off. Seeing that had been impressive. It had taken a couple of days to get everything squared away, but they'd been back here for a full day and a half and Aiden thought he could make her wait to jump his body.

He was clearly out of his mind.

She nipped his bottom lip with her teeth. "Why tonight? Why not now?" Dusk was only a couple of hours away, but she didn't want to wait.

Tensing, he slightly straightened, but didn't pull back from his embrace. "I just met with Connor and he's already started the plans for building us our own home."

She frowned. "That's a good thing." Aiden hadn't told her why he'd needed to meet with his Alpha privately and she hadn't pushed because she trusted him and because she'd wanted to read more of the journal. Even if getting into the head of a madman was frustrating.

"I know. While I was there he received a call from Juhani and Narek. They're waiting outside the main gate and would like to speak to you." His jaw and grip on her tightened at the same time, his fingers digging into her hips.

"About what?" A small sliver of worry worked its way down her spine. She and Aiden's pack had agreed that she would take credit for killing Cornelius and all those hundreds of vampires he'd been controlling. She'd read all about his control in his journal and that male had been sick. He'd forced people to do all sorts of things just for the pleasure of it. He'd said it was to practice his gift, but that wasn't why. He'd been a monster. Even so, it would seem much better that a vampire had killed so many of her own kind rather than a shifter.

"They wouldn't say, but they asked for permission to "retain your audience.'" He used air quotes at the last part, making her smile.

"Then let's get it over with. The sooner they're gone, the better."

"I will tell the truth if—"

She held a finger to his mouth. "Stop. We'll see what they want first. I don't care if you were justified, it's better that a vampire takes the credit for the killings. Your Alpha agreed with me."

Aiden just growled and sent off a quick text. "Come on," he said a few moments later after he received a returning ping. "We'll meet them at the main house."

If the Alpha was letting the vampires into his home, then things must not be as bad as Aiden assumed. But Larissa didn't say that.

They crossed the main yard of the ranch in silence and she noticed how quiet things were. She had no doubt there were shifters out patrolling, but she guessed that Connor had told everyone to remain inside while the Brethren members were here. Once inside the main house they found Connor, Ana, and Liam sitting on one couch, and the two vampire males sitting on another smaller one.

Narek was dressed impeccably in a suit and Juhani looked a bit grungy. She wasn't sure what his style was called, but it was strange and reminded her of a homeless person. They both stood when they saw her before bowing respectfully. She'd met both of them over a hundred years ago, long before her stasis and long before supernaturals had come out to the world. They'd been powerful then, so she knew they were even more so now. Their show of respect helped ease some of the tension building inside her.

Next to her Aiden growled, so she nudged him with her elbow. "That is not necessary," she murmured.

Narek frowned at her as he stood. "Of course it is. You are the last of the Draculesti and Danesti line, a bloodborn. You are true royalty."

She shifted uncomfortably. Yeah, royalty who had no clue how she fit into this new world, no money, and wasn't even sure how she was going to support herself. She had no doubt Aiden would, but she didn't want to depend on anyone that way, not even her bondmate. "Please sit." She motioned to the small couch.

As she did, Liam stood and Connor pulled Ana into his lap so Larissa and Aiden could sit together. The Alpha had a casual pose, but she could see the predator lurking beneath the surface. He did not like these males in his home but he was doing it for her. He'd already told Larissa that she was considered part of the pack because of Aiden. She was still reeling from that declaration.

"Thank you for agreeing to speak to us. It's been a long time and I'm so glad you're well," Juhani said.

"Thank you. Now why are you here?" With vampires it was always okay to get right to the point.

Both males half smiled before Juhani spoke again. "First, I apologize that not all of the Brethren could be here, but we speak on behalf of the four members. Second, I know you are still adjusting to this new world, but no one can negate your power or standing among our kind. Especially considering what you just did with Cornelius and all those vampires."

She frowned at his words. There was something about the way he said it. "What I did?" While Connor told the Brethren she'd killed everyone, he hadn't told them how she'd done it.

The two males shared a hard look before focusing on her again. "We know what the Danesti line can do," Narek said. "If it is true you killed everyone on your own," he said, watching the others cautiously, "then we can only surmise there was one particular way you did it."

She wasn't going to confirm or deny anything. "Okay. What is your point?"

"We want you to join us," Juhani said bluntly.

She blinked once as Aiden let out a low, angry growl. She grasped her mate's hand and squeezed tight. It took a moment for their words to register. Surely they didn't mean . . . "Join you how?"

"Join the Brethren. We've been too lax with our people for too long." Juhani glanced at Connor then. "The New Orleans incident is a prime example." He quickly focused on her again. "We need someone who is strong, feared and . . . your involvement with a shifter is a bonus. The supernatural races need to be joined. What happened in Winston-Salem could have easily spiraled out of control with humans. Even the media coverage of the female enforcer could have been so negative. If it had been . . . We need a new face and you are the perfect candidate. We don't expect a decision right away and—"

Larissa shook her head. "While I appreciate the offer, I can tell you no right now. I don't even want to hear the details. I've just woken from a decades-long coma. I have much adjusting to do and I fear I would be more of a hindrance to you than anything else." When Juhani started to speak, she cut him off. "My mate and I have been separated for a long time and we never truly got to bond in the way mates are supposed to. He is my number one priority and I'm guessing that whatever you're asking me to do will require a lot of time and energy I do not want to give right now. I'm selfish so I must bluntly but respectfully say no."

Next to her Aiden immediately relaxed, but he didn't say anything through their link.

Both males looked at each other again and she guessed they were having a telepathic conversation. A moment later, they nodded and stood. "Don't make a hasty decision now. We will speak again in six months," Juhani said.

She already knew her answer, but didn't think it wise to argue when they were offering something so big. Everyone stood with them, though Aiden wrapped his arm around her in a possessive gesture no one could miss. She returned his embrace as she nodded at the two males. "Thank you for coming to see me. I really do appreciate the offer."

Everyone walked the males outside and as they were watching the vampires drive away a large semitruck rounded one of the bends, slowly coming down the drive. She looked at Aiden and frowned, worried about what it might be, but he had the biggest smile on his face. A pure burst of elation shot through their link. "Stay here with the others, okay?" he said.

Before she could answer he took off toward the gate and reopened it. Standing back, he was practically jumping up and down like a child as he waved the driver inside. The joy she felt through their bond was infectious. Behind her and all around them she saw and sensed everyone coming out of their homes, including Jayce's brother, who was walking hand in hand with Natalia. With all the pack information Aiden had given her over the past couple of days she found that interesting—but not as much as whatever was making Aiden so happy.

The truck pulled all the way through the gate and considering Connor looked amused, Larissa could only guess that he knew what was going on since he was clearly okay with everything.

As the driver got out of the truck, Aiden gave her a look and held up his hands at her as if to make sure she stayed put. She nodded at him and a smile tugged at her lips as he turned around and said something to the driver that was too low for her to hear. With the hum of conversations all around them it was hard to distinguish anything.

The driver nodded and hurried around to the back. From her position she couldn't see him when he rounded the back of the truck. A moment later a long metal ramp slowly rolled out with Aiden walking along next to it. When it finally tilted down and touched the ground, she felt another burst of elation emanate from him.

Seconds later she saw the back of a red car start to slowly descend. Blinking as the entire thing came into view, she could swear her heart skipped a beat.

Her cherry red 1953 Ferrari Berlinetta.

Tears blurred her vision as her throat tightened. She was going to have a breakdown in front of everyone and she didn't care. Batting them away, she raced to Aiden, barely able to make him out through the blurriness.

"You kept it?" she asked as she flung herself into his arms. It was as if the old Larissa had stayed in stasis. She didn't care if she made a big spectacle in front of everyone.

"It was the only piece of you I had left," he rasped out, his eyes suspiciously bright. "It's been in storage up north. This was the soonest they could get it here."

I love you so much, Aiden. With or without this beautiful car. I . . . I can't believe you kept this. Choking back a sob, she buried her face against his neck.

The last one like this sold for over ten million dollars. You can sell it and invest the profit and have enough money to live off the rest of your very long time. I'm not saying you need to or should, but I know you've been worrying about finances. This is your nest egg.

Stunned by his words, she raised her head to meet his gaze. *How did you know?*

He just shook his head. *Because I know you.*

Thank you for this and thank you for loving me.

His expression went dark for a moment. *Just don't ever leave me again.*

Try to get rid of me.

Smiling, he kissed her, soft and sweet. Around them she was vaguely aware of everyone praising the car, but all she could focus on was Aiden. Screw waiting for tonight. As soon as they could find a moment of privacy, they were getting naked and she wasn't letting him come up for air for a long time.

Chapter 27

Aiden started to slow Larissa's car as they reached the end of the long driveway and stopped in front of the two-story brick home. He'd made sure the car had regular maintenance and it purred beautifully.

"What is this place?" Larissa asked quietly, eyeing the house.

They hadn't driven very far, barely half an hour down the main highway.

"The pack just bought it." Even with everything going on, Liam had been diligent about buying up good real estate deals all over the place.

"I think someone's in there," she whispered, tensing.

He could see a flickering of light from one of the windows, but he shook his head. "No, Liam and December got the place ready for us. He just texted me. That truck we passed on the turnoff was them."

She shot him a curious look, but the lust and hunger rolling off her told him all he needed to know. She was just as ready as he was for this. For the past couple of hours he'd wanted nothing more than to bury himself deep inside her, but he'd wanted to do this right.

After she'd spent sixty years in stasis, Larissa deserved it. Aiden had also wanted privacy since there was a full moon tonight. It didn't matter that he and Larissa had already bonded. Once that link broke, the mark he'd carried for her had disappeared from his shoulder. Even when the bonding link had clicked back into place, nearly giving him a heart attack, the tattoo-like symbol hadn't reappeared on him. He wasn't sure if it would ever return and truthfully he didn't care. Larissa's scent was on him and under his skin and wasn't going away. But he still wanted to do the bonding ritual again. For himself, for her, for all the time they'd lost.

He grabbed their bag, then hurried up to the front door. Next to him Larissa was practically dancing with anticipation.

"You're very impatient."

"I'm very turned on," she murmured.

When she'd started rubbing his cock through his pants on the way here, he'd about driven off the road and had to beg for her patience. "Yeah, I got that." And he loved her impatience.

She glanced at him as he opened the front door. "And you're not?"

He laughed. "You know I am." He'd been rock hard since . . . well, for four fucking days. Or at least it felt like it.

As they entered the house he could smell the subtle

scent of lavender and something else he didn't recognize, but it was fresh and crisp.

Larissa's eyes widened slightly as he shut the door behind them. Turning, he followed her gaze to the living room that was directly off to the left from the entryway. The wood-burning fireplace was already blazing and there were a few dozen candles lit all over the room.

What drew his attention was the giant pile of blankets and pillows directly in front of the fireplace. Much better than a bed.

Grabbing the bag from his hand, Larissa tossed it to the side and jumped him, wrapping her legs around him. He stumbled once before his arms wrapped around her petite body and he crushed his mouth to hers.

Feeling like a male possessed, he kissed his mate, flicking and teasing his tongue against hers in a raw, hungry dance.

Larissa clawed at his shirt as he blindly walked them into the living room. Luckily it was a straight shot to the blankets because Aiden didn't have much finesse right now. He lifted his arms to let her pull the shirt over his head.

Her legs tightened around his waist as she held herself up against his body. They had too many damn clothes in the way. Before his shirt had hit the floor, he'd tugged her sweater off and had her flat on her back against the blankets. She wore a lacy blue bra that she removed before he could blink. Her perfect pink nipples hardened under his gaze and his entire body tightened.

Sitting back on his heels he held up a hand when she

made a move to go for the button on his pants. "Let me undress you, enjoy you. Just for a few seconds I want to see all of you," he rasped out. He wanted more than a few seconds but he knew neither of them would last that long without being fully joined.

It had been a long time and he wanted to savor the visual of his mate completely bared to him.

Moving efficiently, he tugged her knee-high boots, socks, and jeans off. As he removed them he realized she wasn't wearing anything else underneath and his cock pulsed. Stretched out on the blankets, Larissa placed her hands behind her head in a casual pose as she watched him with a heavy-lidded gaze. Her dark hair fanned out along the blankets and pillows. Her knees were bent slightly and she spread her legs, giving him a perfect view of her bare mound. Under the candle and firelight, her skin seemed to glow. His throat tightened as he drank in the sight of her completely naked and all his.

"I've thought of this so many times." His voice was a whisper as he remembered all the lonely nights he'd spent without her. Of all the years without his mate.

"You don't have to imagine it anymore," she said, pushing up to a sitting position. Not giving him any more time, Larissa grabbed the button of his pants and ripped it free.

Smiling at how her hands actually shook, he shoved his pants off and had her pinned beneath him in seconds. She arched her back, her full breasts rubbing against his chest. The sensation of her already hard nipples moving against him had him moaning into her mouth.

He gently squeezed one of her breasts as he slid a hand between their bodies and cupped her mound. Using one finger he stroked against her slit and found her soaking wet already. He'd scented her desire the entire ride over, but to feel it made his brain short-circuit.

Dipping two fingers into her, he shuddered at the feel of her slick sheath tightening around him. Her legs wrapped around his waist as she slid her hands down the length of his back and squeezed his ass. Her nails dug into him as she tried to urge him on faster.

That, he could oblige. Part of him wanted to tease her, to drag this out forever, but the hungriest, most primal part of him wouldn't allow it.

He'd been denied his female for too long. As he pulled his fingers out of her, one of her hands reached between them and she wrapped her fingers around his cock. Wordlessly, she arched her back and shifted their bodies so that his cock was aligned perfectly at her entrance. Her breathing was ragged as she waited for him to move.

In one quick thrust he plunged deep into her. Her fangs descended as he buried himself fully inside her. An uncontrollable shudder rolled through him. The feel of being inside her after so long was almost too much. He'd never thought this would happen again, never imagined it as a possibility. His whole body pulled taut as he restrained himself from losing it.

Continuing to caress one of her breasts, he began thrusting into her in an unsteady rhythm. Each time he drove into her tight body, her inner walls squeezed tighter and tighter around him. She feathered kisses along his jaw before she raked her teeth over his neck. The sensation was sending his body into overload.

His own canines descended at the feel of her erotic little nips and kisses. It didn't matter that tradition demanded he take her from behind while sinking his canines into her neck. Tonight he was doing what felt natural.

"Bite me while you come," he ordered roughly.

"You too." A harsh demand from the female he loved.

She was already so slick he knew it wouldn't take long to push her over the edge. He was right there too, about to embarrass himself like a randy cub. He needed her to come first.

Reaching between them again, he tweaked her clit with his thumb and forefinger. As he started rubbing her sensitive bundle of nerves, she moaned before sinking her teeth into his neck.

There was no pain. Only pleasure. As her inner walls clenched around him and she cried out, finding her release, he let go and sank his canines into her neck.

His climax ripped through him, wave after wave seemingly never ending as the orgasm built and then crested into a free fall of pure pleasure. He had no idea how much time passed as they shuddered against each other, as he emptied himself inside her sweet body.

As he came down from his high, he gently licked the wounds on her neck at the same time she licked his, murmuring the sweetest endearments. Nuzzling her neck, he wrapped his arms around her and rolled to the side, but kept their bodies interlocked.

There was no way he was letting her go. As he pulled his head back from her neck, his eyes widened when he realized that all around them a faint blue fire burned. It wasn't burning anything, just flickering around them like a protective shield.

"I couldn't hold the fire back," she murmured as she ran a hand down the length of his spine. Before he could respond, she dragged her body away from him.

His body immediately mourned the loss, until she rolled him over, practically shoving him face-first into the blankets. That was when he realized what she was doing. Her fingers skimmed over both his shoulders before her soft lips pressed against the spot that had once held his bondmate symbol.

He was almost too afraid to ask, but he found his voice. "Is it . . . there?"

She nodded against his back and when he felt wet-ness, he realized she was crying. Turning over, he pulled her on top of him as he rolled onto his back. He cupped her cheek with one hand as she stared down at him.

The love and joy in her gaze nearly overwhelmed him. "It's a small blue flame."

The first symbol had been Celtic knot work symbol-izing unity, but this meant more to him. It was a symbol of her.

"I love you," he rasped out.

"I love you too. Always and forever." As a few stray tears fell down her cheeks, she brushed her lips over his.

There were some unknowns about their future, but nothing would ever separate them again. He wouldn't allow it and he knew she wouldn't either.

Acknowledgments

As always I owe a big thank-you to Kari Walker for reading the early version of Aiden's story! I'm also grateful to my wonderful agent Jill Marsal. To my fabulous editor, Danielle Perez, thank you for your guidance with this series. And to the whole team at New American Library: Ashley Polikoff, Christina Brower, and Jessica Brock, I'm grateful for all the behind-the-scenes work that you do. The art department did a brilliant job with this cover—thanks to cover artist Craig White and designer Katie Anderson. In addition, I'm blessed with a husband and son who put up with my writer's schedule, so more thanks are in order. For my readers, every day I'm appreciative of your support. Thank you for reading my books. Lastly, thank you to God.

Prologue

Marine Corps Scout Sniper motto: one shot, one kill.

Sam Kelly could see his GP tent fifty yards away. He was practically salivating at the thought of a shower and a clean bed. But he'd settle for the fucking bed at this point. He didn't even care that he was sharing that tent with twenty other men. Showers were almost pointless at this dusty military base in hellish sub-Saharan Africa anyway. By the time he got back to his tent from the showers, he'd be covered in a film of grime again.

Four weeks behind enemy lines with limited supplies and he was also starving. Even an MRE sounded good about now. As he trekked across the dry, cracked ground, he crossed his fingers that the beef jerky he'd stashed in his locker was still there, but he doubted it. His bunkmate had likely gotten to it weeks ago. Greedy fucker.

"There a reason you haven't shaved, Marine?"

Sam paused and turned at the sound of the condescending unfamiliar voice. An officer—a lieutenant—he didn't recognize stood a few feet away, his pale face flushed and his skin already burning under the hot sun. With one look Sam knew he was new in-country. Why the hell wasn't the idiot wearing a boonie hat to protect his face? Hell, it had to be a hundred and thirty degrees right now. Yeah, this dick was definitely new. Otherwise, he wouldn't be hassling Sam.

Sam gave him a blank stare and kept his stance relaxed. "Yes, sir, there is. Relaxed grooming standards." *Dumb ass.*

The blond man's head tilted to the side just a fraction, as if he didn't understand the concept. God, could this guy be any greener? The man opened his mouth again and Sam could practically hear the stupid shit he was about to spout off by the arrogant look on his face.

"Lieutenant! There a reason you're bothering my boy?" Colonel Seamus Myers was barreling toward them, dust kicking up under his feet with each step.

The man reminded Sam of an angry bull, and when he got pissed, everyone suffered. He was a good battalion commander, though. Right now Sam was just happy the colonel wasn't directing that rage at him. Guy could be a scary fucker when he wanted.

"No, sir. I was just inquiring about his lack of grooming." The officer's face flushed even darker under his spreading sunburn. Yeah, that was going to itch something fierce when it started peeling. Sam smiled inwardly at the thought.

"You're here one week and you think you know more than me?"

"N-no, sir! Of course not, sir."

The colonel leaned closer and spoke so low that Sam couldn't hear him. But he could guess what he was saying because he'd heard it before. *Stay the fuck away from Sam Kelly and the rest of my snipers or I'll send you home.* Rank definitely mattered, but to the colonel, his few snipers were his boys, and the man had been in more wars than Sam ever wanted to think about. Sam had seen and caused enough death himself to want to get out when his enlistment was up. That wasn't too far off either. He'd been to Iraq, Afghanistan, a few places in South America that weren't even on his official record, and now he was stationed in Djibouti, Africa. Or hell, as he liked to think of it. He loved his job and he loved his country, but enough was enough. Sam just wished he could figure out what the hell he wanted to do if he got out of the military.

He watched as the colonel started talking—loudly—to the new guy. Getting right in his face as only a pissed-off Marine could. Sam almost felt sorry for the guy, but what kind of stupid fucker didn't know that since the environment here was so dirty that staph infections were rampant, grooming standards were *different*? That was one of the reasons he and a thousand other guys his age had relaxed grooming standards in the bowels of this hellish place. But they also cut him slack because he was a sniper. Sometimes he had to blend in with the populace, among other things. He might be stationed in Africa, but he'd just gotten back from—where else?—Afghanistan. He'd stayed holed up for days in that dank cave just waiting—

"Sergeant, in my tent. Now."

Sam blinked and realized Colonel Myers was talking to him. He nodded. "Yes, sir."

The colonel was still reaming out whoever the newbie was, but Sam always followed orders. Looked as though that shower was going to wait. The walk to the big tent in the middle of the base was short.

As he drew the flap back and stepped into the colonel's tent, he stilled when he spotted a dark-haired man leaning against a table with maps on it. He looked as if he thought he had every right to be there too. Interesting. A fly landed on Sam's face, but he didn't move. Just watched the man, ready to go for one of his weapons if need be. He didn't recognize him and he wasn't wearing a uniform.

Just simple fatigues and a T-shirt, which stretched across a clearly fit body even though the guy had to be pushing fifty. There was something about the man that put Sam on edge. He was like a tiger, coiled and waiting to rip your head off. The man's eyes weren't cold, exactly, but they were calculating.

Carefully the man reached for a manila folder next to him and flipped it open. He glanced down at it. "Sam Kelly. Originally from Miami, Florida. Grew up in foster care. No known family. One of the best damn snipers Myers has ever seen. Sniper school honor grad, aptitude for languages, takes orders well, possibly a lifer." He glanced up then, his green eyes focusing on Sam like a laser. "But I don't think you're a lifer. You want a change, don't you?" The man's gaze was shrewd, assessing. Sam didn't like being analyzed, especially by a stranger. And the guy didn't even have an accent, so he couldn't place where he might be from. Nothing in his speech stood out.

Who the hell was this guy? And how the fuck did he know Sam wanted a change? It wasn't as if he'd told anyone. Sam ran through the list of possibilities. He'd been on different operations before, sometimes working for the CIA for solo things, and he'd been attached to various SEAL teams for larger-scale missions, but he'd never worked with this guy before. He did have Sam's file, though—or Sam guessed that was his file in the man's hand. He could just be bluffing. But what would the point of that be? He dropped all semblance of protocol since this guy clearly wasn't a Marine. "Who are you and what do you want?"

"You did some good work in Cartagena a few years ago." He snapped the file shut and set it back on the table.

Sam just stared at him. His statement said a lot all by itself. That mission wasn't in his official jacket, so this guy knew classified shit and was letting Sam know it. But since he hadn't asked a question or introduced himself, Sam wasn't inclined to respond.

The man's lips quirked up a fraction. As they did, the tent flap opened and the colonel strode in. He glared at the man, cursed, then looked at Sam, his expression almost speculative. He jerked a thumb at the stranger. "Whatever this guy tells you is the truth and he's got top secret clearance." He snorted, as if something was funny about that, then sobered. "And whatever you decide . . . Hell, I know what you'll decide. Good luck, son. I'll miss you." He shook Sam's hand, then strode out of the tent.

Miss him? What the hell is he talking about? Sam glared at the man in front of him. "I asked you once who you were. Answer or I'm out of here."

The stranger crossed the short distance and held out his hand.

Sam ignored it.

The man cleared his throat and looked as if he was fighting a smile, which just pissed Sam off. "I'm Lieutenant General Wesley Burkhart, head of—"

"The NSA. I know the name." Sam didn't react outwardly, but the gears in his head were turning. "What do you want with me? I thought you guys were into cryptography and cyber stuff."

"We are, but I'm putting together a team of men and women with a different skill set. Black ops stuff, similar to the CIA, but with fewer . . . rules. I want to offer you a job, but before I go any further, you need to know that if you come to work for me, Sam Kelly will cease to exist. You will leave your past and everything in it behind."

Sam stared at the man, overwhelmed by too many feelings. Relief being one of them. Leaving his identity behind didn't seem like such a bad thing at all. Finishing the rest of his enlistment in shitholes like this wasn't something he looked forward to. He'd seen and caused so much death that sometimes he wondered if God would ever forgive him. The idea of wiping his record clean was so damn appealing. Maybe this was the fresh start he'd been looking for. Except . . . He touched the hog's tooth hanging from his neck. He'd bled, sweated, and starved for this thing. For what it represented. It was part of him now. "I'm not taking this off. Ever."

The other man's eyes flicked to the bullet around his neck, and the corners of his mouth pulled up slightly. "Unless the op calls for it, I wouldn't expect you to."

Okay, then. Heart thudding, Sam dropped his rucksack to the ground. "Tell me everything I need to know."

Chapter 1

Black Death 9 Agent: member of an elite group of men and women employed by the NSA for covert, off-the-books operations. A member's purpose is to gain the trust of targeted individuals in order to gather information or evidence by any means necessary.

Five years later

Jack Stone opened and quietly shut the door behind him as he slipped into the conference room. A few analysts and field agents were already seated around the long rectangular table. One empty chair remained.

A few of the new guys looked up as he entered, but the NSA's security was tighter than Langley's. Since he was the only one missing from this meeting, the senior members pored over the briefs in front of them without even giving him a cursory glance.

Wesley Burkhart, his boss, handler, and recruiter all rolled into one, stuck his head in the room just as Jack started to sit. "Jack, my office. Now."

He inwardly cringed because he knew that tone well. At least his bags were still packed. Once he was out in the hall heading toward Wesley's office, his boss briefly clapped him on the back. "Sorry to drag you out of there, but I've got something bigger for you. Have you had a chance to relax since you've been back?"

Jack shrugged, knowing his boss didn't expect an answer. After working two years undercover to bring down a human trafficking ring that had also been linked to a terrorist group in Southern California, he was still decompressing. He'd been back only a week and the majority of his time had been spent debriefing. It would take longer than a few days to wash the grime and memories off him. If he ever did. "You've got another mission for me already?"

Wesley nodded as he opened the door to his office. "I hate sending you back into the field so soon, but once you read the report, you'll understand why I don't want anyone else."

As the door closed behind them, Jack took a seat in front of his boss's oversized solid oak desk. "Lay it on me."

"Two of our senior analysts have been hearing a lot of chatter lately linking the Vargas cartel and Abu al-Ramaan's terrorist faction. At this point, the only solid connection we have is South Beach Medical Supply."

"SBMS is involved?" The medical company delivered supplies and much-needed drugs to third-world countries across the globe. Ronald Weller, the owner, was such a straight arrow it didn't seem possible.

"Looks that way." His boss handed him an inch-thick manila folder.

Jack picked up the packet and looked over the first document. As he skimmed the report, his chest tightened painfully as long-buried memories clawed at him with razor-sharp talons. After reading the key sections, he looked up. "Is there a chance Sophie is involved?" Her name rolled off his tongue so naturally, as if he'd spoken to her yesterday and not thirteen years ago. As if saying it was no big deal. As if he didn't dream about her all the damn time.

Wesley shook his head. "We don't know. Personally, I don't think so, but it looks like her boss is."

"Ronald Weller? Where are you getting this information?" Jack had been on the West Coast for the last two years, dealing with his own bullshit. A lot could have changed in that time, but SBMS involved with terrorists—he didn't buy it.

"Multiple sources have confirmed his involvement, including Paul Keane, the owner of Keane Flight. We've got Mr. Keane on charges of treason, among other things. He rolled over on SBMS without too much persuasion, but we still need actual proof that SBMS is involved, not just a traitor's word."

"How is Keane Flight involved?"

"Instead of just flying medical supplies, they've been picking up extra cargo."

Jack's mind immediately went to the human trafficking he'd recently dealt with, and he gritted his teeth. "Cargo?"

"Drugs, guns . . . possibly biological weapons."

The first two were typical cargo of most smugglers, but biological shit put Keane right on the NSA's hit list. "What do you want from me?"

His boss rubbed a hand over his face. "I've already built a cover for you. You're a silent partner with Keane Flight. Now that Paul Keane is incapacitated, you'll be taking over the reins for a while, giving you full access to all his dealings."

"Incapacitated, huh?"

The corners of Wesley's mouth pulled up slightly. "He was in a car accident. Bad one."

"Right." Jack flipped through the pages of information. "Where's Keane really at right now?"

"In federal protection until we can bring this whole operation down, but publicly he's in a coma after a serious accident—one that left him scarred beyond recognition and the top half of his body in bandages."

Jack didn't even want to know where they'd gotten the body. Probably a John Doe no one would miss. "So what's the deal with my role?"

"Paul Keane has already made contact with Weller about you—days before his accident. Told him he was taking a vacation and you'd be helping out until he got back. Weller was cautious on the phone, careful not to give up anything. Now that Keane is 'injured,' no one can ask him any questions. Keane's assistant is completely in the dark about everything and thinks you're really a silent partner. You've been e-mailing with her the past week to strengthen your cover, but you won't need to meet her in person. You're supposed to meet with Weller in two days. We want you to completely infiltrate the day-to-day workings of SBMS. We need to know if Weller is working with anyone else, if he has more contacts we're not privy to. Everything."

"Why can't you tap his phone?" That should be child's play for the NSA.

His boss's expression darkened. "So far we've been unable to hack his line. I've got two of my top analysts, Thomas Chadwick and Steven Williams—I don't think you've met either of them." When Jack shook his head, Wesley continued. "The fact that he's got a filter that *we* can't bust through on his phone means he's probably into some dirty stuff."

Maybe. Or maybe the guy was just paranoid. Jack glanced at the report again, but didn't get that same rush he'd always gotten from his work. The last two years he'd seen mothers and fathers sell their children into slavery for less than a hundred dollars. And that wasn't even the worst of it. In the past he hadn't been on a job for more than six months at a time and he'd never been tasked with anything so brutal before, but in addition to human trafficking, they'd been selling people to scientists—under the direction of Albanian terrorists—who had loved having an endless supply of illegals to experiment on. He rolled his shoulders and shoved those thoughts out of his head. "What am I meeting him about?" *And how the hell will I handle seeing Sophie?* he thought.

"You supposedly want to go over flight schedules

and the books and you want to talk about the possibility of investing in his company."

Jack was silent for a long beat. Then he asked the only question that mattered. The question that would burn him alive from the inside out until he actually voiced it. The question that made him feel as if he'd swallowed glass shards as he asked, "Will I be working with Sophie?"

Wesley's jaw clenched. "She *is* Weller's assistant."

"So yes."

Those knowing green eyes narrowed. "Is that going to be a problem?"

Yes. "No."

"She won't recognize you. What're you worried about?" Wesley folded his hands on top of the desk.

Jack wasn't worried about *her*. He was worried he couldn't stay objective around her. Sophie thought he was dead. And thanks to expensive facial reconstruction—all part of the deal in killing off his former identity when he'd joined Wesley's team with the NSA—she'd never know his true identity. Still, the thought of being in the same zip code as her sent flashes of heat racing down his spine. With a petite, curvy body made for string bikinis and wet T-shirt contests, Sophie was the kind of woman to make a man do a double take. He'd spent too many hours dreaming about running his hands through that thick dark hair again as she rode him. When they were seventeen, she'd been his ultimate fantasy and once they'd finally crossed that line from friends to lovers, there had been no keeping their hands off each other. They'd had sex three or four times a day whenever they'd been able to sneak away and get a little privacy. And it had never been enough with Sophie. She'd consumed him then. Now his boss wanted him to voluntarily work with her. "Why not send another agent?"

"I don't *want* anyone else. In fact, no one else here knows you're going in as Keane's partner except me."

Jack frowned. It wasn't the first time he'd gone undercover with only Wesley as his sole contact, but if his boss had people already working on the connection between Vargas and SBMS, it would be protocol for the direct team to know he was going in undercover. "Why?"

"I don't want to risk a leak. If I'm the only one who knows you're not who you say you are, there's no chance of that."

There was more to it than that, but Jack didn't question him. He had that blank expression Jack recognized all too well that meant he wouldn't be getting any more, not even under torture.

Wesley continued. "You know more about Sophie than most people. I want you to use that knowledge to get close to her. I don't think I need to remind you that this is a matter of national security."

"I haven't seen her since I was eighteen." And not a day went by that he didn't think of the ways he'd failed her. What the hell was Wesley thinking?

"It's time for you to face your past, Jack." His boss suddenly straightened and took on that professorial/ fatherly look Jack was accustomed to.

"Is that what this is about? Me, facing my past?" he

ground out. Fuck that. If he wanted to keep his memories buried, he damn well would.

Wesley shrugged noncommittally. "You *will* complete this mission."

As Jack stood, he clenched his jaw so he wouldn't say something he'd regret. Part of him wanted to tell Wesley to take his order and shove it, but another part—his most primal side—hummed with anticipation at the thought of seeing Sophie. She'd always brought out his protective side. Probably because she'd been his entire fucking world at one time and looking out for her had been his number-one priority.

He'd noticed Sophie long before she'd been aware of his existence, but once he was placed in the same foster house as her, they'd quickly become best friends. Probably because he hadn't given her a choice in being his friend. He'd just pushed right past her shy exterior until she came to him about anything and everything. Then one day she'd kissed him. He shoved *that* thought right out of his mind.

"There's a car waiting to take you to the flight strip. Once you land in Miami, there will be another car waiting for you. There's a full wardrobe and anything else you'll need at the condo we've arranged."

"What about my laptop?"

"It's in the car."

When he was halfway to the door, his boss stopped him again. "You need to face your demons, Jack. Seeing Sophie is the only way you'll ever exorcise them. Maybe you can settle down and start a family once you do. I want to see you happy, son."

Son. If only he'd had a father like Wesley growing up. But if he had, he wouldn't have ended up where he was today. And he'd probably never have met Sophie. That alone made his shitty childhood worth every punch and bruise he'd endured. Jack swallowed hard but didn't turn around before exiting. His chest loosened a little when he was out from under Wesley's scrutiny. The older man might be in his early fifties, but with his skill set, his boss could undoubtedly take out any one of the men within their covert organization. That's why he was the deputy director of the NSA and the unidentified head of the covert group Jack worked for.

Officially, Black Death 9 didn't exist. Unofficially, the name was whispered in back rooms and among other similar black ops outfits within the government. Their faction was just another classified group of men and women working to keep their country safe. At times like this Jack wished the NSA didn't have a thick file detailing every minute detail of his past. If they didn't, another agent would be heading for Miami right now and he'd be on his way to a four-star hotel or on another mission.

Jack mentally shook himself as he placed his hand on the elevator scanner. Why was Wesley trying to get under his skin? Now, of all times? The man was too damn intuitive for his own good. He'd been after him for years to see Sophie in person, "to find closure," as he put it, but Jack couldn't bring himself to do it. He had no problem facing down the barrel of a loaded gun, but seeing the woman with the big brown eyes and the soft curves he so often dreamed about—*no, thank you.*

As the elevator opened into the aboveground parking garage, he shoved those thoughts away. He'd be seeing Sophie in two days. Didn't matter what he wanted.

Sophie Moreno took a deep, steadying breath and eased open the side door to one of Keane Flight's hangars. She had a key, so it wasn't as though she was technically breaking in. She was just coming by on a Sunday night when no one was here. And the place was empty. And she just happened to be wearing a black cap to hide her hair.

Oh yeah, she was completely acting like a normal, law-abiding citizen. Cringing at her stupid rationalization, she pushed any fears of getting caught she had to the side. What she was doing wasn't about her.

She loved her job at South Beach Medical Supply, but lately her boss had been acting weird and the flight logs from Keane Flight for SBMS's recent deliveries didn't make sense. They hadn't for the past few months.

And no one—meaning her boss, Ronald Weller—would answer her questions when she brought up anything about Keane Flight.

Considering Ronald hadn't asked her over to dinner in the past few months either, as he normally did, she had a feeling he and his wife must be having problems. They'd treated her like a daughter for almost as long as she'd been with SBMS, so if he was too distracted to look into things because of personal issues, she was going to take care of this herself. SBMS provided much-needed medical supplies to third-world countries, and she wasn't going to let anything jeopardize that. People needed them. And if she could help out Ronald, she wanted to.

She didn't even know what she was looking for, but she'd decided to trust her gut and come here. Wearing all black, she felt a little stupid, like a cat burglar or something, but she wanted to be careful. Hell, she'd even parked outside the hangar and sneaked in through an opening in the giant fence surrounding the private airport. The security here should have been tighter—something she would address later. After she'd done her little B&E. God, she was so going to get in trouble if she was caught. She could tell herself that she wasn't "technically" doing anything wrong, but her palms were sweaty as she stole down the short hallway to where it opened up into a large hangar.

Two twin-engine planes sat there, and the overhead lights from the warehouselike building were dim. But they were bright enough for her to make out a lot of cargo boxes and crates at the foot of one of the planes. The back hatch was open and it looked as if someone had started loading the stuff, then stopped.

Sophie glanced around the hangar as she stepped fully into it just to make sure she was alone. Normally Paul Keane had standard security here. She'd actually been here a couple of weeks ago under the guise of needing paperwork and there had been two Hispanic guys hovering near the planes as if they belonged there. She'd never seen them before and they'd given her the creeps. They'd also killed her chance of trying to sneak in and see what kind of cargo was on the planes.

When she'd asked Paul about them, he'd just waved off her question by telling her he'd hired new security.

One thing she knew for sure. He'd lied straight to her face. Those guys were sure as hell *not* security. One of them had had a MAC-10 tucked into the front of his pants. She might not know everything about weapons, but she'd grown up in shitty neighborhoods all over Miami, so she knew enough. And no respectable security guy carried a MAC-10 with a freaking *suppressor*. That alone was incredibly shady. The only people she'd known to carry that type of gun were gangbangers and other thugs.

So even if she felt a little crazy for sneaking down here, she couldn't go to her boss about any illegal activities—if there even were any—without proof. SBMS was Ronald's heart. He loved the company and she did too. No one was going to mess with it if she had anything to say about it.

Since the place was empty, she hurried across the wide expanse, her black ballet-slipper-type shoes virtually silent. When she neared the back of the plane, she braced herself for someone to be waiting inside.

It was empty except for some crates. Bypassing the crates on the outside, she ran up inside the plane and took half a dozen pictures of the crates with the SBMS logo on the outside. Then she started opening them.

By the time she opened the fifth crate, she was starting to feel completely insane, but as she popped the next lid, ice chilled her veins. She blinked once and struggled to draw in a breath, sure she was seeing things.

A black grenade peeked through the yellow-colored stuffing at the top. Carefully she lifted a bundle of it. There were more grenades lining the smaller crate, packed tight with the fluffy material. Her heart hammered wildly as it registered that Keane was likely running arms and weapons using SBMS supplies as cover, but she forced herself to stay calm. Pulling out her cell phone, she started snapping pictures of the inside of the crate, then pictures that showed the logo on the outside. In the next crate she found actual guns. AK-47s, she was pretty sure. She'd never actually seen one in real life before, but it looked like what she'd seen in movies. After taking pictures of those, she hurried out of the back of the plane toward the crates sitting behind it.

Before she could decide which one to open first, a loud rolling sound rent the air—the hangar door!

Ducking down, she peered under the plane and saw the main door the planes entered and exited through starting to open. Panic detonated inside her. She had no time to do anything but run. Without pause, she raced back toward the darkened hallway. She'd go out the back, the same way she'd come in. All she had to do was get to that hallway before whoever—

"Hey!" a male voice shouted.

Crap, someone had seen her. She shoved her phone in her back pocket and sprinted even faster as she cleared the hallway. Fear ripped through her, threatening to pull her apart at the seams. She wouldn't risk turning around and letting anyone see her face.

The exit door clanged against the wall as she slammed it open. Male voices shouted behind her, ordering her to stop in Spanish.

Her lungs burned and her legs strained with each pounding step against the pavement. She really wished she'd worn sneakers. As she reached the edge of the fence, which thankfully had no lighting and was lined with bushes and foliage behind it, she dove for the opening. If she hadn't known where it was, it would have been almost impossible to find without the aid of light.

Crawling on her hands and knees, she risked a quick glance behind her. Two men were running across the pavement toward the fence, weapons silhouetted in their hands. She couldn't see their faces because the light from the back of the hangar was behind them, but they were far enough away that she should be able to escape. They slowed as they reached the fence, both looking around in confusion.

"Adónde se fue?" one of them snarled.

Sophie snorted inwardly as she shoved up from the ground and disappeared behind the bushes. They'd never catch her now. Not unless they could jump fences in single bounds. Twenty yards down, her car was still parked on the side of the back road where she'd left it.

The dome light came on when she opened the door, so she shut it as quickly as possible. She started her car but immediately turned off the automatic lights and kicked the vehicle into drive. Her tires made a squealing sound and she cringed. She needed to get out of there before those men figured out how to get through the fence. She couldn't risk them seeing her license plate. Only law enforcement should be able to track plates, but people who were clearly running weapons wouldn't care about breaking laws to find out who she was.

She glanced in the rearview mirror as her car disappeared down the dark road, and didn't see anyone on the road or by the side of it. Didn't mean they weren't there, though. Pure adrenaline pumped through her as she sped away, tearing through her like jagged glass, but her hands remained steady on the wheel.

What the hell was she supposed to do now? If she called the cops, this could incriminate SBMS and that could ruin all the good work their company had done over the past decade. And what if by the time the cops got there all the weapons were gone? Then she'd look crazy and would have admitted to breaking into a private airport hangar, which was against the law. Okay, the cops were out. For now. First she needed to talk to her boss. He'd know what to do and they could figure out this mess together.

headline
ETERNAL

FIND YOUR HEART'S DESIRE...